ACRE'S BASTARD

(Part 1 of the Lucca le Pou Stories)

WAYNE TURMEL

Published by Achis Press©

THE HOLY LAND
A.D. 1187

Chapter 1

City of Acre, AD 1187

"Lucca, what do you see?" Poor, fat, Murad stood off to the side, watching us. Since he wasn't strong enough, like Berk, to help lift me, nor small and nimble like myself, he was off to the side bouncing from one leg to the other like he had to pee. He did that when he got nervous—which was whenever things started to get fun. He and Fadhil stood lookout, watching and wishing they were seeing what I was going to see. Women. Hopefully, naked women. If I could get up high enough, that is.

I risked life and limb standing on Berk's broad shoulders. My dirty fingernails clung to the stone windowsill and my feet scrambled for purchase on the wall. And for what? To stare at a bunch of girls. At ten, I didn't know that was nothing worth endangering your life over. Later, I'd realize some men never learned that lesson, but I was always a fast learner.

"I see a wall and not much else. Berk, lift me higher." My filthy bare feet shifted on his shoulders, dust-caked heels digging in mercilessly. The behemoth was the son of a Turkish mason, and even at eleven had all the makings of his late father's broad body, brute strength and slow wit. He made the perfect ladder.

Berk spit as my filthy toes brushed his face, searching for a climbing place on the sandstone. "Ow, be careful." He whined in Turkish.

"Be quiet," Fadhil hissed. "We'll get caught, and you guys get me in enough trouble as it is." Fadhil was the only one of us with an actual father; a Syrian carter. The old bastard was known to be overly strict, and poor Fadhil had shown up bearing the marks of his father's displeasure more than once. To my shame, my quest to see naked flesh outweighed any concern for my friend.

I managed to pull myself up a few more inches; enough to relieve Berk but not enough to actually get my elbows up on the sill. I gave it one more grunting try but felt my fingers slip. "Look out," I shouted, and scraped my knuckles against the coarse rock on my way back to the hard ground.

Fortunately, Berk got out of the way this time. Sometimes he didn't.

Dusting myself off, I looked around for signs of witnesses but saw no one. The alleys were deserted except for my friends. We all grinned guiltily. Even Fadhil allowed himself a smile. We hadn't gotten caught, so there was no need to give up yet. We still had another half an hour or so before darkness fell and people began to show up at the brothel.

My friends and I were famous, if that's the word, as The Lice. We were small, annoying, and constantly in someone's hair. Berk was Turkish, Fadhil and Murad were Syrian—supposedly converted Mohammedans—which is why they were allowed to live in town. They all had parents (or at least a mother) they constantly disappointed.

Then there was me. I was shorter and skinnier than my friends, and a year or so younger. My parentage, or at least what I knew of it, was written all over my brown, sharp face. At first glance I seemed purely Syrian; dark brown skin and a long beak of a nose, but my green eyes showed the other half of the tale. Depending on which story you believed, my mother was either a local whore got with child by a Frankish Knight, or a pure, innocent Frank woman, dishonored by a pillaging Mussulman. The idea that my parents might have actually liked each other and wanted me never seemed to be a credible part of the tale. I preferred to think of my mother as a whore, giving me claim to really being part of the ruling class by virtue of my father's nobility, because of course he had to be noble if he was really a knight. Either way, their union left me with the best—or worst, depending on who told the story—features of each.

My mother died before I could remember her, and I was raised at the orphanage that was part of the Hospitaller charter house, another sign that I wasn't the get of some mere Syrian slut. They gave me the name Lucca, and to tell me apart from the three other Luccas, they gave me the additional name Nemo. Lucca, was fine—a perfectly good Frankish name. But Nemo meant "no man," or "nobody." Lately I'd taken to calling myself Lucca *le Pou*… Lucca the Louse. It made me feel good to have a choice in something, and no one else seemed to care what I was called as long as I answered when called.

At the far end of the alley, I spied a beggar in a grey robe

3

squatting in what little shade there was, watching us. He chuckled, shaking his head in amusement. I'd seen him around before. I suspected he was simple-minded, and no threat to tell anyone since he was enjoying the show so much. He shouted to us, "You boys aren't giving up already are you?"

He obviously didn't know us well. The Lice never gave up until we succeeded gloriously, which was rarely, or failed miserably. Failure resulted in beatings from our intended victims, parents, or priests, depending on who got to us first. In this case our mission was to see a woman without clothes on so we were prepared to take some lumps.

I don't recall exactly how the conversation started, but it never takes anything too specific to get young boys wondering about the opposite sex. I think Murad claimed to have seen his mother's breasts. Of course, mothers didn't count as women, so that began a round of lies about who had seen *real* girls naked. Fadhil and Berk had the best claim to it, with sisters and all. Since I lived in an orphanage run by priests, the only women I saw were either nuns or other people's mothers and the opportunities to see them without clothes were both limited and slightly horrifying. At any rate, we finally decided to solve this terrible lack in our educations.

We had to find a place that not only had women—a rare commodity in a military city—but women likely to be undressed. That left only the baths, which were too crowded and well patrolled, or the brothels. Most of those establishments were located near the port or out in the suburbs past the gate. At this hour, respectable citizens

4

would be heading home for supper, and the unrespectable ones waiting for the comforting cover of darkness.

The house we chose was known as The Harem. This was supposedly named for the beautiful dark haired women, mostly Armenian or Syrian, employed there. Many suspected it was what supposedly celibate warrior monks imagined Saladin's harem must be like. Why good Christian soldiers would want to indulge themselves like unbelievers was a question no one dared ask out loud.

Egged on by the beggar's challenge, I set my mind to solving the problem. How could I get up and through the rear window? "We could get a ladder," offered Murad.

"Excellent plan, do you have one?" I'm glad Fadhil asked. He was always the voice of reason, and managed to sound smart without annoying the other person, a gift I most certainly didn't possess. Everything I said grated on someone.

We pondered a few more seconds. We needed to make Berk taller, so I could get a better grip on the window. Murad pointed in the direction of the beggar. "What about his box?"

We followed his chubby finger to where the man in grey sat perched on a wooden crate. It would suit us perfectly, but how would we get him to surrender his seat? After some discussion Fadhil nodded. "Right. You ask him, Lucca."

"Why me?"

"You're good with grownups." This was true. I was the only one of our group who didn't shake at the idea of adult authority. In fact, it amused me to watch grownups try to act like they knew more than I did, and little made me happier than proving them wrong.

"Okay, fine." I summoned my courage and strutted to the end of the alley. The shadows were lengthening, leaving our audience completely in shade. He wouldn't be in a hurry to surrender that cool corner of paradise.

As I neared him, I quickly considered and discarded one excuse after the other before I settled on something that might work. "Excuse me. May we borrow your stool for a moment?"

The man looked up from under his hood. I stopped dead. His eyes weren't blood shot and glazed as you'd expect from someone sleeping rough and eating rarely. Instead they were clear blue, and seemed to see right through to the back of my head. "And why would I do that?" he asked.

I tried to think of the most extravagant lie I could come up with. It was my experience that the more complicated the story, the more likely people are to believe it—or at least act like they believe so you just stop trying to explain it. "You see my friend there, the fat one? His sister has disappeared, and we have heard she might have been sold by Unbelievers to the owner of that house."

His smile vanished. "You can do better than that."

"Excuse me?"

He snorted. "Your big friend there. If his sister is anything like him, no one could carry her away. Also, she's a Syrian convert. There aren't a lot of those in the city these days, so everyone would know her. A real slaver would take her far away. She'd be whoring in Damascus or married to some wandering camel seller by now. No, you'll need to do better

6

than that. Now, why do you want to borrow my nice, comfortable seat?"

I swallowed hard and scanned his face, looking for a clue to the right answer. He was obviously no fool. In fact, as his eyes squinted at me, I thought he may be the least foolish adult I'd ever encountered. "We need to stand on it, sir."

"Why?"

"So Berk can boost me through the window."

He bit his lip and nodded as though considering this new information. "And why would you want to get in a window? You're not a thief are you?"

"No sir, not a thief." It was true. At least for the moment my soul was clean of that sin. It hadn't been that long since the priests last made me confess.

"Then why do you want to get in that particular window?" Those terrible blue eyes sucked the truth out of me. I looked down at my shoes in shame. Then I thought how amused he'd been watching us, and how it might not be as much fun to see us give up and go home. I did something I rarely attempted and told him the truth.

"We want to see girls with no clothes on." He threw his head back, barking out a deep laugh.

"Now there's a reason any man can relate to, although it can only lead to misery. Believe that, Master le Pou." He knew my name. Perhaps we were famous after all.

He stood with a groan and held his wooden crate out to me. His left hand was covered in a thick kidskin glove. It was far too warm to wear gloves. Maybe his hand was deformed, and that's why he was reduced to begging. It might explain why he wasn't working or fighting like the other men in town. He caught me looking at his glove, and his eyes trapped mine again as if daring me to ask. It was a dare I chose not to take. "Thank you, sir. We won't hurt it. You can see us from here. We'll give it back to you."

"Yes, you will, or I'll find you. Okay, get on with it before someone comes. I'll keep watch." I nodded as politely as possible and took the crate. I ran back to my friends. He was right, time was not on our side.

"All right, Berk. Let's do this." I placed the crate in the dirt and patted the top. Berk took his position, a good foot or more so higher than before. "Help me up." Murad and Fadhil each took an arm and helped me scramble up Berk's back onto his shoulders.

It was perfect. My eyes were now directly level with the stone windowsill. It would be a simple matter for Berk to get me close, then pull myself up so my elbows hooked the stone sill. Then I could climb through. I took a deep breath, preparing for the small leap I'd need. That's when I heard them.

Female voices from inside the room drifted like birdsong out the window and into my ears. There were actually women in there.

"What do you see?" Murad asked again.

"I hope it's better than what I see," said Berk. I realized from beneath me he could see straight up my sack cloth tunic. "Hurry up."

I looked over at the beggar, who watched, amused. He nodded as if giving me permission, although I hadn't asked for any such thing. With only a little effort, my elbows landed on the sill and my fingers hooked the inside of the window. I pulled up to see something I'd never imagined.

There were half a dozen women sitting on lush pillows, talking and laughing. I was a little surprised to see they were all clothed and acting quite normally. That disappointment vanished, though, when I realized they were young and perhaps the most beautiful creatures I'd ever seen. They gossiped and laughed without a care. One was brushing her dark hair, another buckled a sandal on delicate, spotlessly clean feet. Their voices tinkled like bells.

Berk shouted from beneath me. "Well, what do you see?"

I grimaced, knowing I wasn't the only one who heard that braying voice. Conversation stopped in the room and a pretty dark-haired girl directly across the room from me gasped. A delicate hand with brightly painted fingernails covered beautiful glossy red lips. I could feel them all looking at me. I offered as innocent a smile as circumstances allowed.

"Good evening ladies."

My view of the angels was immediately blocked by a wall of rich blue cloth. I craned my neck up to see another woman; older, rounder, harder looking, although still richly dressed and beautiful. She had golden hoops in her ears and carefully painted black circles around slightly wrinkled eyes. Her crimson slash of a mouth curled up in an unexpectedly warm smile.

"Well, hello. We aren't open yet, if you're looking to conduct business," she said in perfect French. I felt my cheeks burn as the women all laughed. I would have slunk back, but I was too far in. My head and upper body were hanging over the sill in the room, and my feet kicked helplessly in the air over the alley.

I gave her my best innocent street urchin smile, the one that often got me out of trouble with the matrons in the market place. I replied in the same language, "My mistake then, Madame. Maybe I'll come back later, when you're open." Another round of laughter led me to believe I'd earned my escape. I risked a look back, hoping to see my human ladder waiting for me. The alley below was empty except for the abandoned crate, too far below to offer salvation. The Lice had deserted me.

The older lady showed even more teeth and offered her hand. I took it, gratefully, as the stone was starting to press uncomfortably into my middle. She braced herself and pulled me into the room. Another wave of laughter washed over me as I fell in an undignified heap at her feet. I stood up as quickly as I could, dusting myself off.

"I'm sorry, I….." I was, for once, at a loss for anything clever to say. I didn't think it would matter, though, because the woman reached out and stroked my hair kindly.

"It's quite all right little one. You're not the first young man to let curiosity get the best of him…." Her voice was warm and soft as her hand tousled my hair. It felt marvelous and I relaxed just long enough for her to find my ear and twist it brutally.

"Owww," I let out a yell and fell to my knees. The old hag twisted even harder and the women's laughter struck me like stones.

"Maybe we should keep him," one woman honked.

"I've got a couple of customers that would prefer him to me. Give him to them, we could make a fortune," someone else offered, and another round of harsh laughter filled the room.

From my knees, I could see the women who moments ago seemed so angelic, now laughing like demons. The older woman, who I presumed was the Chatelaine, clamped onto my ear and was more likely to tear it off than let go any time soon. My eyes filled with tears of pain and shame.

"Out with you, you little maggot. You're lucky I don't send you out the way you came in." She pulled me out of the room, down a narrow hallway past other open doorways. Through beaded curtains, I saw angry, shrieking women of all sizes and shapes. Then I was hauled ear-first down a steep set of stairs to the front door. There we were met by a hulking Armenian with scars all over his face and shoulders.

The monster looked surprised to see a male, even one so young, in the grasp of his employer. "Mistress, I saw no one come in…." His sputtered apology was cut off by the wave of a bejeweled hand.

"Save it. The little bastard came in through the window. Just get rid of him. Turn him over to the Watch, then get back here. It's almost opening time." She spun me by my throbbing ear into the fur-covered arms of the doorman. As I was propelled out the door, I heard her shout, "And next time you come you'd better have a stack of coins taller than that thing between your legs."

The Armenian lifted me by the back of my tunic so my

11

bare feet hardly touched the ground and the cloth cut into my throat, making it hard to breathe. "You're lucky I don't kill you, boy."

"I'm lucky SHE didn't kill me," I responded. He laughed, gave me a crooked, three-toothed smile and lowered me enough so I could catch my breath.

At last he found a patrolling city guard and turned me over. With a wink and nothing more said, the furry ogre lurched back to work. The guardsman pushed, kicked and swatted me all the way back to the orphanage.

It was worth it, though. I could swear that on my way through the corridor, one of the women had neglected to cover her chest as I was dragged past. I'd seen a woman without clothes on. Confession would be a small price to pay.

Chapter 2

I knew the routine by heart. They'd drag me in to see the priest, probably ancient Father Dominic. He'd stay awake long enough to hear my confession—or at least the most entertaining parts of it—and try not to laugh. Then I'd brew up some tears, act contrite, promise to say Hail Marys that would go mostly unsaid, and be out with my friends before the old man woke up.

I wasn't much concerned for either my health or my soul. As transgressions went, this was somewhere between throwing a rotten orange at a beggar—a minor offense—and theft of the orange in the first place, stealing being a greater sin than simply being a terrible person.

This time would be different, though. I could see it in Gilbert's face when he came to get me. Gilbert was another orphan, a year or so older than I, and an enthusiastic acolyte. A tall Frankish boy, he was blond and almost pretty, thus the target of a lot of teasing. He actually enjoyed helping the priests and wearing the bright white robes. He could have it. Still, he was a good audience, and usually gave me a heads up on what to expect on any given day.

Under normal circumstances the Watch turned me over to whichever monk was on duty at the door of the Hospital Charter House. From there, depending on the time of day and the seriousness of the offense, I'd be escorted to the priest on duty to make my confession. There might be a minor licking or a few smacks on the side of the head on the way to the chapel.

Sometimes, that was a long walk. The Charter house was huge. It contained the administrative headquarters of the Order of the Hospital and St. John, as well as military barracks and the actual hospital itself. You could take quite a licking by the time you got where you were going.

Today, though, something was different. I could see it on Gilbert's face when he came to get me. He looked distracted as he led me towards a room in back of the sacristy, rather than the chapel itself.

"Where are we going?" I asked.

Gilbert looked straight ahead and his voice was strangely flat. "You're to see Brother Idoneus before confession."

"Brother? A monk? Not even a priest?" This was unusual, and more interesting than ominous. "Who is he? And what kind of name is Idoneus?"

"It's Latin. It means 'worthy'." Gilbert loved any chance to show off the Latin he picked up since it made him smarter than us. Instead of looking smug, though, he moped along, avoiding my gaze. "He's newly arrived from Rome."

That could explain Gilbert's mood. New arrivals were always suspect, especially those who left a place like Rome. Either they'd done something wrong and were sent to Acre as a punishment, in which case they worked diligently to redeem themselves in the eyes of the Church and scurry back home, or they were here voluntarily. That was worse. Those of us born in the Kingdom of Jerusalem had no choice in the matter, and tended to live our lives as simply and trouble-free as possible. Those who came out of a sense of mission were usually rabid believers.

Their type went out of their way to turn every interaction with the locals into a chance to prove themselves to God. They were a nuisance and the source of most of the trouble with the local Saracen population. Franks, Turks, Syrians, Armenians, Copts, Maronites—the dozens of nationalities claiming Palestine all got along just fine when left to ourselves.

Most of the trouble in the Kingdom could be traced to the differences between those born in Outremer, and those on Crusade. Those knights, priests and soldiers arrived from France—Angevin or Lombardy—full of the Spirit. Led by King Guy de Lusignan, they raised as much hell with the local population as possible. Their stated goal was to kill as many Saracens as possible before returning to Gascony or Iberia or wherever, leaving the locals to clean up their mess. A new arrival trying to make points with The Almighty was not what I needed that day. Vigilance was called for.

Gilbert dragged his feet, like he was in no hurry to deliver me, while I just wanted it over with. Also, he wasn't his usual inquisitive self. As a rule, he insisted on a version of the story closer to the truth than what I'd tell the confessor. Not today, though. He was being no fun at all.

"So what's he like, this Idoneus?" If Idoneus meant worthy, that meant two things. First, he'd chosen his name himself. Secondly, he'd work extra hard to live up to it. He was probably a zealot, which didn't bode at all well.

We arrived at the oak door. Gilbert turned and grabbed my shoulders. He was half a head taller, and he leaned down to whisper in my ear. "Look, don't spend any more time with him than you have to. And for God's sake, don't get him angry at you. Just be polite and get out. Okay?" He was paler than his acolyte's robes as he turned, without waiting for an answer, and left me standing there. He never looked back, and left a whole lot faster than he brought me.

My vast experience in getting into trouble taught me that worrying was always worse than facing punishment, so I knocked three times loudly on the door. A surprisingly friendly voice boomed, "Come in."

I lifted the iron hasp on the door. It creaked as I stepped inside with a little swagger. Best to let the good brother know what he was in for. Whatever I expected Brother Idoneus to be, though, this wasn't it.

The monk sat behind a desk made of planks. There were papers there, perfectly piled as if they were purely decorative. The man himself was equally perfect, at least on first impression. Brother Idoneus was tall, well over six feet, but slim. Most knights were huge across the shoulders and neck, the result of wearing heavy armor and swinging a solid chunk of metal at Saracen skulls. Instead, while obviously strong, he was built like a taut bowstring, rather than a club. His head was almost completely bald. His hair formed a natural tonsure halfway down his shiny scalp. His skull was completely egg-shaped, coming to a shiny point at the top. He looked like no warrior monk I'd ever seen.

But he was a Hospitaller, to be sure. Rather than the robes most warriors wore when not on duty, he was in full uniform even in the brutal heat and humidity of summer in Acre. His sword was hooked on the back of his chair, casually and slightly against regulations. Under his cape, which had to be incredibly uncomfortable, was a perfectly white, starched tunic with the black multi-pointed Hospitaller Cross emblazoned across the front.

He rose and I froze in my place. Good God he was big. At least he was smiling, which was a relief. "Ah, you would be Lucca. Where's Gilbert?" He looked around me for my guide, but to no avail.

"He, uh, left. He had something else to do…. Sir." I had no idea what his actual rank was, but it was always wisest to start as high as possible and be found guilty of flattery than to guess wrong and accused of disrespect.

His smiled and that grin was as perfect as the rest of him. He had all his teeth, and they were white as his tunic and glinted in the sunlight like his head. He showed every one of those choppers as he waved to the soft divan in front of the desk. "Please, Lucca, have a seat." He sat crossing his legs under him Outremer-style.

I walked over slowly and with a little less swagger than earlier, waiting for the trap to spring. Patiently, he patted the cushions and waited. I sat down on the far end, folded my hands meekly and waited for hell to break loose. Instead, he shook his head and chuckled.

"You are something of a legend around here, Monsieur Nemo."

I tried not to show how much that pleased me. It was always best to find out where the conversation was going before committing yourself. Otherwise you were likely to say something to get you into even deeper trouble.

"Nothing to say? The way I hear it, you're quite the storyteller." He studied my face for a moment. "Well, there's time for that. I wanted to meet you in person. This seemed as good a time as any."

"You did?" I didn't mean to speak, but I couldn't help myself. His smile widened.

"Indeed. I'm taking over some of Brother Francis' duties at the Orphanage. One of my main interests is the fate of the boys in our care. I served a similar function in Rome, with the boys. How old are you, Lucca?"

"They tell me I'm ten. Brother." Where was this going?

He nodded. "Ten? You're small for your age. That's rather a problem. You see, we have to make some decisions about your future." He leaned back on the cushions, looking me up and down appraisingly and biting his bottom lip, as if those decisions were imminent.

Truthfully, at ten you don't think about your future much, except that you're reasonably sure you have one. As a nameless orphan, even that was debatable. I knew what fate didn't have in store; I'd never be a knight, never own property, and certainly never marry a woman of good station. As to what did lay before me, I hadn't give it much thought at all.

Most of the orphans wound up either serving as the lowest level foot soldiers, or sold to tradesmen as apprentices. A few, like Gilbert, were bound for the priesthood, or at least church life in one of the clerical orders.

"I don't suppose you've given any thought to serving the Church?" He asked seriously. My mouth hung open and Idoneus barely finished the sentence before he laughed at the idea himself. "No, I rather thought not. Although it's not a bad life. Young Gilbert, there, seems to enjoy it." I'd just been with Gilbert. He hardly seemed ecstatic. The friendly monk rattled on, "But no, I suspect that's not for you. So, something else then."

I wondered what he was thinking. If not the priesthood, that left either the military or being shackled to some miserable tinker or tanner who could afford the few pennies the Church would demand for taking me off its hands. Would they really kick me out of the House? It never occurred to me that this would be the stunt that finally pushed me out the door. Suddenly, I was now paying very close attention to Brother Idoneus.

He laid a clean, surprisingly strong hand on my shoulder. "Relax, my friend. We're not deciding anything today, we're just talking." Up close, his eyes were a little red, and hint of stale wine accompanied his words. *So drink was his weakness? That might explain a few things.*

I relaxed a little. At least I wasn't going to be sent away today. "What do you think of a career in arms, Lucca?"

Like any boy, especially those raised in a military city, I had my share of warrior fantasies. Boys played at smiting Mamelukes, defending the helpless, or saving women and children from bandits to their eternal gratitude and our own glory. I also had enough experience with real soldiers to be skeptical. Men of my station usually wound up with a shovel in their hands, the only question was would we be mucking stalls or digging latrines. Horses or men, shit was shit. With my fear of horses—the huge, nasty, smelly creatures—well I'd gladly take latrine duty. Those who didn't wind up digging found themselves in the front lines with a warped spear, a second hand sword and little chance of a proper burial. No, the military wasn't for me. Not if I had a choice in the matter, at least. Whether I had that choice seemed open to debate.

I never got the chance to answer. Brother Idoneus gave my slim shoulder a friendly squeeze and left his hand there. "I'm guessing not. You weren't blessed with a soldier's size and strength were you?" I hated to be reminded how small I was for my age, but facts were facts. If it kept me out of the way of a Turkish sword, maybe it was more of a gift than I cared to admit.

"Which leaves us with finding a trade for you. You know, part of my job is to match young men with masters who will train them for honest work. What trade might you be interested in, Lucca?" He turned fully towards me now, his hand still on my shoulder, but his face kind and inquisitive, like he really wanted to hear my answer.

I sought desperately for a response that would make him happy. Certain trades were obviously out, either because of my size—like blacksmith—or the amount of sweat and filth involved, like tanning. My stomach lurched at the notion of spending the rest of my life reeking, pouring piss onto animal skins and dodging flies.

"I don't know, Brother. I guess whatever you think best." His red eyes crinkled at the corners, which comforted me a little. He wouldn't choose anything too horrible. He seemed to like me, which was an unusual situation in which to find myself in those days. He also seemed to actually care, which was even more extraordinary. I allowed myself to relax.

"Give it some prayerful consideration, Lucca. Let me know where you think God is leading you. I would love to find the right situation for you, of course. But you know, it's also important that we're fair to the tradesmen. They're looking for good men who will be obedient and help them make a profit. It wouldn't do to make a bad match between apprentice and master, would it?"

There was an awkward pause, until I realized I was supposed to respond in some way. I offered a sullen, "no, Brother. I guess not." This must have been the right answer, because it earned me another shoulder squeeze. I shrugged uncomfortably but couldn't shake his hand off.

"Good lad. Okay, so next time we talk, we'll discuss your future some more. Now, then, about today's little escapade…"

Here it was. How much trouble was I in? At least he used the word "escapade". That was the kind of word grown-ups used when discussing something amusing and not too serious. I could get to like this Brother Idoneus, except for the wine on his breath. I shifted a bit and his hand dropped from my shoulder to my upper arm. His hands were sweaty. Neither of us spoke for a moment. Finally, I pulled away so we weren't touching and turned toward him.

With a sad shake of his head, he asked, "Lucca, why did you do it?" I did what any clever ten-year-old in that situation would do. I shrugged and said nothing. I was staring sullenly at the floor when he took a finger, put it under my chin and turned my head up towards him. His red-veined, wet eyes pinned me to the cushion.

"This is a serious matter, and I need you to be honest with me. Can you do that?" I nodded, not sure I could, but it was the correct answer. Brother Idoneus pursed his lips thoughtfully. "It's perfectly natural to be curious about women. It's not like we see a lot of them around here, do we?"

I couldn't argue with that, and he didn't seem to be angry. Maybe if he found this amusing enough I'd be able to skip confession. I felt a conspiratorial smile spread across my face. "No, Brother."

My relief was short-lived. The monk was talking in my direction but over my head, looking into nothing. "But that doesn't mean you can sneak around like a thief. Nor does it mean you can just indulge your curiosity any time you want. You can't simply give in to your desires. That's a terrible sin." His hand found my arm again. I wanted to pull away, but wasn't sure how he'd take that so I let it rest there.

"Young men get... feelings.... around women. Do you know what I mean Lucca?"

The wine vapors on his breath were becoming oppressive, and I avoided his gaze, stalling for time. I looked at the wall behind his desk." Not really."

Of course I knew what he meant. Every boy knew those

feelings. Sometimes it happened unbidden, for no reason at all. Other times a sudden flushing and swelling accompanied a glimpse of a woman in the market, or when you first woke up in the morning, or when a sudden breeze moved your tunic the wrong way across your stomach. It didn't take much. But I really did not want to discuss it with this old stranger.

Brother Idoneus seemed oblivious to my discomfort. His voice deepened, drawing me into intimate conversation. "But those feelings often lead men to temptation, and to sin. We must be vigilant against them." I said nothing. Father Dominic had given me this same lecture, although through the confessional screen. He hadn't been sitting so closely. I squirmed a few inches further away, but the hand tightened slightly on my arm.

"When you saw those whores... did you get those feelings?" His bleary eyes wouldn't release me, no matter which way I turned. I felt them burning into my skin. He must have thought I was wiggling out of embarrassment at the question, because he gripped tighter and leaned in as if sharing a secret. "It's natural if you did."

The truth is, while I had those feelings occasionally, in fact almost constantly, I didn't experience them at that time. When we hatched the plan to spy on the women, it was more out of a desire for adventure than genuine curiosity about the female form. The women were just a convenient target. Certainly once I got to the window, there was no time to indulge any thoughts beyond shock at actually succeeding, then having my ear nearly ripped from my head. Even the sight of the half-naked woman in the hallway didn't elicit any of *those* feelings.

The grip on my arm tightened. "Don't lie to me, boy." Brother Idoneus' voice changed. It was deeper and raspier. "I know you had those feelings. What did you think would happen in there? Were you going to indulge those sinful desires?"

"No, Brother. Really…" I tried to wriggle away, but his hand had a vise grip on my sleeve and he tugged sharply, pulling me closer.

"I told you not to lie to me, you little bastard. We can't be friends if you won't tell me the truth. Sit still, blast you."

His voice and face had transformed. The friendly Brother I was chatting with moments ago was now sweaty and red-faced. "I know they tempted you. It's what they do, women like that. Make you think horrible…. sinful…. thoughts."

I wanted to get away as quickly as possible. Instead, I sat pinned to the cushion by my arm and those eyes. I felt myself shaking and I desperately needed to pee. Brother Idoneus was oblivious, though. He kept up the interrogation, not waiting for answers, nor really directing the questions at me.

"What did you think you'd do… stick your little prick inside them? Is that what you thought?"

God in Heaven, no. That idea hadn't even occurred to me. I desperately wanted to tell him that, but could only shake my head. This only increased his anger.

"Yes you did, you filthy little liar. You wanted to shove yourself inside them and indulge yourself, didn't you? And with what—this?" Like a striking snake, his hand left my arm and fumbled between my legs, through my tunic. He squeezed me and I struggled to pull away. "You think you're man enough yet to take a woman's most precious possession?"

I heard myself cry out. A callused hand covered my mouth, pushing me back against the cushions. His face loomed over me, that voice hissing through clenched teeth. A spray of spit landed on my forehead. "You think I don't know what kind of sick, perverted thoughts you have? You are far too young for ideas like that. You don't even have the right equipment. This... now this is a man's prick."

I screamed even louder into his smothering palm as his other hand grabbed my wrist and pulled it against him through his tunic. I felt something hot and hard. I knew exactly what it was and wrenched my hand away, but he held me tight. "That's right, that's a man's cock. You like the feel of it don't you. So much better than touching your own pathetic little...."

His hand slipped on my slobbering mouth, and I found myself able to move my jaw. First, I tried again to shout, but couldn't. Then I did the only thing I could think of. I clamped my teeth down on the soft flesh at the base of his thumb. I bit him. Hard.

Brother Idoneus pulled back, giving me just enough room to slip to the floor and scramble away. Desperately, I sought the door, but felt him grab the back of my tunic and yank me backwards. I spun towards the desk, and slammed into it. The hard planks pushed against my stomach, my face rubbing against some of the papers. I felt him looming over me. His hot rancid breath scalded my ears and neck as I disappeared into his shadow.

His arm pressed across the back of my neck, pinioning me to the rough table top. "Do you think you're the first sinful little street rat I've had to tame? There are so many like you. Oblivious to how your sins put your soul at risk. But you don't know what you're doing… what it leads to…" I felt him shift behind me, but could see nothing but the papers and splintered wood.

The voice became a mumble, as if he weren't really addressing me. "You think you're man enough to take a whore? You think she wants you shoving yourself inside her? What kind of woman would endure that? And you'd gladly inflict it on her, wouldn't you? How would you like it?" His arm pressed even harder into my neck and I heard the rustle of clothing behind me.

I squirmed and cried. "No, Brother, please…. I…." Another jerk of his arm choked the cry from my throat. I gagged, gasping for some measure of relief, but he didn't seem to notice. The huge monk just kept ranting, quieter now, as though directing it at himself.

"You think you'd like it? Maybe if you knew how it felt you wouldn't be so eager to do it to some innocent woman… some poor little girl…" I felt the back of my tunic being lifted and hot, wine-soured breath on my neck.

I thrashed wildly, kicking, flailing without any control or real hope of success. I was blinded by tears of shame and anger. I couldn't get away, and his words kept bludgeoning me. "I'll show you…. You won't be in such a hurry to…" I couldn't really hear what he was saying. The blood pounded in my ears. Snot and tears dripped onto the tabletop as I felt him press against me. I felt cold air as he exposed my flesh and the weight of his body against me.

With a last, desperate, cry I pushed back hard, allowing me the few inches I needed to squirm away. Ducking low, I felt his fist whistle past my head as I lunged for the door.

My luck wasn't that good, though. I was flung backwards, slamming into the table, knocking the wind from my lungs. Those neat stacks of paper flew everywhere. Grabbing onto the desk to catch my balance, I felt something else. My hand brushed the cold metal of a candlestick.

The heavy pewter was in my hand and I swung blindly with what little strength I had. I heard a crunch and felt my arm shiver with the force of the blow as I caught my attacker in the forehead. Idoneus pulled back, clutching at his forehead.

Blood trickled from his forehead and he dropped to one knee. "You little bastard. Look what you've…" but he never got a chance to finish his curse. With both hands I swung again, catching him over the right eye. He crumpled to the ground, and I swung downwards once more with all the strength I possessed. This time there was a spray of blood against the white walls and for the first time in my life, I heard the sickening crunch of metal against bone.

The monk fell to the floor with a single fading groan. A ragged bloody seam ran across half his face from eyebrow to lips. Blood gushed into a pool beside him. A single white tooth lay in the growing puddle on the floor. I dropped the candlestick and wretched loudly.

Brother Idoneus didn't move. Thick crimson liquid bubbled in his mouth. The only sound in the room was my own desperate panting. A voice inside my head screamed *move you idiot. Now.* Somehow I obeyed the command.

I flung the door open, only to see Gilbert standing there, silent and pale as a ghost. "Lucca, what have you done?" I looked down at my tunic spattered in blood. My mouth flapped up and down, but nothing came out.

Gilbert came to his senses first. Grabbing my arm he pulled me back inside. "They're all on their way down for Vespers. You can't go out there. He looked down at the man on the ground, then at me. He took a deep breath. "You need to get out of here."

My friend pointed to the window. "Quick. Hurry, before someone sees you." He bent and cupped his hands low. Taking the hint, I put my bare foot into the stirrup and he lifted me to the windowsill. I looked outside. It was the only possible escape.

I turned to thank him. "Gilbert, I..." but he had already turned his back. He stood over the monk's body for a moment, gave it a pathetic, feeble kick, and walked out.

There was no time to think. I threw open the shutters and climbed over the window ledge and dropped a few feet. My legs started pumping before my bare feet hit the dusty ground. I ran as quickly as I could, with no idea of where I was heading. It didn't matter how fast I was, I'd never outrun the truth.

I'd killed a Brother of the Hospital.

Chapter 3

I ran up the alley away from the Hospital as fast as I could. I couldn't see for the tears and snot and muddy dust in my eyes, but knew every twisty lane and street by memory. My legs pumped and pumped, my bare feet slapping the packed dust and stones until a stabbing pain in my side forced me to a sniffling, whining halt.

I paused, panting, to take my bearings, I knew I couldn't be too far from the Damascus gate; nearly as far from the port and the Hospitaller headquarters as I could be and still inside Acre's walls. The deep lowing of oxen and the angry braying of an ass confirmed I was near the carter's district, where caravans coming into the city paid their taxes, then unloaded onto smaller carts to disperse their loads for delivery to the port and throughout the city.

The sun was almost touching the sea now, and the low walls of an animal holding pen offered the perfect dark spot for me to sink to the ground, hug my knees, rock silently, and consider what to do next.

I'd killed a Hospitaller monk, as mortal a sin as was ever invented. I always knew I was never a *good* boy, but I wasn't bad. Now I was a murderer. Not only would I go to Hell—something I'd never taken seriously before—but I'd never be able to return to the Brothers. The smart thing to do would be to leave the city forever, get as far away as possible—maybe to Antioch or even Jerusalem. But to a boy who'd never known anything other than the streets of this one city his whole life, the world outside the gate held terrors both real and imagined.

Even though the kingdom was intact and all appeared well, Salah-adin's troops were rumored to be everywhere all at once, and poised to attack at any time. Children were put to bed with threats of being fed to him if they didn't behave. The mood outside the walls was reported to be ugly; the local Turkish and Syrian farmers were to be trusted less than ever. Rumor had it they'd as soon sell you to slavers or simply kill you to appease the Butcher of Damascus and save their own hides. At least that's what the priests at the Hospital told us.

Bad as it normally was, that was before the zealous idiot Reynauld de Chatillon took to attacking caravans in spite of an informal truce. No Christian was safe outside those walls alone, and I was as alone as anyone could ever be.

But I wasn't really alone. Even though most of the business for the day was done, the corrals were busy with carters feeding their stock and settling things down after a long day. A whirlwind of Arabic, Turk, Armenian and French—mostly curse words and threats—swirled around me. Besides the human chaos, animals of every description paced back and forth in the dust. Once-white sheep with matted clumps of filth in their wool took panicked steps one way then the other in a futile bid for escape. Camels bellowed their frustrated "haw-wonk" at anyone nearby. Everything was mud and dung and chaos. Just another day in Acre.

I looked down at my tunic. It was a filthy, coarse thing, camel brown and splattered with crusty brown streaks of Brother Idoneus' blood. It was all I had in this world. I had two shirts back... back where I could never go again. My only sandals were also tucked beneath my cot, for all the good that did me. Wherever I was going, I wouldn't get far bare footed and covered in a man's blood.

Just then, a familiar voice overcame the chaos. "You whoresons better not leave this cart here. You think I have so many I can afford to have one stolen?" It was the voice of Firan, Fadhil's father. Normally, I avoided him whenever possible. While he'd never done anything to me but glare, I knew how swift and inescapable his wrath could be. Still, I was happy to hear his voice. It meant Fadhil wasn't far away.

Sure enough, a moment later I saw my friend trailing his father, head down and three steps behind like a frightened, mute duckling. The two of them stopped about a hundred feet from me, at the western edge of the enclosure. Firan faced the pen and away from my hiding spot, sending arrow flights of colorful, perverse threats in every direction.

I silently prayed my friend would turn around, but he stood watching his father abuse someone other than himself for a change. I had to get Fadhil's attention so I picked up a small white stone and hurled it sidearm. Normally I was a good aim, but this time I was too good. The stone hit him in the middle of the back. This elicited a sharp "unngh."

Firan turned around and snapped at him. "Shut up, or I'll give you something to complain about." This, at least, made Fadhil turn away and finally saw me waving frantically. He checked that his father was fully occupied and skittered over. "Lucca, what are you doing here?"

"I … I ran away…" was all I could spit out.

"Your clothes… is that blood? Are you hurt?" He was always the mother hen of our pack, which made him the perfect person to help. Or as close to perfect as I was likely to find.

"I'm fine, but I'm in trouble. I need some clean clothes and a place to hide." Of all my friends, Fadhil was the only one close to my size. If it was Berk or Murad, I'd be wearing a small tent.

"Can't you go back to the Hospital? Lucca, what did you do this time?"

My parched mouth couldn't form an answer. How would I tell him? I could never tell anyone. Ever. "I can't…. but it's bad."

Fadhil did what he always did when faced with the need for immediate action—absolutely nothing. He just stared down at his feet.

I grabbed him by the front of his tunic and shook him gently a couple of times. "Fadhil, I need clean clothes… and a place to sleep. I need …" *What did I need?* "Help…please." Maybe he understood what I was trying to say, or I really looked as tired and frightened as I felt, but finally he nodded.

"Okay. Yes…" He looked around to make sure his father couldn't see. My friend bit his lip, looked upward for a moment, as though seeking an answer written in the dark sky but couldn't find it, and heaved a sigh. "I'll get you some clothes. There's a place you can hide. I go there sometimes when.... When I have to." I knew what he meant.

In the farthest corner of the loading area were stacks of damaged, abandoned crates. We'd played among them, pretending that the cheap splintered timber was the fortress wall of Kerak and someone else—usually poor Berk—was the enemy to be tormented and abused from behind the barrier. I knew, too, that from time to time Fadhil slipped behind them, finding a dark space to crawl into until the storm of Firan's rage blew over.

"Good idea," I patted his shoulder. "But no one can know, all right?" It wasn't the first time one of us had hidden from adults. He probably thought I was trying to avoid punishment for today's fiasco, and I wasn't going to tell him different. Hiding a friend from a good whipping was just a normal part of childhood. Sheltering a murderer was something altogether different.

He nodded solemnly, then trotted off to catch up with his father, falling in behind as if he'd been there all along. He may have turned to look for me, but I was already padding around the enclosure to my new hideout as fast as I could go.

I still had to pick a nest out of the jumble of crates. The secret to a good hideout is not just finding a place one can't be seen. You also have to have a means of escape if you're spotted. Every child remembers finding the perfect dark spot to hide, only to be trapped and at the mercy of the seeking grownup when we are inevitably discovered. I knew I could crawl deep inside one of the crates and curl up for the night, but there'd be no way out.

There was also the matter of rats. Vermin was a natural part of any city. Add in the port and open sewers everywhere, and you seldom found a dark corner you weren't sharing with something brown, furry and bad-tempered. You didn't want to startle one and get bitten for your efforts. Poking around, I looked for an uninhabited cranny.

I finally settled on a small opening at the rear of the pile. It wasn't as comfortable as being inside a box, but I could see through the wood around me, and the way the stack of boxes shook when I moved told me the heavy crates could become their own means of defense if I chose to bring them toppling down on a pursuer.

The tears, dirt and snot had long since caked dry on my face. I scratched at it, trying to clean up a bit. That offered a few precious moments to think clearly for the first time. I could certainly spend the night here, but what then? Acre was a huge city, the second largest city in the Kingdom with over twenty-five thousand souls living within its walls. I could easily hide for a day or two, although how I'd eat or what I'd do after that I couldn't imagine. Now that I had stopped running, my growling stomach insisted I'd better address that problem sooner rather than later.

The first order of business, though, was to get through the night without being caught, or there'd be no tomorrows with which to concern myself. I settled in the comforting blanket of darkness between two of the more rickety crates on the pile. The gaps offered me a view—at least a partial one—in every direction.

Soon it was fully dark. I heard City Guardsmen close the

gates for the evening with clanking metal and groaning oak, accompanied by shouts of "Watch your feet, you idiot," and "that'll hold the buggers at bay for another day." The animals began to settle down as well. The tired snorts, whinnies and moans of the livestock became less frequent.

People passed by, but no one was close enough to worry me. I felt, rather than saw or heard, someone pass directly behind my nest, and spun my head in time to catch a glimpse of a long, grey robe as it swept out of sight. Otherwise I sat, hugging my knees, alone with my thoughts. That was a mixed blessing.

I was focused on what to do in the morning, rather than the insistent rumble in my stomach, so I didn't realize Fadhil had returned until I heard him whispering sibilantly in the dark, "Lucca... Lucca... where are you?"

He stood right in front of my hidey hole without seeing me, so I took a little pleasure in leaning close to his ear before I answered. "Where'd you learn to whisper, in a blacksmith's shop? You're the loudest kid I know."

I was rewarded with a little squeak of fear. "That's not nice, you scared me. Hurry, I think my father saw me leave..." He handed me a soft brown bundle. I recognized one of his tunics.

"There aren't any shoes," I said. It sounded far less grateful than it should have.

"Do you think we just have spare sandals laying around? Oh, and I got you this..." He held out a small crust of bread, with little pinch-marks where he'd thoughtfully picked off the mold.

I think I took the time to thank him before sinking my teeth into the brittle crust, cutting my gums a bit but not caring. After the second bite, I wish he'd also thought to bring some water with him. There was no time for a third bite, though.

"What are you doing you little thief? Think you could steal the bread from your family's table and no one would notice?" That shout and a quick "smack" of a palm against my friend's head announced Firan's arrival. In the walk from his house to here he'd built up a full-fledged rage. He practically breathed fire.

A gigantic fist grabbed the neck of my tunic and pulled me out of my hole. Splinters stuck into my bare legs as I fell in a rumpled pile at his feet. "Well," he bellowed, "What is it this time? What kind of trouble are you getting my worthless son into? Huh?" He stopped in mid shout when he got a look at the state of my clothing.

He squinted and for a moment lowered his voice to a mere growl. "What in God's name have you done, lad? Are you hurt?"

"No sir, it's... not mine. And Fadhil was only loaning me that shirt until I get back to the Charter House to change. In fact, they're expecting me...."

The furious carter waved a sausage of a finger in my face. "No lies, you lousy little.... louse, you. What devilment have you been up to? I thought you'd be at least a grown man before you graduated to cutting throats." He swung his palm at my head, but I was faster and shorter than he thought and his hand struck one of the crates. That did nothing to endear me to him.

"I'm going to take you down there myself, and we'll just see. Whatever it is, you're not dragging my boy into it…." He lunged, making a grab for me, but I ducked low and to the left. I stepped backwards slowly, trying to reason with him, and having as much luck as arguing theology with a charging ram.

"I'm going… right now. Back to the Hospital, that is. Fadhil had nothing to do with it, really." Keeping my eyes on Firan's face, I took another step towards safety, backing directly into someone standing there. I twisted over my shoulder to see the beggar from the alley.

He wore the same filthy grey robe and the glove on one hand as the last time I saw him. He stood taller though, so much taller than I'd first thought. He clamped the ungloved hand on my shoulder so I couldn't run. I stared up at him, but his eyes weren't on me. Those piercing ice-colored orbs were locked firmly on Firan.

"Is there a problem I can help with?" His Syrian was as good as his French.

Firan let out a bull-snort of a laugh. "Not from the looks of you, there isn't. I'm taking this little rat back to the hole he climbed out of, so he can get what's coming to him."

The beggar, if that's what he was because I had my doubts, looked down at me. "Do you wish to go home?" I just shook my head, daring to say nothing at all. "Then I guess you're not taking him there, sir."

Fadhil blanched. No one called someone like his father, "sir," except in jest, and Firan hated being the object of a joke. This was going from bad to worse. If the stranger was trying to help, he was doing a terrible job of it. I tried to squirm away before I got someone else killed, but his hand tightened on my shoulder and I relented.

Firan's fists clenched in anticipation of fighting someone a more appropriate size than his runt of a son. "What are you going to do about it… sir?"

"I'm going to take the boy, is what I'm going to do. How about yourself?" He spun me around to face him. "Seems you should have a say in this. Do you want to go with him or me?" The man raised one eyebrow playfully, like this was all some kind of game. Of course, if I had to choose between Firan and anyone—even this man I didn't know—with a sense of humor, it was an easy choice to make.

"With…you?" it came out as more of a question than an answer, but the stranger seemed satisfied with it. Firan was much less so, but said nothing.

"There you go. It's settled then. Lucca will come with me, and you and your son will return home, with his apologies for any trouble he's caused. Isn't that right?" The question was punctuated by another overly firm squeeze of my arm.

I was an old hand at playing along with adults, even when I had no idea what they were up to. "Yes, sir. Very sorry." I nodded excessively and hoped I looked sufficiently contrite.

The tall beggar patted my arm. "Good lad. Now, return the man's property to him." His gaze indicated the clothes Fadhil brought me. "Don't worry, we'll get you a clean shirt." For the life of me, I couldn't imagine where he'd get me clean clothes, given his own attire. Nor could I imagine who "we" were. Still, I meekly handed the wadded up tunic to my friend who took it wordlessly before backing away in silence beside his father.

"There now, you see? All a misunderstanding, and everything's all right." That last sentence was said with his pale, cold eyes drilling holes into the other man, daring him to argue. After an interminable pause, Firan nodded.

"I don't really care what happens to the little bastard, just keep him away from my boy." Firan aimed his finger at me. I didn't have many friends, and the thought of losing Fadhil, and probably Murad and Berk since they were inseparable, stung. Still, I didn't have much choice and nodded my agreement. My eyes burned, watery and red as the carter put his arm possessively around his son's shoulders and they turned for home. I feared for my friend, but could do nothing.

"Come on, lad. Let's go get you some clean clothes and something to eat." I turned to my rescuer. He wore a beggar's rags, but there was something entirely different beneath that obvious disguise, although for the life of me I couldn't figure out what it was. His hand hadn't left my arm, and a sudden cold shiver went through me as I remembered Brother Idoneus touching me in much the same way.

I shrugged my shoulder away, glaring defiantly. He raised his hands in surrender. "All right, fine, but you're still coming with me. Yes?" I offered a sullen nod and without another word, we walked into the street.

After several blocks of silently struggling to keep up with his long strides, the man came to a halt in front of a door which led down into a cellar. He bent down to lift the door and gestured me inside. It was pitch black and smelled of old vegetables and dirt.

Panic and confusion must have been written across my face. He knelt down so his face was level with mine. "I'm not going to hurt you, boy. No one is going to hurt you."

I wanted to believe him. "I don't even know who you are."

He nodded. "Fair enough. You can call me Brother Marco." Another monk, but not like any I'd seen outside the Hospital or the Temple. He had a Hospitaller's bearing but none of the trappings. And as kind as he seemed, there was nothing at all appealing about that dank hole in the ground.

"Look…. I'm offering you a clean shirt and a hot meal and a bed. If you want it, it's down there." He pushed past me down into the cellar, then turned back to me. "Are you coming?" I took a deep breath and followed.

The cellar was just a cellar, but ominous nonetheless. I was about to turn and run when Brother Marco gripped some wood that lay against one wall. Behind it was another low, dark tunnel leading somewhere even darker and scarier. "Pull the door shut and follow me." Heaving a sigh, I did as commanded, plunging us into total smothering darkness. "Just follow my voice, and keep your head down." I heard feet scuffling in the dirt, leading us further underground to heaven only knew where.

"It's not far, but it gives me a chance to be a little…. discreet…. about my coming and going." It was dark, and getting stuffier. Whether it was the fear or an actual lack of oxygen, each step forward took more courage than the last. "Not much further," he said about three more times before we finally stopped. I heard him knock on wood. The creak of hinges meant it was a real door and as it opened, torchlight momentarily blinded me.

The door led into a stone hallway now, obviously part of a large building. Well-carved stone steps led up to yet another door. Torches flickered smokily in iron sconces on either side of the stairwell. Marco shook the dirt from his cloak and gave me a smile. "Impressive isn't it?"

Without looking to see if I followed, he strode up the stairs and knocked twice, then twice again. The metal hasp lifted up, and the door swung inwards. He turned back. "Coming?"

I hesitated. "What is this place?"

Marco didn't look back, just passed through the door as he casually said, "It's the House of the Order of St. Lazar."

The blood rushed from my cheeks and a chill clawed up my spine. My new sanctuary was a leper hospital.

Chapter 4

Everyone knew the Order of St Lazar was a place to avoid. We took it as an article of faith that the whitewashed building in the furthest, filthiest corner of the city was no place for a Christian. We Lice occasionally slunk close enough to catch a glimpse of something wonderfully grotesque, as boys will, but even we knew better than to get too close. Simply looking on a leper could result in God striking you down. Now I was not only near, but inside the very disease-ridden bowels of the place.

Brother Marco slowly removed the grey cowl and wiped the sweat from his forehead with a filthy elbow. His hair was cut short, black with flecks of white in it, especially over the ears. Those eyes of his—cold blue—shone from sun-crinkled sockets and glinted in the flickering orange torchlight. Although streaked with dust, he had a strong face; tanned and angular, with a square chin. Certainly there were no visible signs of sickness or despair. His was a face built for command.

Feeling curiosity that overwhelmed my fear, I examined him closer. The ratty, badly mended robe was obviously a disguise, but what lay beneath it, I couldn't be sure. He offered me what was clearly intended to be an encouraging smile then a bit more softly asked, "Well, what do you see?"

My confusion was written on my face. "Go on Lucca, you must be wondering what's going on. What am I? What do you see when you look at me?"

"I don't know what you mean…. Sir." He had to be noble, so it was a safe bet he'd answer to the title.

Pursing his lips, he scowled then nodded. "Good, so I'm not just some beggar off the street. What am I, then?" I hesitated for a moment, but could see in those eyes there was no escape until I'd satisfied him. I took my time and looked closer. *Start with the obvious, Lucca.* "You're a knight, aren't you?"

An encouraging nod was all I got in response. *What else does he want?* My gaze lowered to take him all in. He gripped that thick wooden staff with the ease and confidence of a practiced warrior. It wasn't the staff of a beggar, I now saw, but a perfectly straight, polished oak quarterstaff. So far, so good. On his right hand, the kidskin glove showed from beneath a gaping sleeve and a mix of knowledge and fear rushed through my body. He was a lot of things, this Brother Marco, including a leper.

"Well, say it."

I looked away, ashamed for him and his plight. "You have… you're a…."

"A what?" The voice was calm and unoffended, but insistent.

"You were a knight. Now you're a…"

"A leper, yes that should have been obvious. What gave it away?"

I motioned in the direction of his right hand, but couldn't

find the words.

"Say it, boy. How do you know?"

"Well, you live… here." That got me an exasperated "tsk", so I offered more. "And your hand. You keep it hidden and you're never without that glove. I thought it was just injured, but now…"

Another nod. "Good, took you long enough. What else do you know about me?" *What in the name of God does he want?* I concentrated now, eager to appease him. "You were a knight before…."

"I still am, a Knight of St Lazarus." I knew what he meant. The Order of St. Lazarus was made up of knights and monks who were still committed to their vows, but whose illness didn't permit them contact with their Brothers in the houses of the Hospital and the Temple. "What order? What order of knight was I?" While he had the arrogance of a Templar, his smile and the fact he hadn't backhanded me yet, told me he wasn't one of those haughty bastards. Plus, most of the members of St. Lazar were associated with the Hospital. I offered a tentative, "Hospitaller?"

"Are you asking me, or telling me?" It was the impatient voice of the brothers who watched the boys at the orphanage. I spit out, "Hospitaller… Sir."

That earned me another curt nod. "You're a smart lad, Lucca. That's why I've been watching you." I felt my head cock to the side like it does when I'm figuring out a puzzle. *What does he mean he's been watching?* "Let's get you some supper and a bed. We'll talk again in the morning."

Without another word he turned his back to me and

walked down the hall to a rough door and opened it. Sensing my hesitation, he just nodded his head in the direction of the room, and my feet followed before I could stop them.

We were in a monk's cell, tiny but clean. It was long enough to hold a small bed and a table, but so narrow Brother Marco could have reached out and touched both side walls. A small tallow candle sat on the rough table, offering a faint, smoky alternative to total darkness. A simple wooden cross hung over the bed. No other ornamentation, no window and only one way in or out. The knight stood in that doorway now, pointing and careful to touch nothing.

"You can spend the night here. I'll have some food brought down. Whatever you're hiding from, you'll be safe enough and we'll talk again on the morrow."

I looked at the bed and wondered how many sick, scabby bodies had lain upon it. I must have been thinking very loudly, because he just said, "It's all right. That's a new blanket, and only the healthy stay down here when they…. visit. You'll be fine. Really."

Exhaustion washed over me, and suddenly I couldn't have continued standing if I'd wanted. I gratefully plunked myself on the edge of the bed. My mind buzzed with a thousand questions for this stranger, and ached to ask every single one of them, but all I could muster was a single, quiet, "Why?"

Marco slowly went to one knee, so our eyes were of a height with each other. He reached out his good hand to stroke my head, I suppose, but I jerked away and pushed well into the bed, my back against the wall and my knees pulled up to my chest. He seemed surprised at my rejection of his comfort. "It's all right, this hand isn't the problem." He couldn't know that any touch felt infectious to me after the night before. Leprosy wasn't the worst thing I'd encountered in the last day. "As I say, I've been watching you, and you'd have wound up here eventually. The good Lord's just decided the time is now. I'll send down some soup, and you get a good night's sleep. We have plenty of time to ask questions. We both have them."

With a grunt, he rose again to his feet, turned towards the door and pulled it shut behind him, leaving me alone. The "snick" of a lock, metallic, loud and ominous, was the only sound except for my own breathing. Propped against the wall, I let my head drop forward in exhaustion and despair.

I must have dozed off, because it seemed like only the next moment I heard a key in the lock, then a soft female voice asked, "May I come in?"

Taking my stunned silence for assent, a slim white hand appeared, gripped the door and pushed it open. It was a Sister, but none like I'd ever seen. She was slight as a bird, and wore the white habit of a nurse Sister, wimple covering her hair and forehead but also a veil across her face like a Muslim woman. Only the slim bridge of her nose and her wide, perfectly round brown eyes were visible. I could tell she was smiling by the way the faint lines around those eyes deepened and turned ever so slightly upwards. In her other hand was a steaming bowl of soup.

"Hello, you must be Lucca. Are you hungry?" I was, or at least more hungry than curious, because all I noticed at that moment were the large chunks of turnip and even some shreds of chicken in the yellowish broth. I nodded enthusiastically.

She offered another eye-smile and placed the soup and a small, round wooden spoon on the table next to the smoldering candle. I looked at the nun more closely. Her spotless white habit and barely-callused white hands marked her as a Sister, or at least a novice, probably of noble birth. I had never seen a Christian woman with a veil though, and it confused me until I realized why she wore it. She, too, had to be a leper or she wouldn't be in this house. Christ alone knew what horrors lurked behind that thin piece of white gauze.

If the repulsion showed on my face, it wasn't acknowledged. She simply placed the bowl onto the table and quickly stood back as far as possible. "There you go. It's quite safe, I assure you."

My cheeks burned from shame. This woman I didn't know had brought me the most delicious looking—and smelling, as the aroma filled the tiny cell—food I'd seen in a long time, and all I could think of was what ugliness lay behind that mask. I forced myself to be polite. "Thank you.... Sister."

Her eyes crinkled again. "You're most welcome. My name is Sister Marie-Pilar. Eat and get some rest, we'll talk again soon." She backed slowly out of the room, closed the door and locked it. Through the wood, I heard a soft, "Good night, Lucca. Sleep well." I couldn't remember the last time a woman had wished me goodnight, and it sounded like a lullaby from a long forgotten dream.

I waited only a moment for the fear of contagion to pass and then fell on the soup like a wild dog. The chicken was plentiful and tasty, and the broth actually had salt in it, along with firm chunks of turnips and other vegetables. It tasted like heaven and, like all visions of paradise, was gone in a flash.

I lay on my back, rubbing my uncomfortably full stomach and tried to make sense of what was going on. The enormity of that task, though, proved too much and I fell into a deep sleep, only occasionally troubled by dreams of grasping hands and grunting, bug-eyed knights.

There was no window in my tiny room, and I'd fallen so deeply into slumber that the first indication of morning was the clank-tick of a key in the lock. I sat bolt upright, pulling the blanket to me in a silly, childish attempt at protection. If what was coming through that door was the same monster that haunted my dreams the night before, that thin layer of wool would serve little purpose.

Brother Marco stood silhouetted in the doorway. His voice echoed, loud and masculine in my chamber. "Are you planning to sleep all day? Didn't you hear the bell for matins?" I hadn't, but then I often slept through the bells at the Hospital as well. I seldom made an appearance at Morning Prayer. In fact, he was the first person in quite some time to care about it. Over his bad arm, Marco had a clean tunic, the other hand held a pitcher and a bowl. "Wash up and join me. We have much to discuss."

I looked down at myself. The blood from the day before

had caked into a flaky crust, leaving crusty brown patches. I looked up, guilt written all over my dirty face. Marco's mouth turned up ever so slightly as he held out the camel-colored tunic. "It's all right, we're quite used to burning clothes around here."

Splashing cold water into the bowl, then onto my face, I managed to remove a tolerably high percentage of the dirt from my face, neck and hands. Most people would still consider me a mess, but by ten-year-old orphan standards I shone like a new gold bezant. Marco tilted my head to the right, then the left, inspecting. I must have passed muster, because he offered a soft grunt and turned, gesturing for me to follow.

We went right down the hallway two doors. A shaft of sunlight shone through the grill in a door to the left making four squares of light on the tiles. With his good hand, he pushed it open. I followed into a large courtyard, bare but for some benches that ran along the perimeter. The sun was barely high enough to crawl over Acre's city walls, let alone this building, but after the dark of the cell, it was more than welcome. I turned my brown face towards the East, gratefully accepting the faint warmth, soaking it in.

Brother Marco plopped down onto one of the benches and closed his eyes to the sun as well. He was wearing a different robe this time—a white cassock with the green cross of St. Lazarus across the front. From his sleeve, he pulled out a crust of coarse brown bread, still warm from the oven. He handed it over without a word, then re-closed his eyes and continued basking in the early morning warmth.

I muttered a quick "thank you," or at least I think I did, and bit into it. Warm bread was a rare treat, and it occurred to me that even lepers ate better than the orphans at the Hospital. Marco allowed me to eat in silence for a moment or two. Then with his eyes still closed, he spoke quietly.

"It seems we aren't the only ones who had a little adventure last night. They had quite a night over at the Hospital." I froze, a wad of bread still inside my cheek. Brother Marco didn't seem to notice or care about my reaction, he just kept talking calmly as if discussing the weather. "It seems a *hashishin* broke into the Charter House and tried to kill one of the knights... a new man named Idoneus. Do you know him?" Blue eyes had turned my way and I avoided his gaze, shaking my head none too convincingly. "Didn't think so. He's new, just arrived from Rome. Apparently someone thinks he's important, although no one that would be worth the Old Man in the Mountain taking notice. Anyway, this killer broke into an office at the House, attacked Idoneus, and fled without getting caught."

If I looked more curious than horrified at such a brazen assault on the Hopsitallers, he never noticed.

"So he's... alive?" I asked.

"Oh yes. Took a sword slash to the face. Nearly cost him an eye. They say it's a miracle he's alive, although he'll have a nasty scar to remember it by. Claims it's a sign of God's mercy and protection he survived at all, and the Saracen whoreson vanished into thin air. Have you ever heard such a thing?" I didn't look at him, but those eyes pierced my skull anyway. I gave my head a quick, unconvincing shake and tried not to choke on the oversized ball of bread that suddenly refused to go quietly down my throat.

On the third try, I succeeded in swallowing the bread. "Was there anything else? Are they looking for... anyone?"

Eyes closed serenely, Marco replied, "You mean have any of the boys been reported missing? A knight of St. John was attacked in their own Charter House. You think one little half-bred orphan is going to matter? It will be days before anyone admits they have misplaced... you."

My shoulders slumped in relief and I took another—more manageable—bite of the crust. My brain spun in dervish circles trying to make sense of everything. *Why was Brother Idoneus lying about what happened? Doesn't anyone care what happens to me?* The answer to the first question was far more of a mystery than the latter.

There was a long silence, and the longer it went, the more tempted I was to start screaming questions and confess everything that had happened. Finally, just to preserve sanity, I asked, "How did you know where to find me last night?"

Marco neither opened his eyes nor moved a muscle. He simply sat with his back against the wall like a contented lizard on a hot rock. "I didn't. I assumed you were still at the House getting your hide tanned or going to confession. Mostly likely both. I just happened to be walking by when I saw you climbing behind those crates. Then when that Syrian bully threatened you, I stepped in." He paused. "I hope you didn't get your friend in too much trouble."

I had, of course, and more than usual. Fadhil was used to being in trouble, so that would pass quickly—at least until the next time. I did feel terrible about it, though. *What else could I do? What would Marco have done in my place?"*

Instead of continuing to ask questions I couldn't answer, I asked him one. "You said you'd been watching me. Why?"

"You're smart, Lucca, even if you don't have the sense God gave a goat." That paradox made no sense at all, but I let him continue. "You notice things, and you puzzle things out. That's a rare gift. Especially among us Franks. If we thought more, most of us would still be in France or Lombardy begging our older brothers for scraps from their table instead of here dying in the desert." We'd spoken in French until now, but he suddenly switched to Arabic. "How many languages do you speak?"

I answered back, *"Thalaatha."* Three. "I speak Latin as well, because of the Brothers. A bit, anyway." It was a harmless exaggeration, but I was getting better, and I wanted to impress the knight.

"Turkic? Armenian?" Those eyes were again digging around in my head.

I shrugged. "A little. Mostly the bad words." That brought a snorting laugh.

"Cursing in a language is the quickest way to convince people you're one of them. Always start with the worst words first, especially anything scandalous about their mothers. You can't go wrong." He said this in pretty good Turkic. Back to French, he asked, "Can you read?"

I shook my head. Languages you could pick up anywhere—the market, the street, the caravanserai. To read you had to spend time in the last place I ever wanted to be;

a classroom. "Not, really. No."

Brother Marco went to pat my leg but stopped himself when he saw me flinch. He pulled his hand back and dropped it into his lap.

"How'd you like to stay here for a while? Just until we figure out what the next step is?"

Until that moment I'd managed to forget that my little haven was, in fact, the country's largest leper hospital. I didn't want to sound ungrateful, but the notion of spending a lot of time here wasn't all that reassuring, either. "Is it safe?"

"Absolutely. This is literally the last place anyone would look for a healthy young man. In fact, even if they knew you were here, no one would dare come inside...." He stopped, realizing that wasn't what I'd meant. "Yes, some of us... them... are contagious. We keep them separate from the others. Leprosy actually doesn't spread once you reach a certain point. In fact, some of the most disgusting cases are the ones you have to worry about least."

"But King Baldwin..." The poor cursed King of Jerusalem had only died a year or so before, the subject of many macabre imaginings about his disfigurement. Berk, in particular, would invent particularly graphic and imaginative narratives about what body parts were affected and which had actually fallen off.

"The King was a rare and sorry case, God rest his soul. And his leprosy was still less of a curse to him than that sister of his." He crossed himself and went on, "Most people have one infected area, then the disease passes. It rarely gets as terrible as you imagine, although it's bad enough."

While he'd been talking, my eyes darted to the kidskin glove on his left hand. I didn't realize I was staring, until I heard him ask, "Do you want to see it? I'm surprised you waited this long."

I gawked in childish fascination as he pulled the glove off with his good hand. Holding my breath anticipating the horrors to come, I was fascinated. Rather than a gnarled, scabrous stump, there was a perfectly normal hand, with coin-sized patches of white, dead-looking skin on both the back and palm. Two fingers were visibly bent and immobile. I was a little disappointed, truth be told.

"I came here to be a knight- a killer for Christ. Along the way I became a healer, too, and a good one. Then God decided I should be neither, and gave me this. Not enough to kill me, just enough to take my life away." He didn't sound grateful.

I hesitated, then heard myself ask, "What do you do now?" My curiosity was constantly putting me in awkward situations. This would have been one of them, had Marco smiled. The distant tinkling of a bell interrupted us. That meant the Chapel service was about to end and the courtyard would be filling up.

"I think we should go out for a walk tonight. What do you say?" What could I say? I nodded. "Oh, and Lucca. You must stay within the walls unless you're with me. You can stay in your room, or anywhere on the ground floor, except for the new patient ward. They're the most infectious. No one will bother you, as long as you don't make a pest of yourself. And one more thing…we don't cover up here. When we go out into the world we cover ourselves, and wear those damned bells, and shout to the world--mainly to spare the delicate constitutions of the citizenry. In here, we are who we are. We don't find ourselves disgusting, and God made us like this, let Him look upon his handiwork, if he cares. The point is, be polite. You're our guest here."

The notion of being cooped up inside all day used to be the worst thing I could imagine, but the last two days reminded me things could always be much, much worse, even when you thought you were in the safest place there was. I answered with what I hoped was a reasonable amount of enthusiasm. "Yes, Brother. Of course."

Brother Marco nodded and slipped his glove into his sleeve, not bothering to put it back on in the comfort of his own sanctuary. "Good lad. Make yourself at home, and we'll see you tonight."

Chapter 5

It was a mystery to me how someone as large as Brother Marco moved so quickly. By the time my eyes completed a quick circuit of the courtyard, watching people shuffle in from the chapel service, he was gone. I was alone on the bench with the sun pulling itself over the eastern wall and bathing me in its warm, yellow glow. I shaded my eyes and took another, more intense look around.

There were perhaps a dozen people in the courtyard, all tilting their faces up to the healing light for a few blessed minutes before the sun turned hot and cruel. Most of the attendees were men, although two women walked closely together nodding to the men but keeping their own company.

From my seat a few yards away, they appeared to be normal, healthy people, like any villager strolling the town square. Then I looked closer. Gnarled hands poked through ragged sleeves. Oddly shaped feet were wrapped in cloth bandages that took the place of sandals. One older man with his hair shaved close to his skull caught me looking and turned towards me. He was one of those with bandaged feet. His left foot dragged behind him as he turned and took three hopping steps towards me.

"You. Boy. What are you looking at?" His eyes dared me

to respond. In fact, what I was looking at was apparent. The Hospital was full of men just like him. He was of middle age, scrawny and bent, with a stubbly, scabby scalp and a wicked scar down his right cheek that showed bright white through the tan and dirt. His French was pure, so he was a Frank, but not one of high birth. The fact that he was here meant he'd been attached to one of the Orders, probably as a common soldier, before he took ill. No, the command apparent in his voice meant he'd probably been a sergeant. They were known to have the least sense of humor of anyone in the army, at least when it came to small boys who got in the way of their duties. I'd taken a sandal to the arse on more than one occasion for being an obstacle to progress.

He conducted a quick inspection, and didn't like what he found—or rather, or what he didn't find. I was obviously not suffering from the same ailment as he and the others, and his eyes squinted suspiciously. "Asked you a question, lad. What are you looking at?"

I didn't have time to formulate a good answer, so I settled for the worst possible. "N-n-nothing sir." Anyone who has ever been challenged on the street knows never to respond with what will inevitably give cause for further argument.

"Nothing? I'm nothing am I?" His hand shot out as if to slap me, and I flinched, which is exactly what he expected and wanted. His hand, covered in grey scabs and with a scabbed stump where his ring finger should be, stopped inches from my face. "What are you looking at now? Huh?"

My natural disdain for adult authority began reasserting itself. While I felt for him in his condition, at that moment he was just another bullying soldier picking on me. I smiled, showing just enough teeth to irritate him and said, "Someone in need of a bath and some manners." The calm in my voice betrayed how badly I needed to pee at that moment.

He was stunned for a second, then pulled his hand back to deliver a proper swat but was restrained by a calmer voice behind him. "Leave the lad alone, Jacques."

Sergeant Jacques seemed terribly disappointed he couldn't swat me like a fly, but thought better about dragging someone else into our discussion. His hand dropped but he kept his eyes on my face, searching for more insolence, knowing he was likely to find it. "What're you doing here, lad?"

Figuring I'd avoid creating an even worse situation, I dropped the smile and my eyes in what I hoped was a properly submissive way. "I'm…. visiting…. Sir."

He snorted. "Yes, we all came here for a…. visit…. And we liked it so much we stuck around." This brought a few laughs from the others. I looked over Sergeant Jacques' shoulder to see three or four decrepit people standing in a tight semi-circle. For a group that didn't want to be stared at, they had no reservations about gawking at me.

The man who prevented my getting a whooping stepped forward. He was Armenian, judging by the thick black pelt on his arms that ended at the back of his hands in dead, smooth, white skin. "I'm Vardan. What's your name, lad?"

I put on my most ingratiating smile and my best get-along-with-grownups voice. "Lucca. My name is Lucca… Nice to meet you." This drew another derisive snort from

Jacques, but he said nothing else.

This led to an eager flurry of introductions, as if everyone had grown tired of each other's company and craved contact with someone new, even if that someone was a mere boy. Most of the names sailed over my head, gone as soon as they were uttered, but the two women elbowed their way through and immediately took possession of me, clucking like biddy hens.

Sisters Agnes and Fleure were complete opposites but formed one chattering, overwhelming ball of womanhood. Agnes was tiny and blond, while Fleure was sturdily built and darker. Both wore simple white habits with scarves on their heads, rather than full wimples. The two of them pelted me with questions I had no time to answer and tsk'ed and cooed incessantly. At one point, Agnes lost herself in a moment of maternal instinct and reached out to stroke my hair, but retracted her scaly claw of a hand before I could react with the expected horror and aversion. I simply gave her the endearing-orphan smile that served me well.

At the moment, my love of attention, particularly from two women, overrode any sensible concern for my health. If I could sleep in a room by myself, eat like this and get fawned over, the risk of a digit or two didn't seem like such a bad trade.

The distant bell from the church down the street drew everyone up short. Vardan and a few of the others waved farewell and left the others standing in the growing morning heat. "Where are they going?" I asked.

"They're going to change clothes and head out for the

day." Sister Agnes said simply.

I was confused. "They can leave? I thought once you were here…" This earned me an indulgent smile from Sister Fleure.

"They can leave for a few hours, as long as they're back before dark. They're going to put on their bells and their rags, and go out begging alms for the House." I thought of the times I'd seen leprous beggars in the street, calling for good Christians to toss them a coin or two. They never failed to be as filthy and horrific as possible, covered up and reeking of disease and God's most inventive punishment upon them. But then who'd give their hard earned money to the perfectly normal and only slightly damaged people I just met? I felt a deep appreciation for the theater of it all. Not for the first time, and certainly not the last, I was aware that life in Acre was not as simple as I believed.

The two mother hens offered to show me around the House of the Order of St. Lazarus, and since their offer satisfied not only my need for curiosity, but to be the center of attention as well, I gladly accepted. It was a short tour but most thorough, since they felt a desperate need to show off every square inch of the place. Whether they were really as proud of their lodgings as they acted, or they just wanted to prolong our time together, I couldn't really say, and it didn't matter much.

Because the house was so small, the men's and women's lodgings were only a corridor apart. I'd never seen that before, since the other Military Orders strictly separated the sexes. The Templars, of course, didn't let women inside their charter house at all. The Hospital, where I lived, had a small number of nuns attached to it but they were kept strictly segregated except in the medical ward itself, where they mixed with the Knights only in the performance of their duties. Of course, we boys were in the tender care of the monks, so we seldom crossed paths with the Sisters. When we did, we responded with a dread of the unknown as if they were a different species from us altogether.

Unlike the Hospital, where women were there at the sufferance of the Knights and behaved accordingly, the female residents of the Leper House acted as if they ran the place. I'd never seen this, except in the few real families I occasionally spied on. My friends' mothers acted in much the same way—officially obedient to the men but ruling their domain with the occasional shriek or threatening wave of a wooden spoon. The kitchen, in particular, was a wonderland of high pitched laughter and gossip—unlike the solemn mess halls I was used to. If the quality of the last night's meal was any indication, good humor was at least as important as salt in preparing delicious meals. I could get used to that.

It was among the steam of pots and aroma of fresh-baked bread I crossed paths with Sister Marie-Pilar again. Her dark eyes smiled at me, although her nose and mouth were still covered by the grey veil. Since everyone else I'd encountered went uncovered—and I thought of a few of them could have benefitted from some discretion—again I couldn't help visualizing what lay underneath that thin covering.

"Lucca, I'm glad you're here." Words I'd not heard often sounded even sweeter from her. "Fetch your bowl and spoon and come back here, please."

"I'll come with you," offered Sister Fleure, as if something awful might befall me before I could return.

"Nonsense, Fleure. The lad has to get used to fending for himself and that starts now. Go, get out of here." Marie-Pilar waved that spoon like a scimitar and I got as fast as I could. My exposure to women was limited, but a lot of those interactions included the wielding of wooden cooking utensils.

Two quick lefts and a right brought me back to my cell, which I now noticed was one of three "guest rooms" completely separate from the rest of the living quarters. Apparently they wanted to protect visitors from infection. The segregation extended elsewhere as well. Back in the kitchen, Marie-Pilar, closely followed by Agnes and Fleure, showed me where the dishes were kept.

"This is your bowl and spoon, and only your bowl and spoon. Can you write your name?" I shook my head no. Apparently reading and writing were more useful skills than I imagined. Most people, even knights were illiterate, but I suddenly felt ashamed that I couldn't do something so basic, especially when it was obvious most of these women read and wrote. I couldn't imagine such a thing, yet there it was.

If Marie-Pilar thought any less of me for this glaring lack, she didn't show it. She simply handed me a nail and instructed me to scratch my mark into both the wooden bowl and the soup spoon. I knew my name started with an "L", so I took the point and etched two reasonably straight lines into the dishes.

The twin hens clucked approvingly. "Yes, Lucca starts with 'L', you are more talented than you let on," Sister Fleure cooed as if I'd made the blind see or the lame walk instead of scratching a badly made initial into the bottom of a bowl.

I was a little disappointed that Marie-Pilar didn't acknowledge my genius. She simply pointed to a blank spot on the shelf. "Keep your dishes there. From now on, you're the only one that touches them. You'll serve yourself, wash them yourself, and keep them away from everyone else's understand?"

"Yes, Sister."

That earned me a nod of approval. "Good. You eat with the rest of us. If you aren't here, you go hungry. Understand?" I did. Those rules didn't change no matter which Chapter House you lived in, and I'd missed many a meal when distracted by something more interesting. Of course, the food wasn't nearly as good at the Hospital, so I promised myself to make more of an effort in the future. Besides, the odds of missing a mealtime weren't great since I was essentially a prisoner.

Once I'd seen the sleeping quarters, the kitchen, and the courtyard, the only place still on the itinerary was the medical ward. I was astounded by the difference between the Hospital of St Lazar and the formal Hospital. First of all, it was much smaller; maybe a dozen beds lay close together in two tight rows. Only three of the beds were occupied, which meant that unlike the chaos and constant moaning, groaning, puking and screams I associated with healing, the place was sundrenched and quiet. More unusual still, it was spotless.

No blood or clumps of God-knows-what on the floor, the sheets all clean and fresh-looking, and one of the sisters with a nice smile but a grey smear of scales across her nose moved busily from one person to the next without them shrieking for attention. Again, I thought that if she was unembarrassed by her disease, how maimed was my favorite nun?

"It doesn't look much like a Hospital," I said to Sister Agnes.

She smiled. "What makes you say that?"

"Well, it's so… "*What was so different?* Then it occurred to me. "…Clean. It's clean. And sunny."

This earned me a smile. "Yes, it is. It's much more like a Mohammedan hospital than a Christian one. It's Brother Marco's idea. Since they've lived here longer, maybe those people know a thing or two about treating the sick who live here, eh? Do you know they have entire books just about treating leprosy?"

Actually, I couldn't imagine entire books about anything. With the exception of the Scriptures and some simple devotionals the priests hoarded, I'd never seen one. Why you'd need entire books dedicated to a disease perplexed me, but I nodded sagely and tried hard to keep my big stupid mouth shut.

Out of nowhere, one of the patients began thrashing and gasping for breath. My guide and two of the other nurses ran over to him. I followed silently, maneuvering for the best view. I know I should have felt pity, or fear, or something other than the simple, overwhelming curiosity of a child witnessing something forbidden yet thrilling.

The patient was a man, I could see, and his sparse, matted hair indicated he was of middle age. Other than that, it was impossible to gauge much else. Where his nose should have been was a sunken hole, lined with grey-brown scales, as if tiled with pebbles. He pounded gnarled fists on the sheets, demanding breath that wouldn't come. A horrible, wet sucking sound issued from his chest. Sister Agnes, despite her size, efficiently flipped him on his left side and pounded on his back, which brought momentary relief as he spat up thick chunks of bloody phlegm, but the relief was short-lived.

I came to learn later that leprosy seldom had the decency to kill its victims outright, preferring to condemn them to an otherwise long, healthy life. When the disease took hold of the face, though, the nose and soft tissue sometimes collapsed in on itself, and the victim got some kind of infection that usually spread to the lungs, like pneumonia. The poor fellow in front of me was obviously in the last stages of a losing battle, but the Sisters and one of the Brothers weren't about to surrender without a fight. Listening to the gurgling, retching panicky gasps, I wasn't sure that commitment to prolonging his life was as much of a blessing as they seemed to think.

Discretion overcame my curiosity and I backed out of the medical ward, finding myself alone in a cool stone corridor. *What was I supposed to do with the rest of the day?* Brother Marco said he'd see me after dinner, and that meant I had a whole day to kill. Then another day, and days after that. The notion of so much boredom was more frightening than the obvious terrors of the place. So I did what I always did—got up to no good.

I was an old hand at sneaking around kitchens, so I went back there to scout the scenes of future crimes. I had to learn where the fresh bread was kept, and who minded the pots of simmering soup. While so far everyone had been very kind, you never knew when a raid on the food stores would be in order.

Additionally, I wanted to know who I was sharing accommodations with. By afternoon, I had met most of the residents, and categorized them by sex (about three to one, men to women) as well as by the severity of their disease. Most had varying degrees of problems with their hands or feet—usually one or the other—and a very few suffered scarring and problems with their faces. All in all, as grotesque disfigurement went, it wasn't that much worse than the medical wards at the Hospital, where amputations, scars and ulcerous diseases were everyday sights.

Surprisingly, not everyone was a leper. There were two sullen priests, unhappy but unscarred, assigned as chaplains. Whispers suggested they came seeking martyrdom, and were mildly annoyed God was taking so long. There was also an able-bodied caretaker who must have been down on his luck indeed to take the job.

I was always terrible with names and sometimes couldn't tell one adult from another. Often I simply gave them nicknames based on their obvious characteristics. A carpet seller in the souk I called "Flat Face" for obvious reasons. Until I got to know them, the residents of St. Lazar went by

"No Nose" or "One Finger." Eventually they all became real people and had real names.

Finally, after a delicious dinner, where I only got my knuckles rapped once for sneaking a second helping, I went back to my little cell to await Brother Marco. The long shadows from the lamp danced on the wooden crucifix on the wall, and I watched them play until I heard a single rap on my door.

The door creaked open. Brother Marco stood there in the same cloak as yesterday, with his glove back on his hand. "You ready?"

Before I could nod, he'd already turned and disappeared down the tunnel. I hopped off the cot and chased him, eager to get back onto the streets of Acre.

Chapter 6

Brother Marco pushed the cellar door open an inch or so and listened carefully. I held my breath, but heard nothing except my blood rushing around in my skull. Satisfied no one saw us, he used his good, ungloved, hand to push the door open and hustled me up into the alley. Clean warm air stroked my face, welcoming me to the outside world. I'd only been in the leper house for less than a day, and already was feeling cooped up. I shooed a rat away and turned to offer my assistance to my companion, but he gruffly brushed me aside.

He pushed his staff through the opening, pulled himself up behind me, and carefully let the door fall back into place. Standing and stretching to his full height, he placed his hands on his hips, swiveled them back and forth to remove any kinks, then he pulled his hood over his head and stooped low. The beggar was back, gripping his staff low as if for support.

I restrained myself long past the point I thought I would simply explode into a thousand curious pieces, and could hold back no longer. "Where are we going?"

He shot me a look designed to freeze me, and it did for a moment, but then said. "For a walk." He offered me his elbow. "A poor beggar can't hardly walk without the aid of his helper, can he?" Without having the slightest hesitation, I took it and led him into the fainter light of the main street. He paused at the entrance to the alley and looked around. By this time, I knew better than to ask where we were headed. I just waited for him.

Like any military port, Acre was a maze of narrow streets and narrower alleys, with three wide main boulevards leading from the three main gates to the docks. One led from the Damascus gate past my former home in the Hospital of St. John and their Charter House to the waterfront. A second led from the Edessa Gate, (which was its formal name, although the local Syrians called it the Bayrut Gate, and that's what I usually called it) and allowed the Templars a direct, easy march to their own headquarters. The third, the Jerusalem Gate, or King's Gate, was smaller and traffic usually consisted of commercial trade. In a desire to be as close to the main body of Templar knights—and as far from possible bandits as possible—many supplies for the Holy City arrived at Acre and were escorted south. Even at this time of night, it was crowded and noisy. With a silent nod of Brother Marco's head, that's where we headed.

Sprung from captivity, I wanted to sprint in every direction at once, but Brother Marco shuffled slowly and I didn't dare let go of his arm. We followed the hubbub a few steps to one of the cross streets where there was torchlight and human activity.

I stretched my arms to maintain contact with his elbow while silently willing him to hurry. As always, my eyes darted everywhere at once. There was so much to see, and each sight promised some kind of fun. There were soldiers, pack animals, screaming peddlers... so much potential amusement and I wouldn't get to any of it moving at Marco's pace.

Finally, tired of my antsy-ness, the man grabbed my hand in his. Through clenched teeth, I heard him hiss, "Slow down. What draws more attention, a beggar moving slowly or a beggar in a hurry? Where would he be going to?" He was right, of course. Besides, there was no real sense hurrying, since I had absolutely no idea where we were going, or what we'd do when we got there. I settled for gawking around, taking in the sights.

Nearing the King's Gate, I noticed it was unusually busy for that time of night. In fact, it was chaos. Soldiers dismounted sweaty, whickering horses, loudly swearing and yanking reins to calm the beasts before they kicked some innocent citizen. A bearded commander shouted orders and waved his hand wildly, hoping in vain someone was actually listening. Foot soldiers helped pull carts out of the way, shoving people and kicking at donkeys, clearing the road so the knights could get back to their stables, hot food and clean beds.

Local merchants, mostly Armenians and Syrian converts, hustled from wagon to wagon. They cast covetous eyes over the goods of their compatriots, loudly bemoaning the state in which their wares arrived and cursing whatever poor soldier happened to be closest. The merchants grabbed the nearest caravan member, and dragged them over to their wagon, complaining about the shoddy state of their goods, and the lateness of their arrival.

I watched with delight as one young driver, probably the son of the caravan's leader, tried to deal with a particularly nasty couple of cloth merchants. While the husband tried politely to carry on a conversation, his harpy of a wife shouted curses and threats. "Are you going to let him get away with this? How are we supposed to sell this shit?"

The merchant gave a weary smile. "I am sorry young man; I know this isn't your...."

"What are you apologizing for you worthless, ball-less dog? They're stealing from us and you're saying sorry..." She swatted a callused and spotted hand across the back of her husband's head, obviously not for the first or last time.

The young man couldn't decide whether to be offended or horrified, so settled for simply standing dumbfounded with his mouth hanging open. The merchant laid a comforting hand on the boy's shoulder. "I have known your father for twenty years. You're honest men, I know that. But really, the cloth is filthy and torn. You know if it were up to me..."

"If it were up to you, you worthless idiot, you'd kiss him and give him extra money just to be nice. What are they going to do about this? Huh?" Spit flew from where one of her front teeth should have been as she harangued her spouse.

The young man's shoulders sagged. "I'm sorry. You know if it were up to me.... But my father. You agreed to the price...."

"For cloth delivered so we could actually sell it. What are we supposed to do with..." the rest of the sentence ended in unintelligible shrieks.

The husband meekly held up a hand. "Please, *jan,* sweetheart, it's not the lad's fault."

"No, it's mine for marrying a useless *chent* like you. You're not going to pay the boy, are you?"

I looked over my shoulder to see if Marco was enjoying the show as much as I was, but he wasn't even watching. His eyes were on the soldiers. I squinted in the same direction, hoping to see what he saw, but nothing stood out. Just soldiers being soldiers. Living in a military city and practically in their barracks, that wasn't even worth mentioning.

I wasn't the only one noticing Marco's attention. A hulking brute of a soldier with the crest of the Kingdom of Jerusalem, the four crosses inside a larger cross, also saw his curiosity. "Hey, what are you looking at?" He slammed his pike on the ground menacingly, and when we didn't scatter like rats, took two steps towards us.

I had no idea what Marco was up to, but was pretty confident it didn't include unfortunate run-ins with soldiers. I ducked out of the knight's grip and ran up to the evil-smelling, hairy man. "We're seeking alms, sir. Obviously, the Lord watched out for you today, care to return the favor by helping others?" This elicited the expected response.

I heard, "Get out of here. Beat it" as I ducked, unharmed, under a slow backhanded slap.

While retreating, I shouted a quick, "I hope the Mamelukes get you for being a cheap bastard." That, of course, is what any self-respecting child beggar says under the circumstances and hurried back to Marco, tugging on his sleeve impatiently. The soldier watched us hobble away, then returned to his job; glowering at people doing real work.

As soon as we turned the corner, Marco pulled off his hood and hissed at me. "What was that?"

Without thinking, I put my hands defiantly on my hips. My voice was an insolent mockery of a moment ago. "What draws more attention, a beggar begging or a beggar not begging?" Since this just made him snort once, rather than hit me, I presumed I wasn't in trouble.

"Since you're so clever, then, Professeur le Pou, what did you see back there?"

Excitedly, I began to tell him about the cloth merchants. "I can't believe you didn't see it, these two… a husband and wife ganged up on this…." He held up his gloved hand to stop me.

"Lest you think I'm an idiot, I did see that. But that's an everyday occurrence with those two, and you know it. Did you notice anything unusual?" My confusion must have been written across my face. He took a breath and looked me in the eye. "Any dolt can see what's going on around him. Only a well-trained…observer, let's call it…can see what shouldn't be there and figure out why. So, let's go through this. What was all the fuss about?"

I knew this to be some kind of test, and out of sheer stubbornness, I refused to fail. I squinted my eyes shut as hard as I could, as if squeezing an answer out of my brain, but nothing came. Naturally, that didn't stop me from talking. "Well, it was a caravan arriving…"

"Good. What was different about it? Anything?" He was

in no mood for hesitation, because he immediately snapped, "well?"

My mouth moved before my brain did. "No, nothing. It was just the usual… and not a very big caravan—just cloth and vegetables, the usual."

"Very good. So if the caravan itself wasn't unusual, what was?"

There was more squinting, but not much more thinking. "It was later than usual?"

"Asking me or telling me?"

"It was later than usual." That earned me a nod and a "hmph," nearly as good as actual approval.

"So this pathetic little caravan with nothing special in it arrived later than usual. Who was in the caravan?"

"Merchants and soldiers. Just like always." This time his head shook.

"Not like always. What soldiers?"

"The King's soldiers. Jerusalem soldiers. I saw the gold crosses," and I drew them across my chest with a finger. This got me another nod. *Why should that matter? What was so special about that? Because that's not who it should have been.* Normally, caravans were accompanied by troops of either the Hospitallers or Templars, it's how the Houses made their money, and the caravans were more or less certain of arriving at their destinations. King's men usually stayed in the cities and helped keep order.

"They weren't Hospitallers or Templars… Why were the King's troops escorting caravans of no value?"

Marco's eyes flashed. "Exactly. Very good, you've asked

the right question."

"But what's the answer?" I asked.

Marco shrugged. "I don't know yet, but you can't know what's really going on until you ask the right question, and now we know what that is. Come on, there's more to see." Rising, he once again offered his elbow. This time, we headed down the broad boulevard towards the port shuffling all the way.

His notion of asking the right question bothered me, because I had so many of my own, and wasn't sure which—if any—were the "right ones". *Why is he looking out for me? What does he want? What are we doing out here?* None of them seemed exactly right, yet each of them mattered. Whatever the answer, the one thing I felt in my bones was this was some kind of test, and I was determined not to fail. It was vital I not fail the mysterious Brother Marco. For one thing, if I did, I might have nowhere to live.

Soldiers of all kinds patrolled the streets. There were the city guards, surly, stupid looking commoners with staffs and pikes in their hands. More importantly, Templars with their cloud-white tunics and dark red crosses, and Hospitallers, their black eight-pointed crosses emblazoned on their tunics and cloaks also roamed the streets, walking slowly up the broad, populated boulevards, then down the streets and alleys. *There are so many tonight, and their groups are too large.*

Marco noticed the puzzlement written across my face, because he shuffled over to a dark alley and leaned back against the wall, sliding to a squat in the dust. He gestured me to sit as well.

"Well, my little louse. What is going on in that head of yours?" I shrugged casually. He wasn't buying it. "You see something, what is it?"

I wasn't entirely sure how to describe the feeling. It was a vague nagging, like a mosquito buzzing around your bed at night but never quite landing so you could squish it. I knew that wouldn't satisfy my companion, though, so I started slowly, hoping it would make sense if I said it out loud.

"Something's not...right. On a normal night in this part of the city you'd see City patrols. They chase us all the time... But the Orders have real knights out... they're looking for something." I paused, checking Marco's face for confirmation I was on the right track, but I may as well have checked out the brick walls behind him. "And they're not in pairs... there's three and four of them. That means real trouble." I knew in my gut I'd spotted the problem.

Marco grunted, which probably meant I was right, but that didn't mean he was done with me. So I kept going. "Maybe they're still looking for the *hashishin*, After all, he broke into the Hospital and attacked a knight." That sounded reasonable, if the story were true, only it wasn't. I shook my head before he could respond. That didn't explain the Templars. *One more or less Hospitaller wouldn't matter to those arrogant bastards. They probably arranged it.*

"Normally, they patrol in pairs. There are too many of them. They're looking for someone." *Maybe they're looking for me?* I knew the idea was ridiculous. I might have a worried monk or two concerned about my health, but the Brothers themselves wouldn't have given a single solitary shit about one half-caste orphan boy, especially a trouble maker like the Louse.

A trio of Templars paused back to back, surveying the street. One of them caught sight of us and elbowed his compatriots before pointing a gloved finger at me. "You, boy, and your ugly friend. Come here." Out of reflex, I jumped to my feet. It was best to respond immediately and correctly when spoken to by a full-blown knight of the Order of the Temple. Then I remembered Marco was supposed to be sick, or old, or incapacitated at least, so I bent down while he slowly, amid loud groans, rose unsteadily to his feet, then I led him forward by the elbow. We moved too slowly for the guard's liking, but fast enough to show frightened compliance.

A short knight with shoulders wide as a wagon's axle glared down at me. "What are you doing here?"

Marco began to cough loudly and wetly, bending over in order to catch his breath. As expected, the knights took two steps back. You never knew what you'd catch from street vermin like us. I assumed the role of caretaking nephew I'd used back at the King's Gate. "Seeking alms from good Christians, sir. My... uncle is......" Fortunately I didn't have to complete the lie. I was interrupted by a barking, hacking, cough from Marco, who spat the fattest gob of phlegm I'd ever seen onto the sidewalk three paces in front of the Templars.

The other two soldiers desperately wanted to move on, but Shoulders held his ground in the face of likely contagion. "You look like a poor excuse for a Christian, lad. More like one of those murdering Camel-Kissers. Have your uncle show his face." Marco held the cloak tightly around his chin, pulling it back only to reveal an obviously Frankish nose, mouth and eyes. He managed a thin line of drool from his bottom lip.

"We are Christians, my lord, but my sister was not a woman of…. high virtue or discretion. This lad is all we have left of her. A constant reminder of her sin…. But a good boy, for the most part."

The tallest knight set aside his revulsion long enough to examine Marco's half-exposed face. "Do I know you?"

The only answer was the mightiest cough yet, and another truly impressive gob flew at them. Marco shook his head, as if trying to catch his breath. Between wheezes and pants, he managed to choke out, "We're just newly arrived from Caesarea. Salah-adin and his mongrels…."

"Yes, we know what happened there. Why are you here?"

I stepped in protectively. "If you're going to beg, you have to be where there's money to be had. He was a tanner before…." I hoped I looked properly sorrowful. "All this…. Are you looking for someone?" I was, after all, a ten-year-old boy, and no one my age ever saw a group of soldiers without asking what was afoot.

"There's talk of spies about. Nothing out of the ordinary." The first statement might have been true. The second certainly wasn't but I nodded. "We'll keep an eye out for anything, sir. You bet. Is there, maybe, some kind of reward…?"

"Find shelter for the night, or your only reward will be to

become guests of the King. Get him out of here and away from honest people. " Shoulders nodded to his colleagues and they strutted off towards the port.

I led Marco back to the corner. He played his part as he let one more grand, hacking, phlegmy cough echo down the street. We resumed our seats in the dusty darkness. A curious rat squatted and chittered angrily a few paces away, but otherwise we were alone. He let out a sigh of relief. "Well done, Lad." He couldn't see my smile in the dark, but must have known it was there. "That's nearly enough for one night. Let's head back."

It took us most of an hour, winding down one alley, up the next street, shuffling and bent over the whole way to make our way back to the secret cellar door. The farther away from the port, the fewer soldiers we saw, until the streets were once again quiet and dark. Marco stood and stretched himself out before holding the panels open and then following me quickly inside.

As he closed the doors behind him, casting us into deepest blackness, he allowed himself one small chuckle. "Not bad for a first mission, eh?"

Mission? What mission? But that was all he said and we shuffled the rest of the way home in the dark.

Chapter 7

"Stop sniveling, boy. If ye'll hold your position, ye won't get hit." Sergeant Jacques swung his cane again. There was a loud crack of wood against wood, and the hard tip landed, adding yet more blue and yellow-green to the tattoo of bruises up and down my right arm. I dropped the piece of olive wood serving as my sword with a yowl of pain.

The ugly soldier waggled his walking stick—his sword for this morning's purposes—at me to pick mine up as he got back into position. His face was stone, and while there were no visible signs, I suspected he was enjoying himself immensely. I sniffed back a gigantic snot bubble, wiped my sleeve across my eyes to remove any stray tears and tried my best to assume the defensive stance he showed me; left foot forward towards my attacker, right foot behind and turned out for balance.

"Christ's blood, Sergeant, give the boy a break," said Vardan from the shady comfort of his bench.

"Ye're right. I'm sure the Turks won't run him through if he lets them know his arm hurts." He slowly pulled his good left arm back and, with a lazy looping motion, swung his "sword" at me again. Crack. Whack.

"Owww."

"Hold position and ye'll not get hit. Again." Crack.

Whack. Sniff.

"Hold position and ye'll not get hit. Again."

Another swing, this time I somehow willed my tingling arm forward a few inches. I was rewarded with a loud "crack" and a shiver up my arm, but his weapon never struck me. This earned me a grunt and a nod. "See? Ye hold position and you don't get hit. Again."

We did it again, this time I didn't hold position, and as predicted I got hit. "Again." Once more he grabbed my right hand with his cracked, scabrous hand and pulled it forward to the right spot. Then he took his cane and touched my elbow. "See this here, that's ye're position," he said and his cane touched my side, "about that far from yer body. Again."

Boredom makes boys do terribly stupid things, and when a good thumping from Sergeant Jacques was better than doing nothing all day, I was very bored indeed. It had been three days since Marco's and my first excursion. Even though he came every night after dinner and we spent hours roaming the dark streets of Acre, the days started early and left a lot of hot, dull hours to fill.

It didn't take long for me to investigate and memorize every inch of the House of St. Lazarus. It was a big, square building of two stories—three if you counted the basement tunnels which no one admitted were there—with cells, the hospital, and the kitchen, and the chapel making up the four sides. In the middle was the courtyard, serving as a place for socializing and recreation. Most importantly, it was the only way most of the lepers who lived there ever got to feel the full warmth of the sun on their faces. What few windows it had were small, barred squares designed to prevent contagion from escaping to the civilized world.

The kitchen was quickly and thoroughly reconnoitered; the hiding places for various goodies identified and noted for future raids. Not that I was able to do much about it, since the Sisters guarded their domain jealously, and wielded wooden spoons with nearly as much ferocity as Sergeant Jacques swung his cane. Cells were empty during the day, so that left the courtyard, the infirmary and the chapel as places to kill time. The chapel held no more interest here than it did anywhere else, and the sight and sounds of the sick were enough to overcome even the murderous boredom. That left the courtyard, and my fighting lessons.

I accepted Sergeant Jacques' offer to "make a man of me." I should have been suspicious when he seemed so glad to help, but it was too late to back out now. Besides, only my right side was bruised and battered from swordplay. Vardan's attempt to teach me to wrestle had the muscles everywhere else begging for mercy. I had the day off from that, at least. Tomorrow I was all his.

Jacques threw his cane to the ground with equal parts disgust and relief, put his hands to his knees and breathed deeply. "Kicking your buttocks is hard work. That's enough, lad. Get out of here. Let a sick old man get some rest." Except for having to use his left hand, being sick and old didn't seem to affect his swordplay, and I could only imagine what shape I'd be in if he were his old self.

"Thank you, Sergeant." I remembered to say, this time. The last time I ran off without expressing gratitude for my bruises I took a cane across the backside that I still felt at breakfast. The lesson, if I remember correctly, was that the sergeant's job was to keep my worthless hide intact so I could be "useful more than once." Gratitude for that miserable task was a small price to pay, or so I was told.

I managed to walk upright and slowly until I got to my cell. Then, when I was sure nobody could see or hear, I crawled onto the cot left side down, faced the wall and let the throbbing spread through my body, allowing myself the luxury of a good, cleansing cry. God knows I had seen Fadhil do this on many an occasion, and his bruises were much more cruelly earned, coming as they did from his own father.

The dinner bell yanked me from a deep sleep. I got up so fast that I was halfway down the hall before the first aches and pains caught up to my body. To a young boy nothing is as encouraging as the idea of a good meal, though, so my bruises and I straightened up and limped to dinner.

I felt better with a belly full, and stronger and happier still when I watched Sisters Fleur and Agnes tear into Sergeant Jacques. They were the dogs and he the poor, confused bear trapped in the pit. Those two biddies clucked and nagged, calling him 'brute," and "monster," and "bully," and other horrible names until he begged for their mercy as well as that of God and the Saints. It was the perfect dessert.

I heard Brother Marco laugh. He leaned back in his chair against the wall, arms crossed, appreciating the drama playing out before him. He was ungloved and without his cloak, looked like the jolly landlord of a tavern surveying his establishment. He happily bit into a slightly bruised, overripe orange persimmon, and wiped his sleeve across his mouth. He acknowledged me with a smiling nod, but otherwise ignored me completely.

My enjoyment at Jacques' discomfort had pretty much ebbed, and I was eager to get going on the night's adventure, but Brother Marco showed no sign of ever leaving this spot. At long last, my gaze drew his attention. Pulling the juicy fruit's short leafy stem out of his mouth and laying it on the table in front of him, he turned and simply asked, "What?"

"Aren't you getting dressed?" I asked.

"No. Why?"

"Aren't we going out tonight?" I cringed at the desperate disappointment in my voice, but if he heard he didn't seem much bothered.

"I'm not. You are, though." He unashamedly licked his fingers, even on his infected hand and I shuddered.

"What do you mean?"

"I'm staying in tonight. You are going out by yourself. That's all right, isn't it?"

I summoned up all the ten-year-old bravado I could muster. "Of course. What do you want me to do... by myself?" I hoped I didn't sound too much like a whiney girl. Naturally, I could go out by myself, I'd been doing it all my life, but it occurred to me that I didn't much want to. In a short time, I'd grown accustomed to spending hours in the city streets with Marco, sharing laughs and even a companionable silence I had never really known before.

"I want you to find one person you think is interesting, and follow him all night. Come back and tell me everything about him... or her. Your choice. You seem to like women well enough..."

My nose wrinkled. "You mean what they wear, where they go..."

"Of course, that. But one more thing." He leaned in and those icy blue eyes pinned me in place as his voice dropped to a whisper. "I want you to tell me their secret."

"What do you mean?"

He grunted at the stupidity of that question. "Have you learned nothing the last few nights? Everyone has secrets. There's what they want the world to see, then there's what they really are. I want you to tell me what you see, even though they think you can't." It was obvious I wasn't understanding, and equally clear he was disappointed in me, which hurt worse than my arm. "Look, when we went to the port the other night, what did you see?"

Now I knew what he was talking about. I scrunched my eyes closed, recalling the scene. The port was extremely crowded and chaotic, far busier than usual. He forced me to listen to the noise as well, until it became clear that nearly every voice spoke the guttural Italian of Venice, and the gold lion atop the red Venetian shield flew from every mast. He questioned and prodded and we talked until the secret emerged. Everyone knew that Venice had the exclusive rights to trade with the kingdom of Jerusalem. Usually, though, there were other ships—Genoan, Norman, Portuguese—in the harbor. Now the taverns, gaming houses and chandleries were full of none but the arrogant, perpetually angry sailors of Venice. By talking to some of the sailors, particularly those deepest in their cups, we discovered what was really going on.

It wasn't that Venice was doing so well, it's that no one else was interested in our trade. The rest of the world was avoiding Acre, and in fact the entire Kingdom. No fresh troops, no families coming to start businesses. That things were dire outside our city walls was no secret, the surprise was how wide-spread our desperate status was known to the rest of the world. We were being abandoned by all but the country with the biggest stake in our survival. Everyone else was off seeking easier rewards elsewhere. Acre had become too big a risk, even for those used to betting everything on the vagaries of wind and sea.

I opened my eyes. "Do you understand what I'm asking?" I nodded. "You're sure?" I nodded again. He waved his hand. "All right, off with you. I'm going to get a good night's sleep for once. Try not to get arrested or killed or anything."

Sister Marie-Pilar gave me a warm smile over her veil and shooed me away. "You heard the man. Scat." I wouldn't swear to it, but I thought I saw Marco give her a wink before he reached over to the fruit barrel to pull out another persimmon. I do know I very clearly saw him take a quick whack to the back of his hand for his trouble. I laughed out loud, earning myself a dirty look that sent me on my way in a particularly good mood.

Back in my cell, I put on a ratty tunic we'd found on an earlier excursion—sufficiently old and smelly that I'd be noticed but no one would want to actually look at me twice—then headed down the stairs to the cellar tunnel. It took several attempts to hoist the oak door open. It was heavier than it looked, designed to keep people out as much as aid in escape. On previous nights out, Marco always opened and closed it. It took considerable effort to crack it open enough to let my skinny frame through into the pitch black tunnel and more effort to quell the panic that arose when it slammed shut before I was ready. If I ever had to get in and out in a hurry by myself, it might be problematic.

I groped my way down the earthen tunnel, fingers lightly touching the walls that felt closer than ever without the bigger man's torch to show the way. It seemed to take ages longer than usual and I fought the fear I could feel hanging all around me. I nearly went back, but demonstrating cowardice bothered me more than not being able to see where I was going, or what I might run into along the way, so I just kept going.

At last, when I was about convinced I had made a wrong turn somewhere because I *must* have traveled half way to Jerusalem and back, I felt the ground slope up and my sandal nudged the bottom step. The thinnest sliver of moonlight wormed its way through the door that covered the cellar entrance.

I crouched so my shoulder pressed against the planks and heaved against it. I almost let out a scream as the reminders of Sergeant Jacques' swordplay throbbed, but I bit down and blew the pain through my nose rather than let it escape as noise. I raised the door enough to get a good grip on it, and lifted it a few inches. I paused, listening for anyone around, but the only noise was the clatter of cart wheels, the sad, slow clop-clop of unshod horse hooves on the street, and the occasional peddler shouting desperately, long after any decent trade was home for dinner. For once being small was actually an advantage, since I didn't have to raise the planks far in order to squeeze through.

Emerging into the alley, I tried to slowly lower the door but it slipped from my fingertips, scraping them raw, and dropped with a solid ca-thunk. I froze, looking around to see if I was noticed but I seemed to be alone. In fact, more alone than I'd been in some time and while part of me thrilled to be master of my actions again, I also felt the absence of my protector and guide. The desire to have fun and do whatever I pleased lost out to my wish to complete my assignment.

I wasn't entirely sure where I was supposed to go. I slunk to where the alley met the street and looked around for inspiration. Where was I supposed to find someone to follow—and one with a secret worth bringing back? I stood with my hands on my hips, just swinging back and forth as if inspiration would pull me one way or the other, when I heard the creak and clatter of a wooden door. I looked back down the alley, but didn't see anyone. I knew that didn't mean no one was there, though. I suspected I wasn't alone as I thought. The idea made me smile.

Now I needed to find someone with a secret. In all my running the streets and getting in trouble, I learned that the place to find the secrets of adults were the very places most expressly forbidden to us. There was only one real choice— the vice dens of the suburb of Montmusard. Because the area just to the north and west of the Hospital Charter House was expressly off limits, I spent more time there than was wise, and I knew it fairly well. Surely there would be something worth seeing.

I walked slowly, then realized I was no longer forced to crawl for the sake of my "poor crippled uncle," and did something I couldn't do in the halls of the St Lazar House... I ran. Joyfully, aimlessly, darting in and out of the citizens of Acre, spinning, and laughing like a maniac. If Marco was indeed following me, he'd have to move fast. Laughter burst from my chest, drawing some looks, but who really pays attention to a happy child that isn't theirs? I felt fully free for the first time in what felt like ages.

That feeling ended when I saw the roof of the Hospital looming ahead. In order to get through the gate to Montmusard, I had to pass within a block or two of the Hospital. The upper windows glared down at me accusingly. Until that moment I hadn't actually felt much of anything for my old home, but I was suddenly both homesick and terrified of discovery. As much as I was curious about the goings on there—Gilbert's angry face suddenly appeared in my mind's eye—I didn't want to be seen. Even though Brother Idoneus was alive, I doubted how much Christian forgiveness was on offer.

Avoiding the Hospital meant going a block or two out of the way, and as I rounded a corner by a fruit stall, I froze with my hand half extended to a particularly ripe and tempting fig. A familiar face in a kaftan walked by, head down. It was Charles, a Syrian clerk to the Hospitallers.

His real name, of course, was not Charles but

Muhammad. He changed it upon converting. Keeping a Muslim name, especially that one, would create some question about the state of his soul. Many of the converts took Western names, and the shakier their faith, the more the outward trappings of their new life mattered. Charles usually dressed in Frankish clothes, with a large wooden cross around his neck. It didn't really help. His true lineage was written across his face as plainly as it was mine.

If anyone had unknown depths, I thought, it would be this man who spent all day huddled in a dark room with parchment and ink, but left at night and often didn't return for hours. His biggest secret was badly kept—he was a gambler. Like so many converts he found Christianity more accommodating to the sins of the flesh than the Way of the Prophet. Sure, drunkenness, whoring and violence against one's neighbor were sins in both religions, but Christianity offered confession. If one had vices, at least there was a path to salvation.

I may have been spotted, because Charles/Muhammad looked back in my direction as if to confirm he'd seen what he thought he saw. By that time, though, I was already crouched low beside a vendor's stall, ready to run and wiping sticky fig juice from my mouth with a filthy sleeve. Not seeing me, the clerk lowered his head and picked up his pace, heading for the gambling dens of the suburb.

I followed at a safe distance as he passed several of the closest taverns. They were also the establishments most likely frequented by people he knew, so that made sense. At last he turned into a "tea house," which served tea only when the authorities were watching. These tea houses were Syrian run, and the customers were almost entirely Turks or locals. To be sure, fraternizing with infidels was the least of the ways one's soul was at risk in a place that also provided liquor, dice and women, but it was an odd choice for one associated with one of the Orders. I'd found my subject for the evening.

It was a hot night, so the doors and shutters were thrown open, comfort being more important than discretion. I found a nest between two rain barrels, and looked across the narrow street into the belly of the tea house. The clerk fidgeted nervously at the end of a table and pulled out some coins, slapping them on the table.

The local gamblers usually played dice, rather than tables or chess for money. This teahouse used Frankish dice, rather than camel bones. Not that it mattered much what they used, Charles was well known for being a first rate clerk, and a terrible, snake-bitten gambler.

I tried to use all the observation skills Marco drilled into me. *What did I see?* There were three others at the table, two other converts and one fat merchant type who was clearly a Mussulman and unashamed of it. I recognized none of the other players, but closed my eyes and tried to memorize what they wore and how they acted, so I could give a full report. I was, after all, here on business.

What was out of the ordinary? At first, nothing. It was just another night in Acre. Gamblers avoided all the other available temptations as if only able to concentrate on one deadly sin at a time. Charles brushed aside a pretty whore, and drank actual tea. It looked to be a rather dull night.

After the dice roll changed hands a few times, the fat one reached down and pulled out another handful of coins. I couldn't hear anything, but I saw him look upward as if beseeching Allah to grant him at least the chance to win his money back, then laugh and push two coins towards Charles, who nodded graciously and piled them neatly in front of himself.

That's what was odd. *Charles was winning. He never wins.* But he steadily added to the growing pile in front of him, occasionally running ink-stained fingers up and down the stacks as if to ensure himself he wasn't dreaming. The other two participants would occasionally groan as the dice fell Charles' way, or gesture wildly, and one let out a shout I could hear from my hiding spot across the road. The fat one merely shook his head and pulled out more silver. The fact that he was losing—badly—to the clerk didn't seem to bother him in the least. I couldn't imagine how many times he must have said "*inshallah*" and just kept playing.

At one point, the merchant, who I christened *al Sameen-* The Fat One-- because I had to call him something and it always sounded funny—asked for something to drink. There was the usual huge pot of tea, and a small flask of something else placed discreetly in front of the clerk. Fatso poured a bit for each of the players. I don't know what it was, but from the way Charles' face scrunched up it was strong and intoxicating. They kept playing, and the clerk kept winning. Twice he tried to leave, and al Sameen placed a comradely hand on his shoulder, poured more wine and called for another roll of the dice.

Before long, the inevitable happened; Charles began to lose. It was only every other roll or so at first, but then two out of three, and as fast as the piles were built, they were dismantled and transferred across the table. One of the other players got up to go to the privy out back and never returned. Shortly after, the second man, who looked like a convert as well, did the sensible thing and went home.

Less than an hour later, the poor fool was digging into his purse and pulling his own coins out. With the same friendly smile he had on his face when losing, al Sameen graciously accepted them.

By the time the street was deserted and pain shot up my legs from being crouched so long, the two men rose from the table. Charles stood for a moment saying nothing just staring at the tabletop. His head hung limply, fingertips touching the edge of the table. The merchant reached over and took him by the arm, leaned in and whispered something. Charles simply nodded and allowed himself to be led to the door.

The two men stepped into the street and at last I could hear them, or at least snatches of Arabic conversation that drifted my way on the feeble breeze.

"How will I ever... I don't have..." Charles was whining through drink-thickened lips.

"My friend, I trust you. You'll repay me." Al Sameen may have been rich, but he was also a fool if he believed that.

Charles didn't believe it himself. "How? I don't have... God help me. How can I?"

The fat man wrapped an arm around Charles' shoulder

and pulled him tightly against his shoulder. "My dear friend, there are plenty of ways to satisfy a debt besides gold."

As they walked away it was getting harder to hear. I leaned nearly out of my hiding spot when two carters, drunk and belligerent, were escorted out of the teahouse and into the street by a stern-looking matron who had each of them by a sharply twisted ear. I wondered if they taught women that move or it was natural instinct.

By the time the complaining and shrieking died down, my two targets were well onto the next block. I darted out from between the rain barrels, scaring the wits out of the two drunkards, and to the corner, making sure I could see al Sameen's broad back.

Fortunately, the closer they got to the predominantly Christian quarter, the slower they walked, their business not quite completed. I tried not to breathe, since even my own huffing and puffing prevented hearing everything.

"You will bring it to me tomorrow night. The same place, yes?" Fatso now had Charles by both shoulders, and while there was nothing overtly threatening in the gesture, I could clearly see the clerk was terrified.

"I can't... I..."

"You can. And you will or you will be exposed, my friend. Who do you think will want first crack at you? The *Firengi* knights for spilling their secrets, or the *Ismaili* who just love to find apostates and take the Prophet's revenge for abandoning the True Faith? And, of course, you'll certainly not be welcome back to that teahouse if it's known you failed to pay your debts." I felt the hair on my neck rise at the fat man's tone. It was as terrible as any threat I'd ever heard, yet delivered in the same calm way one might ask the price of an orange.

Al Sameen grabbed the clerk's arms, forcing him to stand erect. He dusted Charles off and straightened his clothing. "There. Now you look respectable. I'll see you tomorrow night, Muhammad."

Hearing his birth name only added to Charles' shame. It took a shove on the back to start him shuffling, head down, towards the gate back into Acre and the Christian quarter. The guards barely noticed him. It wasn't the first time he'd passed them drunk and penniless. They failed to notice that this time, he was also terrified to his bones.

The fat merchant watched him pass into the streets of Acre proper, then whistled softly through clenched teeth. The other two gamblers from earlier appeared from the shadows and the three men headed north and east, away from the port and into the Syrian neighborhoods of Montmusard.

I had my secret to report to Marco. There was a clerk for the Hopsitallers, owing a debt to a mysterious stranger, and was to bring something tomorrow night that would repay the debt and save his life. Actually, it was only three quarters of a secret, because I had no idea what that something was.

Maybe Brother Marco would know.

Chapter 8

"Come on, lad. Almost had me that time. Try it again."
Vardan wasn't tall, but he looked like a giant from my
position on the dusty courtyard floor. I squinted up at his
monstrous black shadow against the bright mid-morning
sun, and let my head fall back to the earth. Maybe I could
will the air back into my lungs.

If I thought I'd give my bruises a rest to wrestle with the
big Armenian rather than take more punishment to my
sword arm, I had misjudged. Too sore to take any more of
Sergeant Jacques' instruction, I asked Vardan to teach me to
wrestle. So far all I'd learned was how to hit the ground and
still be able to breathe. A valuable skill, I'm sure, but not one
I was looking to develop.

Not only was it humiliating, it was unpleasant as well.
Vardan wrestled shirtless, meaning the thick coarse hair on
his chest and back, matted as it was with sweat, made
grappling with him like hugging a wet dog. My face smeared
into the rank, dank pelt with every attempt, and he was slick
as if he'd bathed in oil. I couldn't grab a hold of him, and
when I did I couldn't let go soon enough.

"You know, if you had a sword—and knew how to use
it—you'd be able to cut him down to size," Jacques offered
from his bench in the shade. Somewhere inside me, I knew

they were trying to help, but their jokes just irritated me more and more. I knew I had to get Vardan down, but how?

From my vantage point in the dirt, I studied my opponent. He was bare from the waist up, if you consider a permanent fur coat bare. His simple pantaloons reached below the knee, and I could see the bandages covering the sores on his left leg, shin to toe.

"Well, Louse. The bigger man has you at a disadvantage. What are you going to do?"

I'm going to lay here til I die peacefully. I looked him over in frustration. *How am I going to knock him down?* The bandage on his left foot was unraveling, and for a moment, I thought about going for his maimed foot, then thought better of it.

I wish I discounted the idea because it wasn't fair or charitable. Actually, it was a strategic decision. If I went for his injured leg, he'd be left balancing on his right—his good—leg. If I could knock that leg out from under him, though, his weight would shift to the left, and I knew he couldn't support himself fully.

I got to my knees, made a show of staring at his left leg and lifted myself to all fours. Roaring like a bull, I charged. At the last moment I shifted direction and launched my shoulder towards his right leg, right behind the knee. If I hit him, he'd drop like a stone.

My plan worked, as far as I'd thought it out. I slammed into thick leg and felt him wobble. That's when I realized that when you chop down a tree, you don't want to be directly underneath it. My satisfied laugh turned to a scream as that fat, hairy, dank shadow landed right on top of me.

It took Vardan a moment to get off me, laughing loudly. From under a couple of hundred pounds of matted flesh I heard Jacques clapping. "That was a dirty trick, boy. I like it."

Vardan pretended to be angry, at least I prayed he was pretending because he hobbled to one leg, then let out a wall-shaking roar. I was grabbed by the back of my neck in one hand, one thigh with the other and was hoisted high over his head. I had a panoramic view of the exercise yard including the outer wall. I feared he might just heave me over it to teach me a lesson about cheating.

"Sergeant, what should I do with this little pest?" Vardan shouted.

Jacques shrugged. "Squish him, toss him and stop wasting your time."

"Ha. Good idea. He's too smart for his own good anyway, it'll only get him killed."

I heard a voice from somewhere way down on the ground. "Before you dispose of him permanently, do you think I could have him for a moment?" It was Brother Marco.

"You sure you want him?" Vardan asked.

Marco shrugged. "The good Lord has a use for everything, no matter how much of a mystery that might be." The knight looked up at me. "Have you had enough, or would you like me to come back later?"

"Now's good," I squeaked. Marco gently lowered me to my feet.

"The little bugger went for my bad leg." Vardan said, wiping his hands on his pants. "There's hope for him yet."

He tousled my hair and gave me a shove towards Marco. "He's all yours."

"Don't feel the need to bring him back any time soon," Jacques offered helpfully.

"Oh, I think we'll find something to keep him busy." Marco turned and walked towards the kitchen. I ran after him, but not before thanking Vardan for the lesson, getting a satisfied growl and a wave in response.

"So when are we…" Marco held up a shushing finger and pointed down the hall towards my cell. I managed to remain silent until we got inside. "So when do we go?" The words burst out of me.

"As soon as it's dusk. I imagine your friend Charles will want to delay his meeting as long as possible, but we need to make sure we're in place. Now, one more time… who is this al Sameen?"

"He's a merchant of some kind. Maybe from Damascus…a big fat man…" I went on to repeat, for the third time, word for word, the story I told him the night before. "… and then he went back to the Hospital. Al Sameen and the other two headed back to Montmusard, and I came to tell you."

Marco plunked on the end of my cot, the back of his head against the cool masonry. "What makes you so sure he'll show up tonight? What if he just tells the Brothers at the Hospital about it?"

"He won't." I was surprised how sure I was.

"Why not?"

How could I explain? I'd seen Charles at work. He had

the pathetic sniveling of your average clerk mixed with a healthy dose of over-caution. Like all newly converted Christians, he knew he was never above suspicion. The price one paid for not appearing sufficiently grateful for the privilege of living among people who hated the sight of you, was a steep one. More than one *convérsi fuéritis muslim* paid with their life for not crossing themselves appropriately, or lapsing into Arabic in a moment of weakness. Fear was his normal condition. What I saw last night, though, was much worse. It was mortal terror. He feared al Sameen, and whatever he represented, far more than he worried about Christians.

"He's more scared of the fat man than the Knights."

Marco nodded, his eyes closed. "He's not stupid at least. What do you think he'll bring with him?"

"Information?" I heard the question in my voice and corrected myself before my mentor could. "Information.... Of some kind. Don't know what though."

"That's what we need to find out tonight. That and who your mysterious al Sameen really is. I don't know about you, but I'm not about to do all that on an empty stomach." He got to his feet and left the room. I followed, hot on his heels.

After a quick dinner of whatever we could scrounge in the kitchen while dodging Sister Marie-Pilar's dirty looks and kitchen implements, we found ourselves in the dark musty tunnel. Moments later, we blended into the purple shadows as the sun retired behind the Templar and Hospital houses and tucked into the sea for the night.

The plan called for Marco to find a hiding place with a

good view of the tea house and the street. That probably meant the roof of the building across the alley. That's what I'd have done, although how he'd fit was a mystery. It was my job to watch near the gate for Charles' approach and follow him from behind.

It sounded reasonable enough, except that it called for the one talent I didn't possess. Without something to hold my attention, I couldn't sit still for two minutes at a time, never mind however long it might take until my quarry arrived. Bored and restless, I nearly failed my assignment before it started.

I was at the gate in plenty of time and looked around for a place to wait without getting into trouble. I needed to be unseen by the soldiers but in clear eye shot of the gate. Against the northern wall was a small scaffold and some lumber. If I could sneak in there, it would be ideal. I squeezed in without attracting the attention of the guards. As crowded as it was I wasn't in much danger of detection. It was perfect. Then the boredom kicked in.

It started with a wiggle in my bottom. Then my hands began beating a faint tum-tum-tum starting at the fingertips, then my palms. The real problem was when my legs started swinging back and forth. On a particularly aggressive kick, my foot struck an upright beam. Horrified, I watched it teeter a moment, then crash into the beam next to it, then the next until I felt the board I sat on swing out from under me. With a terrible crash and a geyser of dust, the boards, bucket of whitewash and one small boy all collapsed to the ground.

I squirmed out from under the pile, right into the legs of

two very unamused city guards. Beyond them I spied Muhammed/Charles, head down and trudging through the gate into the alley beyond. I didn't really have time to notice anything else as I was dragged to my feet and spun around to face the King's justice.

What part of my brain hadn't been scrambled in the accident tried to formulate an escape, but it seemed futile. Each of the burly, garlic-smelling soldiers held an arm and looked like they might tear me in half at any moment.

The smartest looking one snarled, "What in God's name are you doing in there, you little shit?"

Nothing clever came to mind. The dimmer one grunted something equally profane but I wasn't paying attention. I frantically searched for a way to escape. *Holding my current position won't help much, thank you very much Jacques.* They didn't have an obvious weakness I could exploit, and the way they held me at the shoulders didn't give me any leverage for an attack. Little good that would have done against trained, if not very bright, soldiers.

My hand was sticky where the pail of whitewash spilled over it, painting my fingers in thick, white guck. That gave me the slightest glimmer of hope. I bent my arm just enough to grip the arm of my stupidest captor and leave a nasty white streak on his hauberk. He dropped me to wipe at it, "What are you doing, you little bastard?"

With my hand free I backhanded a white swoosh across the front of the other soldier's uniform. He yelled even louder than the first man and, in order to give me a well-deserved backhand, dropped my arm as well. That was the only break I needed. While my leper instructors had been teaching me to attack my enemies, nobody had to teach me how to run like hell. I ducked between them and lit out as fast as my bare feet could carry me. They may have been bigger, stronger and fully armed, but I was small, fast and highly motivated.

I slashed through the crowded street like a mouse across a kitchen floor, zigging, zagging, right underfoot but completely uncatchable. I shouted apologies to the civilians I jostled in my dash to freedom.

When I finally stopped in a panting, bending, groaning heap to catch my breath, I looked around. I was safe from the guards, but now I was still a fair way from where I should have been, and had no idea where Charles was.

I wiped the snot from my nose, leaving a white streak across my upper lip and adding to my feelings of uselessness. Scared, angry and frustrated as I was, I was even more worried about disappointing Brother Marco and pulled my self together as best as I could.

The flow of traffic was to the northwest as degenerate gamblers, drinkers and perverts slowly made their way into the depths of Montmusard for the evening's entertainment. The teahouse where Charles met al Sameen was a few blocks away, so I headed in that direction.

My conscience pecked at me all the way, to the point where I overshot the street. It was just as well, Marco wouldn't see me coming empty-handed and useless. It would be easier to approach the place from the back.

The back was where the privies were. Gamblers and

drinkers spewed the poisons from their bodies into pails for the tanners to harvest. These were kept in wooden sheds behind the inns in narrow alleyways. When the drunk or desperate could make it that far, that is. As I approached, holding my breath against the putrid stench, I clearly heard someone retching their guts into the alley.

It was Charles. The clerk was on his knees in the fetid dirt, alternately retching, sobbing and begging Allah, then Christ, then Allah again, for forgiveness. *But for what? What had he done that was so awful?*

I inched closer, looking for someplace to watch while remaining out of sight. Fortunately there were plenty of badly built structures with chinks in the wall that offered a good view of the gambling house and the alley behind it. Unfortunately, those were the privies and it had been a long night already.

The smell was horrible enough from outside. The thought of hiding inside one of these hell-holes was infinitely worse. I nearly settled for hiding behind one, but saw the fat man and his two accomplices step out of the building. Quickly, I slipped into the first outhouse and dropped the wooden catch. Shooing away a couple of rats, one of whom obeyed, I pressed my eye—and nose—to the biggest crack I could find.

I couldn't hear the conversation, but watched al Sameen tiptoe through the muck to the kneeling, sobbing clerk and touch his shoulder. Nodding, the two assistants each grabbed an arm, pulling Charles to his feet. The fat man took a couple of steps closer, allowing me to hear better.

"A terrible place, but maybe not inappropriate for the matter at hand, don't you think?" The merchant offered a clean handkerchief to Charles and looked away, allowing his victim a moment to pull himself together. "Better?"

Charles nodded.

"All right, my friend. Let's not linger in this horrible place any longer than we need to. Did you bring it?" Charles nodded, slowly reaching into the bag at his side and producing a plain roll of parchment, barely big enough to stick out of his fist.

I was disappointed. *This was what all the excitement was about?* If I didn't appreciate the importance of the treasure, al Sameen's smile told a different story. He unfurled the scroll just long enough to ascertain its contents, then rerolled it tightly and stuffed it inside his robe. Charles looked up at the fat man like a dog wondering if the beatings had finally stopped.

"Are we finished?"

Al Sameen nodded. "Yes, we are. Actually, the Sultan hoped to use your services again, but I told him you were too loyal to those Christian pigs." I caught the glint of a ruby ring as the merchant dropped a pudgy hand to his side. "At first I was afraid you might run back to your masters and tell them what you did… but you wouldn't do that would you?"

The terrified clerk's eyes widened and he shook his head. "I'd never…" This brought another comforting pat on the shoulder.

"I know *sadiqa*, I know you wouldn't." The way he said *my friend* didn't sound at all friendly to my ears, but it appeared to comfort the weaker man. "I don't think you'll say anything. I think you'd rather die first." Al Sameen paused as if pondering an important question. "That's the problem, of course. Suicide is a terrible sin whatever God you answer to. I would hate to think of you doing such a terrible thing. You wouldn't try to kill yourself over this, now, would you?"

"No…. never…."

The big man bit his bottom lip thoughtfully and put his hand casually in his pocket. "Good. I'd hate to see you commit an even worse crime. In fact, let me ease your pain…"

As Charles turned toward him gratefully, al Sameen's hand shot out of his pocket. I caught the glint of a knife in the lamplight as the blade slashed across Charles' throat. Blood sprayed several feet in front of him, some nearly hitting my hiding spot.

The clerk clutched uselessly at his throat as al Sameen grabbed his hair. "Allah is merciful. Even the Christian God forgives, but Salah-adin does not, and I work for him." Then he shoved the gargling, sputtering, blood-gushing body face first into the filthy mud where it twitched twice and stopped.

I had seen a lot of awful things in ten years on the streets of the violent, ugly port of Acre, but I'd never actually seen anyone casually slice another man's throat like that. I gagged, nearly choking to death in an attempt to retch silently. I must have failed, because the skinny accomplice's head jerked like a bird and held up a finger.

"I think I heard something." The shorter man, still

dressed as a *converso* ran off to investigate.

"Look around, Rafi. I have to piss," the merchant said to his thin assistant as he entered the privy next to my hiding spot. I heard clothes rustle as I frantically sought a way out. Pressing my eye to a crack in the wood, I couldn't see anyone. I turned to my right, pressed my eye to the hole and saw... another large, blood-shot eye looking in at me.

Rafi's fist hammered once on the wall, making the whole fragile structure shake. "Come out of there, whoever you are." The door rattled against the single stick holding it shut. Another bang, this time directly on the door itself, nearly snapped it open. Through the gaps in the timbers I watched as he lifted a foot to kick it in, then heard a thumping noise and a grunt as he lay on his back in the muck.

A familiar voice hissed in the darkness. "Lucca, get out of there."

I didn't need to be told twice. I threw open the splintered wooden bolt and leaned out, gasping, into the relatively clean night air. Brother Marco's strong hand gripped my arm and jerked me aside. I hugged him tightly and felt him stiffen.

"What's going on out there?" a voice shouted as the other privy door burst open. The killer emerged slowly, that wickedly curved eight-inch blade leading the way. He stepped cautiously. He blanched on seeing his associate on the ground trying to rise to his feet and clutching an egg-sized lump.

Brother Marco held his staff in front of him, the tip down but not touching the stinking mud that squelched beneath our feet. His head was covered by his hood, and he wore only a dirty grey cassock with strong leather boots.

Rafi struggled to get to his feet. "Stay down, damn you," Marco hissed.

The huge goon ignored the order and as soon as he got off the ground, charged like a bull. Before I could say anything, Marco's staff caught him square in the temple, knocking him face down beside Charles' body.

Al Sameen must have thought it was the opening he needed, because he lunged forward, quicker than one would expect for a man of his size. His blade slashed towards Marco's face, but was met by a cracking blow from the quarterstaff and the knife flew into a foul smelling gutter, nearly skewering an inquisitive rodent.

The fat man held his hands up in surrender and squinted, willing his eyes to see through Marco's hood. In perfect unaccented French, he asked *"qui etes vous, Firengi?"* Marco merely shrugged.

Al Sameen nodded, as if it were a satisfactory answer. He took a step forward, but Marco's staff was held a foot in front of his face. That brought him to a sudden halt.

For the first time, the leper knight spoke to me. "Get out of here, go." I looked from Rafi, to Marco, to al Sameen. The big man's hands were still in the air and his robe hung open. Tucked in his sash was the parchment scroll.

"Not yet," I said and took a couple of tentative steps forward.

"What the hell are you doing?" Marco demanded. The murderer didn't need to ask. His hands instinctively dropped, earning him a quick rap upside the head from Marco's staff.

The big man glared at Marco but obeyed and raised his hands again.

I reached out, my hand still smeared with whitewash. It looked grey and scaly in what little light there was. As I neared the Mussulman, he suddenly gasped and tried to pull away from me. For the first time, I saw real fear in his eyes. Then it dawned on me.

He thought I was a leper. The thought made me grin and I waved my hand at his face, just to see him flinch. In the next moment, I grabbed the scroll from his belt with my clean hand, and stepped back, my eyes never leaving his face.

When I drew even with Marco, I looked at the scroll in my white-crusted hand, then at Marco, then at Rafi, who was trying a third time to rise to his feet.

Marco spit through his teeth. "Ready to run *now?*" He didn't need to ask twice. I tore off into the night, back towards the Acre gate and the safety of the St. Lazar House. I could tell from the heavy footsteps, raspy breathing and heart-felt curses that Brother Marco was right behind me so I didn't look back. On the night breeze, the big spy let loose a string of truly impressive Arabic curses that followed us down the narrow alley.

We didn't stop until we reached our secret cellar door. I was too weak to lift the door all the way up. I squeezed through the gap, then turned and propped it open as best I could while Marco wriggled and grunted his way into the tunnel and the door dropped shut, catching his cloak. Neither of us had the energy to care if anyone heard or saw.

For a minute we just lay panting for breath, grabbing our

aching sides and moaning. It was only after my breath returned and I laid on the dirt floor of our tunnel that I remembered the scroll. I wondered what was in it, and what was worth slitting a man's throat like that?

Chapter 9

"Do you have any idea what this is, lad?" Marco stabbed a gloved finger in the middle of the parchment. The scroll lay unfurled on a wooden trestle table, two of its corners held down with candlesticks. Light flickered across the document, but that didn't help reveal its meaning to me. The room may as well have been pitch black for all the good it did. For maybe the first time in my young life, I resented my inability to read.

So, no, I didn't know what that was. I couldn't answer any of his earlier questions, either. *What was I thinking? Was I all right? Where the hell had I been?* Given the night's chaos I don't think I offered very satisfactory answers to any of those questions and I knew it. I was too exhausted to care much, truth be told.

My head swam as I looked down at the document again and tried once more to focus. A wavy line ran down the left, with what looked like a boat on the edge. The rest of the document consisted of more wavy lines, with the occasional Crusader cross—Hospital, Templar or with the four crosses of Jerusalem near the bottom, and some numbers beneath each cross.

"It's a map… I think." This earned me a terse grin and a single nod of the head.

"So you still have some wits about you. I was beginning to wonder. But a map of what? That's the question." Marco paused and took a deep breath as if readying himself to do battle instead of talking to a ten-year-old. He closed his eyes for a second, then leveled them on me and softened the tone of his voice. I could hear the effort it took not to speak to me like I was an imbecile.

"It's a map of the Kingdom... well both kingdoms, Tripoli and Jerusalem. Do you know how I know that?"

I squinted at it, willing the answer to show itself, but it stayed hidden among the squiggles and numbers. I shook my head.

The gloved finger traced down the left hand line. "This is the sea coast. We know that because....." His voice trailed off expectantly.

"Of the boat." I pointed to the boat. "There's nothing there but a boat, so it must be water."

"Good. So where are we?"

I studied the page, willing it to give up its secrets. There were two large dots along the coast. The one on top had a Templar cross and a rough drawing of Raymond of Tripoli's coat of arms. The lower one had some writing, but both a Templar and Hospital cross. *Acre is the only city besides Jerusalem with an equal number of Templars and Hopsitallers, it's got to be that one.* I put my finger on the spot. "There. This is Acre." Brother Marco just looked at me, and I realized he wanted more. I thought that should have been enough of a trick but I continued. "It's near the sea, it has the same number of both Orders and that other city must be Tripoli, yeah?

"That's Tripoli. Indeed it is."

He may as well have carried me around the room on his shoulders, I felt so proud. Still, the fact it was a map was only part of the mystery, and the easiest part at that. I continued staring down at the chart, feeling it mock me. "What are those numbers under each spot?" I knew those were numbers... Arabic, but numbers.

Brother Marco sighed. "That's the bad news, I suspect. You see this spot here?" He pointed to a small castle, like a chess piece, in an otherwise bare spot on the map. "This is the citadel of Kerak. That bastard Chatillon holds it. This number, the five and the zero.... That's fifty.... Is the exact number of knights he has at his disposal.

I could feel my eyebrows scrunching. "What about the others?"

Marco weighed his words carefully, as if he didn't want to tell me but couldn't be sure of his thoughts unless he expressed them out loud. "Well, I have to check the numbers, but if those are troop counts... and I think they are... "

I couldn't wait for him to say it, so I did. "It's a map of how many soldiers are at each settlement, right?"

Marco bit his lip and nodded silently for a moment. Then, more to himself than to me added, "Perhaps, yes. Do you know why Charles would have a map like this?" I shook my head. "What did he do for the Hospital?"

"I don't know. I mean..... He was just a clerk. He counted bags of flour and things like that. He had nothing to do with the soldiers. They wouldn't give information like this to a *converso.* And what would al Sameen want with it?"

"Imagine you're Salah-adin. Would you be interested in knowing exactly how many troops were at each fort? I suspect your fat friend is a spy for the Sultan."

"A spy? But Charles wouldn't help the Mamelukes, they hated him for converting. And the Brothers were good to him."

Marco shook his head. "People do all kinds of things for all kinds of reasons that make no sense to the rest of us. Maybe he felt he didn't have a choice. At any rate, he paid rather a high price for his sins." That conjured up a vision I had managed to momentarily forget- Charles' twitching body bleeding out into the filthy gutter. I felt my stomach lurch, and for a moment I thought I'd be sick right there.

Marco must have thought the noise was my stomach growling. "It's been a long night. Let's get you something to eat and get you to bed." Both were equally tempting, but when you're ten, food wins every time.

A few minutes later, I sat on a bench in the kitchen slurping an overly-ripe persimmon while Sister Marie-Pilar and Brother Marco whispered together, throwing an occasional worried glance my way. I reached up to wipe my face with my sleeve, and Sister's hand lashed out, grabbing me by the wrist. The flakes of whitewash still covered my fingers.

"What's this?" she demanded.

"Relax, Sister. It's just whitewash," Marco chuckled. She picked at the flakes with her fingernail to reveal unblemished brown skin beneath.

"Ugh, men. You're all filthy pigs." She shot a sideways glance at the knight. "Every one of you." Dropping my hand, she licked her apron wiped my face with it, a little rougher than absolutely necessary. "Clean yourself up before you go to bed."

Bathing wasn't at the top of my favorite things to do, and all I wanted to do was crawl into bed. "But the Templars only bathe once a year, and they do all right."

This drew a snort of contempt. "The Templars don't have to share quarters with women or other civilized people. And you, Master Louse, are no Templar."

Marco stepped in to rescue me. "He might not be a Templar, and let's thank God for small mercies, but he did a man's work tonight. Off to bed with you." He took a couple of deep sniffs. "And wash yourself. You smell like you've been playing in a privy." Then he gave me a playful cuff on the back of the head and a wink.

I struggled to my feet woozily. As I left the kitchen, I saw Brother Marco and Sister Marie-Pilar engaged in a hushed conversation, paying me no more attention.

That night was one nightmare after another. Of course I saw al Sameen slit Charles' throat, only it was Brother Marco murdered in the dream. Then I saw Brother Idoneus' hand reaching up from the terrible stinking pit in the privy to grab at me and force me to see his scarred dead face. I woke whimpering, then drift off only to be attacked again by *hashishins* or Hospitallers with the faces of dogs.

When Brother Marco came to wake me, I furiously clawed at his arms and face as I awoke, crying. It took all his strength to crush me against him, enfolding me in those big arms and holding my sob-wracked body close until I breathed normally.

"All right. You're all right. Stop it now…." As if I were choosing to bawl like a baby. Still, I eventually calmed down and wiped my eyes. "Are you okay now?"

I nodded. "Yes. Thank you… I'm sorry I…"

"No time for that, lad. We've places to go."

"Right now? In the daytime?"

Brother Marco nodded. Then he stopped and sniffed at me like a confused hound. "I thought I told you to bathe."

"You were serious about that?"

"Not as serious as Sister was, but yes. You stink. And you're meeting important people today, we don't need you smelling like a camel's arse."

This was news worth bathing for. "Who are we meeting?"

"You'll find out. And it won't matter if we can't get within a hundred feet of him for the reek. Now go. I'll meet you in the kitchen when you're fit for human companionship. Maybe the sisters can burn this bedding between now and the time we get back."

For over a week, my life had been about not being seen by anyone other than my leprous companions. Suddenly I was going to meet someone worth scrubbing up for. I had a thousand questions, and knew none of them would be answered until I was presentable.

I went out to the courtyard to find a bucket of warm water, some rags, a scrub brush, and Sister Fleure standing a safe distance away pointing to them. I nodded and gingerly dipped the rags into the water and ran them over my hands. I heard a disgusted "Pish..." and her rough hands grabbed mine and my flesh burned as the rags, then the scrub brush scoured my skin.

"Strip," she commanded. I froze in place. *Is she serious? Isn't being naked in front of a nun the worst sin you can imagine?* I realized I wasn't truly given a choice when I felt the tunic being lifted over my head and tossed to the ground. My hands reflexively covered my man parts, which drew a chuckle from the nun. "I bathe men all the time, Lucca. Doubt you've got much to shock me." She might not have been shocked, but I certainly was and I squeezed my eyes shut against my shame.

It might have been two minutes, or an hour and a half, but eventually she pronounced me clean enough to meet her standards. My skin tingled and burned from the brushing and scrubbing. Whoever the mystery person was, they had better be important enough to warrant all that torture. She handed me a clean tunic and my sandals.

As if my shame couldn't get any more intense, I heard Sergeant Jacques' voice from somewhere behind me. "Can I be next, Sister?"

Without missing a stroke of the brush, she shouted back, "I don't have the time to deal with your foolishness today. Besides, there's less of him. With you I'd be here all day and still not get the stink off."

"It'd be fun to try, though, wouldn't it?" I couldn't believe he'd talk that way to any woman, especially a nun, but Fleure didn't seem put off. In fact, she tried unsuccessfully to suppress a laugh. A small one escaped her lips anyway.

"You," she shouted behind her, "can just hush up. And you," she turned back to me. "Brother Marco's in the kitchen. Don't keep him waiting longer than you already have."

As if the day weren't full enough of surprises, when I found Marco in the kitchen, he was dressed –not in his beggar's robes—but in full military uniform. He wore spotless robes and a hauberk with the green cross of St. Lazar emblazoned on it. A two-handed sword with the belt hung low across his hips, and he also carried his quarter staff with him. His head was covered in the *coif* the headpiece worn under the helmet. That he carried under his good arm.

"About time. She scrubbed you within an inch of your life." I inspected my shockingly clean hands. "I'm amazed I'm still brown.

"Well, even a Bride of Christ can't work miracles, can she?"

"Where are we going?"

"To meet someone who is going to want to hear about your adventures. You're going to meet Count Raymond."

He may as well have said I was going to meet the Man in the Moon. "We're going to Tripoli?" Marco shook his head.

"We don't have to go so far. He arrived last night with half his troops. He's waiting for us in his camp outside the city. Come on." Without another word he strode out of the kitchen with me eagerly on his heels.

My excitement and confusion only increased when we left through the front door. "Today's official business," was the only explanation I got, but I gladly followed into the glaring furnace that was mid-day Acre.

Without having to maintain his disguise, Marco strode briskly and I struggled to keep up to him as he headed east on the wide boulevard towards the Damascus Gate. *We're going to meet Raymond of Tripoli.* That should have intimidated me, but the thought that thrilled me to the bones was, *outside the city.*

I had never been outside the city walls. My playground, in fact my entire world, had been the streets, alleys, barracks, churches and stinking gutters of Acre. Outside lay a world of terror: wild animals and murderous Seljuks and Heaven only knew what else. Muslim villagers who would sell me to slavers, if they didn't actually devour me first, were just one minor example of the tales we heard. There were Mohammedans in Acre, of course, and everyone got along well enough, but *out there* was different. Even though Raymond's encampment would be within sight of the city walls, when I passed through the gates I might as well be stepping off the edge of the earth.

As busy and crowded as the broad boulevard was, nothing compared to the chaos in the blocks surrounding the Damascus Gate. The din started before I saw what was going on. Knights and city guards shouted and gestured frantically, trying to manage the traffic in and out of the gate. Porters and carters and their animals were everywhere. Vendors milled about, desperate to capture visitors as soon as they entered into Acre, before their purses were emptied by other, more aggressive peddlers, pickpockets or whores. A wall of noise and dust and odor, at least as high and formidable as the sandstone barricades encircling the city, greeted the newcomer to what was widely regarded as the wickedest city in the world.

We were heading the other way, though, against the current and Marco was in a hurry. He nimbly dodged the carts, civilians and ox-dung, only occasionally checking to see that I kept up. The flow of sweating, swearing humanity slowed down and I could see two Hospitaller soldiers were engaged in a lively but futile battle to control the chaos. They alternately allowed people in, then stopped those entering the city to make way for those leaving. Whenever they'd turn their back to allow the outgoing group to pass, someone or a small group would elbow their way past them into the city, and when the soldiers tried to deal with them, they were almost trampled by those impatient to leave.

One of them grabbed at a young water seller who was shouting to the thirsty and grateful new arrivals but blocking traffic and creating an awful mess. Water skins dripped everywhere, and he couldn't maneuver very well, so he bumped into people both coming and going. The guards demanded that everyone halt until order was restored. Most obeyed, although my guide kept walking, with no intention of slowing down.

The sight of a big, formally dressed, knight barreling down on them got the soldiers' attention. One of them nodded to the other and held up his hand like he was actually going to stop us. "Stay close, lad," Marco said and kept walking, with me now in his shadow to the left. The bravest of the guards actually held his hand up to us, but his partner whispered in his ear, nodded and the look in the guard's eyes widened fearfully when he saw the insignia on Marco's chest. He simply knuckled a salute and pushed the water vendor out of the way.

As we passed, I stood a little taller. How proud I was to be with a knight so important. They obviously recognized the importance of our mission and made way for the esteemed person I traveled with. Only later did I realize that what they recognized was the emblem of St. Lazar. They'd not so much made way for our august personages, as got out of the path of an oncoming leper.

My first steps past the gate were anti-climactic. The dust still choked and the sun still hammered us as it did inside the walls. The ground was trampled hard, so it may as well have been paved. The only difference was there was no shade at all. I squinted at the world around me, past the crowds and saw the horizon over land for the first time. The earth seemed to go on forever, and unlike looking at the sea, I was heading towards it and could keep going, presumably forever. My heart pounded a little harder in my chest.

Slightly to the north, a dozen or so tents were set up. Raymond's coat of arms, a red shield with a gold and red cross, flew on a pennant over the largest. Marco stopped and nodded in that direction.

"That's the camp. When we get there, I do all the talking. If someone asks you a question you answer it as quickly as you can and shut up. If the Count asks you a question, you answer him and say, 'your Grace.' Got it?"

I gulped and nodded in agreement. He was worried about me talking too much. I, on the other hand, was worried I wouldn't be able to speak at all. Marco laid a gloved hand on my shoulder and gave me a gentle shove towards the camp. I was about to meet the man who, if fate had decided differently, might have been—depending on who you asked should have been—our king.

I drew closer to Brother Marco as the number of soldiers increased. I could hear the blaspheming, grunting and cursing that accompanied every army, even—maybe especially—those fighting for a holy cause. The dust they all kicked up coated my tongue. I debated which I needed more, to pee or to get a drink of water and couldn't reach a satisfactory conclusion. Besides, my companion didn't seem particularly worried about my needs. His stride increased as we neared Raymond's pavilion.

Four guards stood near the pavilion. One pair were Hospitaller soldiers in fairly clean uniforms. A toothless sergeant held a foaming, bad-tempered black horse by the bridle. Both men and the horse sweated profusely and looked equally miserable.

The other pair wore Raymond of Tripoli's insignia. Unlike the noble Knights of the Hospital, two of the biggest, most cretinous guards I'd ever seen closed ranks over the flap of the tent as we approached. The one on the right, the less stupid-looking of the two if I had to make a choice, held up a mailed hand. "Hold it." Then after a pause he remembered his manners. "Brother."

Marco took a deep breath, gathering the patience to deal

with this fool. "Please tell His Grace that Brother Marco of the Order of St Lazar is here, and the news cannot wait."

The guard's eyebrows scrunched so they formed one furry line across his face. "It will have to wait. He's in with someone."

Marco's voice held an underlying anger and tension even these idiots must have felt. He hissed through clenched teeth, "So you said. Tell him anyway. Unless, of course, you like the idea of lepers hanging about your camp. This looks like a grand spot for a plague, don't you think?"

"Just a moment.... Sir." He turned inside and bellowed, "There's a fancy leper out here, demanding to see Your Grace. Won't take no for an answer."

A sharp laugh burst through the tent's door. "A fancy leper? Well I haven't seen one of those in a while." His voice dropped, and I barely heard him as he spoke to his guest. "Forgive me, Brother, but I suspect this is important. And even if it's not, this one won't stop pestering me 'til I hear him out."

Five seconds later, the smarter of the two morons emerged. "He'll see you now. Brother." This time the title came a little faster and more sincerely.

Marco offered a deep bow of thanks, the sarcasm of which went unappreciated. Turning to me he said, "Stay here until I call for you. And try not to get into trouble. I'm sure these two officers will keep an eye on you."

The dimmer of the two started to say, "Oh, we're not officers..." but took an elbow in his ribs and shut up. "Stand over here and don't make any trouble." He pointed to an empty spot between the tent and his left shoulder.

I obeyed quickly, partly out of fear, partly because it offered a modicum of shade, and mostly because it put me in a perfect spot to hear everything that was said. I heard the swishing of robes and jingling of mail. As I closed my eyes to focus, I heard the loud voice bellow out a greeting. "Brother Marco, it's been too long my friend."

"My Grace, indeed it has. I'm afraid I come on an errand of some importance, and I must speak to you privately." There was a deference in Marco's voice I'd never heard before. This was someone who could overcome my mentor's natural sense of superiority. I shuddered to think how powerful and terrible Count Raymond must be.

The Count paused, then said, "Of course. Brother if you'll excuse us. I will give prayerful consideration to what you've said." There was a pause and then he added, "Brother Marco of St Lazar, have you met Brother Idoneus?"

I nearly wet myself then and there.

Chapter 10

Brother Idoneus? What's he doing here? Without thinking, I took a couple of steps backwards and tripped over a tent peg. The guard with the least teeth laughed until the other one shut him up with an elbow to the ribs.

"Where are you going?" the dentally blessed one demanded.

"I need to pee," I said, still backing away towards the back of the big tent. That was true, my guts churned wildly. That the latrines were far away from this tent was an added blessing

"Back that way, but make it fast. Your master told us to keep an eye on you. Walk where we can see you." He then promptly turned his back, making that completely impossible, but I knew what he meant. I hustled towards the long, low trench set a hundred yards beyond the Count's pavilion.

Once I reached the nasty-smelling ditch, I hiked my tunic and proceeded to empty my tortured bladder with a loud hiss and splash. Closing my eyes in happy relief, I listened to the crowd around me, not quite drowned out by the fat buzzing flies.

I looked around me. The excitement of the new kept the fact that Idoneus was alive—and right here—from overwhelming me.

The arrival of an army like this wasn't an everyday occasion, but it wasn't rare either. The usual people who benefitted from such events were present, in larger numbers than I'd ever seen. A skinny boy my own age ran from soldier to soldier with a dripping water skin. A thirsty pike man or sergeant would curse him for daring to charge one of the Count's men for something as simple as water, then grin and toss him a coin. After four such encounters, the boy ran back to a cart where his mother handed him a full skin and refilled the one he returned. Water was more precious than wine that summer. I envied him his family, but not his job. It looked like a lot of work for little reward.

Vendors of all sorts walked through the camp hawking their wares. Most were male and older. One was female, young and pretty. What she was selling couldn't be delivered on the spot, though. She'd approach a group of soldiers, laugh and whisper the name of her establishment in the ears of the men for later reference. She even started to walk my way, then reevaluated my possibilities as a paying customer and turned away with a "hmph," which I found both unnecessary and mildly insulting. How did she know what I could or couldn't afford? Didn't she know I'd seen breasts in a whorehouse at the age of ten? I was practically a man.

Fruit sellers, cheap wine purveyors, careworn former soldiers hawking weapons that (like their owners) had seen better days swarmed around the new arrivals. Business people of every sex, nationality and body type moved among the soldiers like flies in a corral chasing each other from one pile to the next.

Looking back at the pavilion, one of the guards frantically waved me back. Hopefully Brother Idoneus was gone. I turned back, although taking my own sweet time. It wasn't so scary outside the wall after all. Same people, same activity, in fact the only difference was that the flat dusty earth spread out for miles in three directions. Only the stone walls of Acre, which I now saw from the other side for the first time, formed any clear horizon at all. The world outside was without limits.

Not in any hurry, and to annoy the guard a bit, I pretended I was on a mission with Brother Marco. Since I wasn't sure what passed for "normal" behavior out here, I looked for anything that appeared wrong. The young whore had made her way to the outer fringes of the camp. Not liking the looks of the men she found there, she was now working her way back to her place of employment in the relative safety of the city walls. Her hips swayed, less now than before. Her work was done, and her walk was simply functional now, not a form of advertising. The family of water sellers was down to the dregs of their barrel and I watched the boy try to tip it without letting it drop on top of his crone of a mother.

A fat Syrian in dusty brown robes stood, hands on hips, looking around him as if seeking someone who'd wandered off. I took about a dozen steps forward when I stopped. He wasn't looking around. He was looking up. Specifically, he looked up at one of the battle flags, which Brother Marco said indicated a troop of 25 soldiers.

I risked a glance back, although I could now hear the guard yelling for me to hurry up. I saw him clearly from the side now. His eyes darted from one pennant to another, and I saw his lips move as if counting. *But what would he be counting out here? What would Brother Marco think?* He was probably taking tally of how many soldiers Raymond brought with him. What else made sense? Then he turned and his eyes dropped to ground level again, just in time to look directly into mine, and suddenly I had to pee again. It was al Sameen.

The spy's eyes widened in surprise, then squinted angrily. Suddenly I wanted to be in the presence of those two wonderful, brave, competent, fellows keeping watch at the front of the Count's tent.

Al Sameen took a step towards me, and that's all it took to launch me into full flight. Running as fast as I could, I left little clouds of dust behind me, hoping they'd obscure me from the fat man's gaze. His eyes burned into my back, looking for the perfect place to plant a flying blade. Miraculously, I got to the tent, panting but alive.

The toothy guard dropped a mailed glove on my shoulder. It weighed a ton, but was as welcome as a mother's kiss. "'Bout time. Lucky for you that Hospitaller ain't stopped talking yet. Can't shut his yap, that one."

I risked a look back, to see al Sameen bent low to the ground but facing towards the pavilion. To passerby he was simply working on fixing a sandal strap. He looked up, the right corner of his mouth curled in a terrible sneer.

From just inside the tent, a voice boomed through the

cloth. "I take leave of you then, Your Grace. Remember though, if God be with us, who can stand against us?" The cloth flap blew outwards and Brother Idoneus strode out, followed by a younger man in ill-fitting squire's garb.

The monk was every bit as tall and bald as I remembered, but otherwise he'd changed dramatically. First, he was in full battle regalia. Over full chain mail, he wore the black *cappae*. The robes were bulky, and more suited to the monastery than the battle field, but Idoneus' managed to wear it like a king. It was brand new, or at least unsullied by battle. His egg of a head was covered in a mail *coif*, despite the mid-day heat. All in all, he presented a far more imposing and military figure than the man I'd met back in that room at the Hospital.

In his hands, he carried a small inlaid box, a reliquary of some kind. He cradled it with both hands then bowed in momentary prayer and lifted it high above his head as if handing it over to God himself. The two Hospitallers immediately dropped to their knees, fervently crossing themselves. The Count's men looked at each other and then did the same, with far less enthusiasm.

Idoneus looked around, and seeing that no one was paying much attention, bellowed at the top of his lungs, "Behold a fragment of the True Cross of our Savior."

He waited for everyone in range to stop speaking. Some knelt in the dust, others just looked at each other in bewilderment then dropped too, just to be safe. An expectant hush fell over the camp, at least for fifty yards around us.

Finally having his audience, Idoneus stepped forward and

yelled some more. "It is my holy duty and honor to be the keeper, and with the help of our Lord Jesus, the Virgin Mother and God Almighty, it will lead us to victory." He turned slowly, displaying the relic to everyone around him. A few more people dropped to the dirt. An excited buzz of conversation developed all around.

Idoneus turned, basking in the blessings of God and the attention of the mere mortals around him, and I got a good look at his face. Gone were the handsome, deceptively kind features I knew. An angry, lumpy red scar ran from above his right eye, down his cheek and into the corner of his mouth. His arrogant smile revealed a missing upper right tooth.

I never much cared for religious ceremony, and often got into trouble for not bowing, or kneeling, or chanting at the right time during services. Now my failure to kneel alongside everyone else made me the only person standing for yards, and Idoneus' piercing eyes easily picked me out.

At first, he saw only a filthy boy, probably a heathen, failing to show the proper awe for the symbol of Christ's suffering and its holy guardian. Then it dawned on him who that someone was. Confusion, followed by recognition, more confusion and finally resolution crossed his face in less than a second. The lines of his mouth changed from grim righteousness to a friendly smile, one I recognized too well, despite the missing tooth.

"Lucca, is that you, son? God be praised, we thought we'd lost you." He lowered his hands now, and spread them wide as if expecting me to run into his arms. "Come now, we'll go home." My only answer was to shake my head and take a step backwards.

The squire, standing silently behind him, looked up. My eyes nearly popped out of my head as I recognized Gilbert. The squire uniform didn't fit him, hanging off limply as it did, but my shy friend looked embarrassed and terribly uncomfortable for many more reasons than that. His eyes registered me, then he refused to look at me at all. Idoneus dropped a claw onto the boy's shoulder. "You surely recognize your friend Gilbert here? He and the other boys miss you terribly. Don't you, lad?" This elicited a reluctant, silent nod. He still couldn't bring himself to make eye contact.

The smug bastard smiled at his two armed companions. "Bring our lost lamb back to the Hospital with us, will you please? He seems a bit confused." The two knights looked at each other and shrugged, taking a step towards me, but I ducked behind the Count's guards, still shaking my head in silent fear. No sound came out of my useless mouth.

The Hospitaller knight said nothing more, just nodded impatiently and held his hand out to me expectantly. Irrationally, I almost reached for it then dropped it to my side. I could feel everyone's eyes on me, and I thought about running away. Then I looked behind me for an escape route. Thirty yards or so away, I saw the fat Mussulman watching the proceedings with more interest than most. I looked back at Brother Idoneus and gritted my teeth. If I had to choose, I'd take my chances with al Sameen. At least a blade across the throat was an honorable end.

I was spared the decision when I felt a familiar presence over my shoulder. Brother Marco gripped my shoulder and ever so slightly nudged me to the tent's entrance. "Brother Idoneus, still here?"

The warm smile never left the warrior monk's face. "Indeed, we just found our dear Lucca here. He's been missing from the Hospital for days. I'm just taking him home with us."

"Oh, I think he'll be fine. He's in good hands." Marco's tone remained as friendly and warm as ever.

"Well, one good hand, to be sure," replied Idoneus. Marco's only response to the jibe was to tighten his hold on my shoulder ever so slightly, but the insult's sting never found its way into his voice.

"He's fine. If he wishes to return to you, I'm sure the Lord will guide him home. Meanwhile, he'll stay with me. We have business with Lord Raymond first." This statement must have shocked the monk, because for the first time he appeared truly nonplussed.

Idoneus gestured for his colleagues to bring his horse over. I watched the two soldiers grab the reins and lead him over, motioning for Gilbert to do his Squire's duty. The ill-mannered beast stomped and snorted and almost stepped on the boy's foot.

Idoneus put a hand on the bridle, then turned and locked eyes with my friend. "What purpose would a leper have for a healthy young boy?" he sneered.

Marco never hesitated. "A far healthier purpose than some I can think of." Idoneus managed not to flinch too much, although poor Gilbert's head dropped even lower and he looked as if wished the earth would swallow him whole. "Still, it's Lord Raymond's business we're about today. The Lord can wait his turn."

Idoneus nodded. "He always does. And he's never denied." With that, the monk climbed up into the saddle, and once again raised the reliquary and the True Cross over his head. "The day of victory approaches!" That drew an unsatisfactory cheer from the assembled crowd, but it was the best he would get.

With an exasperated flip of the reins, the horse lunged forward. Gilbert and the two Hospital knights fell in step behind, towards the Kings gate and the sanctuary of Acre and the Hospital.

My eyes never left them until my companion said, "Well, that was interesting."

I risked a look behind me. Sure enough, the big Mussulman was watching, his hand fidgeting at his belt. Brother Marco steered me towards the tent. "Come on, let's go inside. We've work to do." I meekly followed.

I was already numb from the last several minutes, so my face probably didn't register how shocked I was entering Count Raymond's tent. The pavilion was by far the largest tent I'd ever seen. Somehow it looked even bigger from the inside.

I'd heard that the local landholders adopted Syrian ways, one reason the Orders hated them, but never really believed it until that minute. After all, why would Christians act like Infidels? Yet here was proof.

A low trestle table was set up towards the back, with two oil lamps of local Syrian make burning brightly at each end. Plush cushions in garish colors formed a three-quarter circle on the carpeted floor around the perimeter making for much more comfortable seating than the wooden stools and chairs favored by the Hospital and Templars. One lone stool sat beside the table. Idoneus occupied it a minute ago, eschewing heathen comforts out of sheer holy stubbornness.

Beside the table stood the most impressive man I'd ever seen. Raymond St-Gilles, Duke of Tripoli and Galilee, Count of Tortosa and Tiberias, former Regent of the Kingdom of Jerusalem, and the most slandered man in all of Outremer stood with martial ease, hands behind his back. He wasn't as tall as Brother Marco, nor as striking looking as Idoneus, yet there was no question where the power in this room resided.

Sandy brown hair hung to his shoulders, and his cheeks were clean-shaven, although a neat tuft of beard covered his chin disguising a small cleft. His robes were local style, rather than Military or Frankish, and made of a fine green and red material I'd never seen before. At first glance, he might have been mistaken for one of Salah-adin's nobles, except for the gold crucifix, larger than my hand, hanging around his neck and the finely crafted military sword strapped to his hip. His eyes locked on me. The whites were bloodshot and tired-looking but the dark centers fell on me and stripped me of any desire, or ability, to speak.

I stared at the floor, unsure what to do with myself. I felt Marco's hand on my shoulder and the pain forced me to bend a knee, which I later learned was the proper respect to show such a nobleman. Then my guide eased the pressure allowing me to rise again. My eyes stayed glued to the rich carpet.

"My Lord Raymond, may I introduce Lucca Le Pou." I stifled a grin. So "The Louse" was my formal name now? It beat "No-one" I supposed.

The Count said nothing, although his eyes narrowed. "Le Pou isn't a name you usually associate with such a brown face," he said quietly. Every muscle tightened. *Of course he would hate Syrians, he's a Christian noble. Why should he be any different than any other high-borns?* "Or such a dusty face, either. You must be thirsty my friend." He clapped twice, and a boy, my age but a shade browner, appeared in the doorway.

"Ahmed, bring Lucca here some water, please." *Ahmed- That's a Syrian name. Does he have Muslims working for him?* Ahmed must have been a *converso*, but there was no cross around his neck. When the lad disappeared, the Count gestured to the pillows on the floor. "Take a seat. I would like to learn more about you." My body obeyed, which is good because my brain wasn't at all functional.

I sat mutely as the boy reappeared and quietly poured from a pitcher and handed me a cup made of thick glass. It was the first time I'd ever held such a precious thing in my hands and my fingers suddenly tingled like they wanted nothing more than to drop it. I clutched it tighter and nodded at the servant, while avoiding eye contact. My mouth formed the words, "thank you," though no noise came out. He nodded anyway, gave me a friendly smile and a bow, and retreated to a dark corner of the tent.

I took another sip, more to kill time than because I needed it. Count Raymond eventually broke the silence. "Feel better now?"

"Yes, thank you." I felt a gentle but insistent slap upside the back of my head.

"Thank you, Your Grace." Marco hissed.

"Your Grace. Thank you, Your Grace." I parroted.

This drew a chuckle from Count Raymond. "I suspect your tale is interesting, and I'm eager to hear it, but let's stick to important facts for the moment. How does a Muslim boy come to live with Christian lepers?"

"Oh, I'm not a Mohammedan…. Your Grace." My eyes darted to Marco but there didn't seem to be another slap headed my way and I relaxed. "I mean… I'm a Christian. Always have been. My mother was Syrian but my father was a great knight of the Hospital." I clumsily crossed myself just to make the point.

This earned me a raised eyebrow, but he seemed to accept my story. Maybe this would be easier than I thought. "I used to live with the Knights at the Hospital…." Then I ran out of nonsense. What was I supposed to tell him? That Brother Idoneus tried to use me like a whore? That I almost killed the keeper of the True Cross? "But I, uh, ran away." Boys were always running away from orphanages, hopefully he wouldn't probe much deeper. "Brother Marco took me in."

"A strange sort of refuge, don't you think? Living with lepers, I mean." Raymond's eyes never left mine, although his eyebrow stayed up and he was smiling, so at least he wasn't angry with me. The question hung in the air while I frantically tried to formulate an answer, but he let me off the hook. "And you've been, uh, working with Brother Marco, I understand."

"Yes sir, he's been taking me on… missions." I stood taller and straighter as I said the word.

"Indeed? Tell me about the last one. The one where you procured this?" He gestured to the tabletop, where our map lay unfurled.

I told the story, hesitantly at first, then with more energy, and possibly overstating the importance of skill versus blind luck. I wasn't interrupted, although an occasional confirming glance passed between the two men as I rattled on. That kept me more or less honest. "…and that's when I grabbed the map and ran. Of course, Brother Marco did the hard work, the fighting and all." It was only right I give my partner credit for his part in my heroics.

Both men chuckled. "I am glad you appreciate my efforts, boy. It's my honor to serve," Marco offered a slight bow. They both laughed harder than was either necessary or polite.

"Lucca, this is a great service you've done your king. If he were here he'd thank you himself…. Or would if he wasn't such an ungrateful toad…" My eyes popped wide at Raymond's treasonous words. "Now that this spy is gone, will you continue on your… missions with Brother Marco?"

"But he's not gone. I saw him just outside…"

"Saw who?" snapped Marco.

"Al Sameen. He was outside walking around with the crowd." The look of genuine surprise on their faces told me this was more important information than I thought. I immediately assumed my "reporting to Marco" voice.

"What was he doing?" asked Count Raymond.

"Counting troops, I think…. Your Grace. He was looking at all the…. flag things and counting."

Marco nodded. "That makes sense. He wants to know how many troops you brought with you from Tripoli."

Raymond bit his bottom lip. Hesitantly, he said, "Except that I didn't come from Tripoli. I came here from Tiberias. These troops are mostly household soldiers from the castle there." He moved over to the table and leaned over the map looking at it. Marco followed, as did I. The two men leaned over the map thoughtfully. I raised up on tiptoe see, although I had no idea what I was supposed to be looking at. All three of us bit our lips and stayed quiet.

Finally, Marco spoke. "How many men are left at Tiberias?"

Without looking up from the map, Raymond quietly answered, "A couple of knights and their squads. Two dozen or so men at arms."

"Not a lot, but Salah-adin has never really bothered your lands…."

"You're right, I had an agreement with him—have for years. But that whoreson Chatillon attacked a caravan with the Sultan's sister in it. I suspect all treaties are moot now."

"What's at Tiberius that he could want?"

"Land, of course. My people…. And my wife."

"Excuse me, your grace?" Marco asked.

"I left my wife and household at Tiberius. Things were getting…. too complicated in Tripoli. We felt they'd be safer there, away from the madness." The two men exchanged worried glances as Count Raymond tapped his finger repeatedly over the place on the map. If the numbers on the page were correct, it was already one of the smallest garrisons in the Kingdom.

Now it was practically unguarded. If the Mamelukes knew there was nobody guarding the Count's castle, it would be easy pickings.

The knot in my stomach told me al Sameen knew it all too well.

Chapter 11

About half the sun still hung over Acre's wall bathing it in a golden glow that belied the filthy, fetid and corrupt dung heap the city really was. I'd never seen anything quite as lovely. Brother Marco and I walked slowly towards the gate, squinting against the brightness and the dust.

My companion hadn't said a word since leaving Count Raymond's tent. Our meeting ended abruptly, and Raymond suggested—in that way important people have that isn't really a suggestion at all—that we return to the safety of the St Lazar house as quickly as we could. I whole heartedly agreed. Between al Sameen and Brother Idoneus, the dullness of life behind those walls suddenly appealed to me.

The silence eventually became too much, and the questions gushed out. "What do you think Count Raymond is going to do?" This was met with stony silence, so I tried again. "Do you think he's going to go rescue his wife?" More silence. If anything Marco picked up the pace, walking even faster. The only sound was his long staff striking the ground every other step. "What are we…"

"Stop it! Lucca… just… stop." There was a weariness in Brother Marco's voice I'd never heard before.

"But…"

"Please." The exhausted plea was more effective than the

143

usual slap to the back of my head and I fell quietly in line, saying nothing and trying to time my steps to his out of sheer boredom. With such big strides, it's no wonder he was tired. I tried to imagine what it would be like to be so big you could cover that much ground so quickly.

We fell in with the slow moving crowd funneling its way through the Kings Gate. King's guards tried desperately to control the flow of people into the city, but true vigilance was impossible. Instead, the patrolmen looked each traveler in the eyes, asked a question they never really heard the answer to, and waved them on. They actually stopped every third or fourth person, mostly the poor and disreputable looking, and jostled them a bit to give the impression of being in control. The guard closest to us took one look at Brother Marco and waved us through.

Having passed the gate, it was a simple matter of returning home to St Lazar, some food and a bed. My mind ricocheted wildly from one thought to the next. *Does al Sameen know where I am? Will Count Raymond make me a knight? Would I really meet the king?* Lost in thought, I was surprised when Brother Marco suddenly stopped.

"Good evening, brothers. What can we do for you?" The two Hospitallers who'd accompanied Idoneus earlier stood directly in our path, hands up in a silent demand that we halt.

"Evening Brother Marco."

"Well met. To what do we owe the honor?" He leaned a bit on his staff and I heard him wheezing a bit.

"We are to take the boy home." My blood ran cold and, like a little girl, I stepped into Marco's shadow as if that would hide me.

"That's funny, so am I."

The two knights passed a knowing look and each took a step forward and to the outside, flanking us. "There's no need for trouble. We're just returning to the Hospital what's ours. Although why anyone wants the little brat is more than I can guess."

"Then why not let him stay with me?"

"Orders are orders. You know that, Brother." The one on the left reached out to me and grabbed air as I fell back two steps. Fear being more powerful than shame, I shuffled even further back, leaving Brother Marco to face two Hospitallers by himself.

"Exactly whose orders are these?" Marco asked in that dangerous calm way.

"Not that it matters, but it was Brother Idoneus."

Marco's feet were planted shoulder width apart, and his shoulders raised and lowered as he stretched his neck one way or the other. "He calls the shots there now? I never heard of him until today. What does he want with the lad?"

"Don't know. Don't really care. The bald bastard says the boy is Hospital property and we want him back." As the first knight engaged Brother Marco in conversation, the second one took a few steps to the left, circling almost to my friend's right flank. Any further movement was stopped by a wooden staff at chest height. It didn't touch him, but the message was unmistakable. The guard halted, more resigned than frightened, unfortunately. I watched his hand move slowly to his sword.

Marco saw the movement as well, and turned to face the second knight. That's when the first one struck him across the head with the hilt of his sword. With a loud grunt—more surprise than pain-- Marco fell to one knee. He looked up into the point of a sword.

"Don't. Just… don't." The first knight now loomed over Brother Marco, fully prepared to stake him to the ground, Christian knight or not.

While the two combatants glared at each other, his partner reached for me, but I jumped back just out of reach. "Christ's sake boy, we just want to take you home. It's not like we're going to cook and eat you. You really want to stay with a bunch of lepers?"

Yes, I truly did. I wanted nothing more in this world. I knew there was no point in explaining myself. I couldn't if I wanted to. My friend needed my help, and I was completely useless to him. I felt my eyes burn with dammed up tears and tried to think. There were two fully armed Hospital knights against myself and a leper who was already on the ground and at a disadvantage.

"Come on, Brother. He's hardly worth killing you over. Just let us take him and you can go home," the older knight said with all the calm confidence the situation warranted.

Brother Marco planted his staff upright in the ground and sagged wearily against it. To my surprise he nodded. "Yes, fine. You're right."

The second knight offered a grim smile. "That's that, then." I stubbornly refused to let the tears fall, but I hated the notion. Burning with shame, I sniffed and nodded.

The guard reached out, but we both turned suddenly on hearing a loud "thwack" and the unmistakable sound of a body hitting hard dry ground. I heard a strangled "Lucca, run." Marco was still on one knee, but the first knight was flat on his back, sputtering oaths and trying to scramble to his feet. Chain mail had its disadvantages. My guard, acting out of instinct I suppose, ran to help his partner. If I were a real man I might have done the same. I was ten. I ran.

A few seconds and half a hundred yards later, I turned to watch Marco and the two Hospitallers wrestling. Through my tears and the open spots between the backs of the gathering onlookers, I saw grey-black shadows surround a single dark green blur. The sounds of wood and metal striking mail and the terrible sounds of panting and groaning now mixed with the cheers of the crowd.

Wiping my eyes and nose, I was violently jostled on all sides by people trying to catch a glimpse of the fight. I got shoved to the left, then just as I regained my balance to the right again—nearly off my feet. A hand to the back propelled me a few steps forward, then an elbow—probably inadvertent but no less bruising—threw me backward. I felt my back bump against someone large, but paid no attention. I needed to see what was happening to my friend. Standing on tiptoe, straining for a decent view, I was thwarted; there were too many bodies in the way now. I couldn't even hear the fight all that well, the "oohs," and "ahhs" of the onlookers smothered the thump-thwack-grunt of the struggle.

The body behind me pressed closer, and as I turned to

complain, a cloth bag covered my head and the world became a grey, shapeless void. Strong hands pinned my hands together, and my feet left the ground. I was thrown over unknown shoulders and two voices spoke in Arabic.

"Take the motherless runt to the teahouse." One voice commanded. I knew that voice, but couldn't place it.

"Why not jutht kill him?" another, familiar, deeper, voice slurred, sounding as if his lips were too thick for his face. I felt myself hoisted, then dropped again and the grey world spun one way and then the other as whoever's shoulders I was slung across bounced me around, trying to find a comfortable position.

"Not until we find out what he knows. Now do it." My gratitude at not being killed outright was mitigated by a heavy blow to my head that made my senses swim and the greyness became fully black. Whoever it was may not want me dead, but that didn't mean they wished me well either.

Blood pounded in my head and the blackness under my hood was interrupted by bright flashes of white and purple that appeared with each bouncing step. Eventually I was moved to a wagon or a cart. My body bounced against hard wooden planks and I could feel my skull pressed against the side of the vehicle. My captors spread moldy straw over me.

I wasn't about to go passively. Kicking wildly and trying to scream at the same time, my throat filled with straw dust, causing me to cough and wheeze. A punch to my stomach and another to my head convinced me that curling up into a ball and silently sniveling was a more appropriate course of action.

Shame at my inability to defend myself and the knowledge I probably got Brother Marco killed seared through me and outweighed concern for my own situation. I lay in the bouncing cart sobbing, sniffling and sneezing for who knows how long. Each rut in the road threw me somewhere else. I no longer felt the boards against my head, but my body caromed to the side and made contact there, then back to the middle of the cart bed. I strained to figure out where they were taking me.

The babble of multiple languages was overwhelmed by the creak and rattle of the cart on rutted stone streets. The thick smoky smell of food frying and the reek of moldy straw, sewage and the cloth over my head filled my nose. My head pounded. I was completely lost.

Random thoughts zoomed across my consciousness, only to be immediately replaced by stray notions zooming from another direction. *How is Marco? What's going to happen to me? Was that a mouse that just ran across my leg? Who has me? Where am I going? I'm so thirsty…. Am I going to die? What was in this cloth bag before my head?* It's been said many people go blank when panic sets in. For me it only seemed to increase the number of thoughts I could generate in a short period of time.

My captors never spoke, until the wagon slowed and then stopped.

"King'th guardth," lisped the big one.

"Just be calm. And keep him quiet." I knew very well who the "him" in question was and I wasn't inclined to cooperate. I took a deep breath, preparing to scream bloody murder and bring the king's guards to my aid. Why they would suddenly care was a question I didn't consider. The rustle of straw and a firm prick against my neck of what I assumed to be a wickedly sharp dagger changed the plan.

"Shut up or you're dead," the voice hissed. I shut up.

In perfect French, the leader greeted the guards. "Good evening, sirs. How may we help you?"

A gruff Firengi voice growled, "Where are you off to?"

"Bed, Christ be praised. Too much work, too little money made, but such is life, no?" This friendly speech earned a bored grunt in response.

"You're Christian?"

"Thank God we are born who we are, but can be redeemed and saved from the error of our ways."

My eyes nearly bugged out of my head as I listened. *Are they really buying this?* I knew guards were inherently stupid, in fact I counted on it most days, but this was a surprising level of gullibility. No wonder the Kingdom was losing itself to Salah-adin.

"Maybe we should search the wagon for contraband." *Yes, you should, you idiot. You'd be amazed what you'll find.*

"As you wish," my captor crooned. Of course, all you'll find is straw and empty barrels." A hand thumped against wood just over my head. "Of course, when one has been blessed, sharing your bounty is God's will, no?" I heard the jingle of a coin purse.

The guards weren't stupid after all, simply corrupt. "Get home soon. We don't want to see you in the streets after dark. There are spies about. Not everyone will see you for the good Christians you are... brothers."

"Inside Acre? Surely not? Still, God will defend us won't he?" My captor's piety failed to impress the guard.

The patrolman ignored the question and rapped on the outside wall of my prison. "Get this thing out of here." The wagon lurched forward. I felt my body slide lower in the cart, and my feet touched wood, then air. I'd nearly bounced out of the cart.

Without thinking too much about it, I hooked my ankles over the cart's lip and scooched forward. One bounce, then another, then a sensation of falling and landing on the ground. *If the guards were still watching...*

I took a ragged breath and bellowed for all I was worth, *"Me adiuvate. Sunt interfectores!"* Help me, they are killers, I shouted. My breath expired in a dusty cough and gag, spitting the words out with bits of straw and dirt. Commoners, and especially Syrian converts, didn't speak Latin. I doubted the city patrol guards did, but if they heard that tongue there were two things they'd know: first, that I was Christian, or at least connected to the church. Most importantly, I was important enough to pay attention to.

I felt hands grab my robe, and my backward momentum shook the covering off my face. Rafi glared at me, murder written all over his face. He still bore the marks of Brother Marco's quarterstaff. I yelled again, in French this time, "Help, they're trying to kill me." The tall killer grunted an obscenity in Arabic, and struck me with the back of his hand.

He only got one shot in, though, before the guards screamed at him, "Put the lad down. Put him down or by

God we'll…" I didn't hear the rest as I thumped to the ground and scrambled to my feet. I stumbled several steps away, then risked looking up. Al Sameen—the other man had to be he—was nowhere to be seen. Rafi stood alone, a curved blade in his hand, facing both city guards and their swords.

A crowd of the curious formed an arena around us. "What are you doing with the boy?" the patrolman shouted again. Rafi simply sneered and looked behind him to see that the ring of onlookers eliminated any chance of escape. The jangle of chain mail announced the arrival of several more city guards, and the big Saracen's shoulders slumped.

"Put down the knife, you prick. Do it." Rafi didn't comply. Instead, he lifted the knife and lunged at the nearest guard.

"Allahu akbar," burst from his throat and he swung the blade in a vicious backhand. Two guards moved forward at the same time, swinging their swords. The first caught Rafi's arm on the way down. Both hand and knife fell into the dirt amid a spray of crimson droplets. Rafi's eyes may have registered the loss, but he didn't have time to scream. The second guard swung his sword overhead, striking Rafi's shoulder and slicing through his body clear to his hip.

For the second time in only a few days, a bloody corpse lay at my feet. Rafi's lifeless eyes looked at me accusingly and for a brief moment, everything was silent. Then all hell broke loose.

Hands prodded and poked at me. I was buffeted by questions shouted from all sides. "What was that about?"

"Who were these men?" "What did they want with you?" "Who are you?" I wasn't sure I had the answers at that moment.

Eventually I regained the ability to speak, and managed to stutter out my story. "He's a Mussulman spy." More noise erupted and even more questions followed. Eventually I was able to spew out the bones of the story; Rafi and al Sameen's spying, Charles' murder, why they kidnapped me, who I was.

One sergeant finally asked me, "Where do you live, boy?"

"St. Lazar. The Hospital of St. Lazar." Not only did that shush the crowd, but offered me some much-needed breathing room as everyone took a quick step back. Being presumed a leper had its advantages.

"We'll take you home boy." A short sergeant stepped up. "I've got him."

We walked more or less silently for ten minutes, which was plenty of time for me to wonder about Brother Marco. *Is he all right? What happened to him? What will happen to me? Where is the fat man, and what did he want?* Finally, we arrived at the front door of the Charter House and Sergeant Louis rapped loudly on the door with a mailed fist.

The door cracked an inch, then flew open. Behind her veil, Sister Marie-Pilar's eyes were wide and frightened.

"Pardon me, Sister, he says he lives here…" Louis began.

She barely had time to ask, "Lucca, what in the name of God…" before I shot forward and wrapped my arms around her. Strong, thin arms enveloped me, and her breasts cushioned my head as I collapsed into the most comforting hug I'd ever experienced.

Chapter 12

The cool, damp cloth felt wonderful against my face--almost as good as Sister Marie-Pilar's hands on my skin; comforting and what I could only imagine was motherly. Between strokes and coos she pried the story out of me. I'd only gotten as far as Marco's fight with the Hospitallers, when I had to start over as Sergeant Jacques arrived and began demanding answers I'd already provided, then started over a third time as the kitchen filled up with curious, worried lepers.

"And where is Marco now?" Sister Fleure honked.

I shook my head. "I don't know. He was fighting with those knights and…"

"Wait a minute, boy. You left a comrade behind?" Jacques accusation stung.

"Jacques, he's just a…" Fleure offered.

"He left a friend on the battlefield. Is that what we taught you, you little…"

"Jacques…" Sister Marie-Pilar attempted to intervene, but the old soldier waved her off.

He leaned over me, his crumbly stub of a finger stabbing at my face. "A real soldier never leaves his fellows…"

"He's not a soldier for God's sake, he's just a little boy…" Fleure's excuses struck deeper than Jacques' charges.

"I didn't leave him," I protested, sounding precisely like a whiney little boy. "I was grabbed and thrown in a wagon."

"Who grabbed you?" Vardan demanded. "Everyone just shut up and let the lad tell his tale."

I took a deep ragged breath. "It was al Sameen and Rafi..." I could tell from the confused faces that meant nothing to my audience. I took another run at it. "Two ... spies. A big fat one, that's al Sameen...and a really tall mean one..." I stopped, remembering Rafi's bloody, butchered corpse laying in the dark dusty street.

The questions came faster and more insistent. I sagged under the assault. "Why did they grab you?" "What did they want?" "How in heaven's name did you get away?" The replies stuck in my throat as I opened my mouth uselessly. Unable to drag any sensible answers from me, they turned to questioning each other.

"Where's Marco?" "What does this all mean..."

"It means there's trouble coming," came a ragged voice from the doorway. Everyone turned to see Brother Marco standing there. His dress uniform—so clean and impressive just hours ago now covered in light spatters of blood, the tan dust of the streets and smears of the darker brown mud from the secret tunnel. A bruise on his cheek matched the dark circles under his eyes.

Sister Marie-Pilar's arms disappeared from around me as she leapt towards him. He stood stiffly as she took inventory. A quick look and a slight shake of his head caused her to drop her hands to her side. Pulling herself together she asked, "Are you all right.... Brother?" He took a half step back and gave what was supposed to be a reassuring nod but was undermined by a wince. It fooled no one, but she nodded back. "I'm glad." Then she stepped away from him, wiping her hands on her habit.

Everyone pretended not to see anything for a moment, then Jacques mercifully broke the silence. "Doesn't answer the question. This country's nothing but trouble. What's really going on?"

Sister Agnes's bird-like voice peeped, "Lucca, you go on to bed now. This isn't something…"

"No, sister. He needs to hear this. He's part of it now." Everyone turned to look at me as Brother Marco took a couple of commanding steps to the center of the circle. "It looks like it's finally happened. Salah-adin has tired of mucking about with us and means to declare all-out war."

Vardan coughed. "Why now? I thought he and Count Raymond, had…. you know…. an understanding."

"They did… now they don't. That arsehole Chatillon made sure of that when he attacked the caravan and attempted to ransom the Sultan's sister. The King and the Orders have sided with him and the other Frankish nobles. They want war. Salah-adin's nobles want war. Whatever good will the Count built up between them isn't enough to stop what's coming."

Marie-Pilar asked, "What does this have to do with Lucca?"

"I'm afraid our friend, Monsieur Louse here, helped uncover some of the Sultan's spies hiding in Acre." I met their collective stares with a small grin and a nod, hoping to convince them I had done any of this on purpose. Creating deliberate chaos is one thing, letting things spin out of all control quite another.

Vardan crossed his hairy arms, sucking at his bottom lip with his head tilted to one side like a dog trying to grasp why his dish is empty. "Wait a minute, if the spies are Syrians, why were you fighting with Knights of the Hospital?"

This wasn't a part of the conversation anyone needed to know about. "They wanted me to come with them... and I didn't want to.... Brother Marco stopped them."

Sister Marie-Pilar pushed a dangling lock of hair out of my eyes. "Maybe the Hospital is the best place for you. They have other boys, and you'll be safe..." Her eyes widened as I recoiled at her touch.

"No, I can't. I... please, I can't."

"Oh for heaven's sake, why not?" She spit, in the voice reserved for recalcitrant patients and kitchen thieves. "You're much safer there than you are here." I hugged my knees up to my chest and didn't reply.

Marco softly interrupted. "The lad has his reasons, Sister. But he can't stay here either. It's not safe."

I hated the whine in my voice but couldn't stop myself. "But you said I was safe here. You said I couldn't catch... you know"

"I meant safe for the others, you little brat," Marco's voice was tired, angry, frustrated and quite done with me. I had heard that tone many times before. "For whatever reason, Idoneus has taken an interest in you, and we can't resist them for long. Your... al Sameen as you call him...

Knows you're here too. None of the others are safe as long as you're here."

Most of my life I was getting other people into trouble. Whether it was Fadhil's beatings at the hands of his father or the maternal tongue lashings poor Murad endured on my behalf, I was constantly creating turmoil and it never bothered me much. It seemed to be the price others paid for basking in my presence; and one they willing paid. Even at my young age, I knew that when a house full of lepers was worse off simply because of your presence, you'd messed up very badly indeed. Perhaps beyond repair.

"But where will he go?" Fleure twittered.

"Just let me think, woman. Damn it." A startled hush fell over the room. Even Jacques, who uttered more or less the same phrase twenty times a day was shocked at the knight's outburst.

"She was just asking... Sir. Seems like a fair question." An embarrassed nod and wave of a gloved hand served as an apology. For a moment, the only sound was the tap, tap, tap of the knight's wooden quarterstaff on the kitchen floor.

"I have an idea, maybe, but I won't know for sure until tomorrow. For now, let's call it a night." Brother Marco's suggestion was met with begrudging murmurs of assent that rippled around the kitchen.

Sister Marie-Pilar gently patted my arm. "Off to bed with you."

I shuffled out of the kitchen, down the hall to my room. The notion of running away occurred to me as it had about three times a day for most of my life. *Where would I run to, though?* The streets and alleys of Acre had always been my refuge, to run its back lanes and rooftops until whatever trouble I was in blew over. Now that was no longer true.

I'd only just slipped under the blankets when I heard a soft rap on my cell door and candlelight oozed around the edges. The door opened a crack. Sister's long pale fingers, then her face appeared. "Lucca, may I speak to you?"

It took two tries, but I finally managed to croak out, "yes, Sister," and scooched across the bed, my back to the wall and the blanket over my lap.

The nun smiled over her veil, reaching into her sleeve and pulling out some fat dates. "Would you like some?" My eagerness was met with a laugh and she sat on the end of my bed, a discreet distance away. She held one of the sugary treats out to me, which I gratefully shoved into my face in one motion. This earned another laugh and the nun took one herself. I watched her lift her veil with her left hand and bring the date to her mouth. The delicate bite was met with a most indelicate moan of pleasure. "Mmmm. I love dates."

I was still dealing with the concept of nuns enjoying anything, so I wasn't prepared for her next question. "Lucca, why won't you go back to the Hospital?"

"It's …. Not safe for me there." How can I explain this to her? How would she know what happened to me? How I feel? "It's just better here."

"Did someone try to hurt you? Was it one of the other boys?"

I felt my cheeks burn. *She'd never understand.* Maybe just part of the story would suffice…. "No, it was an adult. He tried to… he tried to hurt me, but I hurt him instead. Badly…. And I can't go back because…. I hit a Brother Knight with a candlestick… and…. He was hurting me. I didn't want to," The words clogged up my throat and I tried to shake them free with another of Marie-Pilar's dates.

The little nun said nothing for a moment. She lifted her veil enough to spit a date seed into her hand, then set it on the blanket beside her. She made even that act seem delicate and bird like. I was beginning to think women were a wonderful mystery that I really needed to explore more fully. Not like at the brothel. Although that, too, I supposed, when the time came.

"He must have tried to do something terrible, for you to do that." It wasn't a question, and I didn't feel compelled to provide more information. I nodded and concentrated on sniffing a huge booger back into my nose where it belonged.

She took a deep breath. "You know, whatever he did…. or tried to do…" That came out as a question but I just hugged my knees closer to my chest, and after a long moment, she continued. "That could happen anywhere. Can I tell you what happened to me my first week here?"

I lifted my eyes up, trying not to seem too eager. "Mm-hmm."

Sister leaned against the stone wall and paused, taking a deep preparatory breath. "I was just newly arrived here. It was just after I got …. sick, you know…. And it was my first day in the sickroom, helping out. I didn't wear…" she waved a finger at her veil, "…yet. I was just changing bandages and offering drinks of water. One of the patients, a Templar, newly arrived… we'd been talking. He seemed kind enough, and offered to help me refill my bucket. When we got to the rain barrel, though, he pushed me against the wall and tried to…. to touch me…."

I tried to imagine how horrified she must have felt… as a young nun to feel a man's hands on her must have been terrifying… and scabby, deformed, leprous hands at that… and in a House of God….

"What did you do?"

"Nothing. I stood there like a cornered mouse and just let him…. Someone came and pulled him off me. One minute he was there, pawing at me, and the next…"

"It was Brother Marco, wasn't it? Who saved you?" I offered, sure I knew how the story ended. Of course it would be Marco to the rescue.

She shook her head. "No, Sergeant Jacques. Really. Brother Marco pulled the two apart and probably saved the man's life." I knew what the bad tempered soldier was capable of when he was just trying to help and tried to imagine what he would do to someone he was actually motivated to hurt.

"Do you think he should have touched me, Lucca?"

"No."

"So why did he do it?" I was bewildered. She was a Bride of Christ, not some tavern wench. And scarred… it's not like she was so beautiful he couldn't help himself. I mean he was sick too, so it's not like he'd have caught anything but still…. And a Templar, sworn to his own chastity although everyone knew how knights of every order were about that particular

162

oath.

"You didn't deserve that," I offered. She didn't, either. I was outraged on her behalf.

"We don't deserve the bad things that happen to us, any more than we deserve the good things that happen. Some people.... men particularly," she added with surprising venom, "Are going to do terrible, sinful things. It's not the fault of the mouse that the cat tries to eat them. It was no fault of mine that he thought he could touch me in that way, and..." Her hand dropped to mine. It felt cool against mine as she gave it a soft squeeze, "...whatever that man tried to do to you is not your fault either."

She continued speaking, but I couldn't hear the words. My head pounded with heat and guilt and shame and fear and anger and suddenly I started sobbing. Ladles of tears seared my cheeks and my chest heaved convulsively; so hard it felt like I was retching.

Sister Marie-Pilar's cool hand just rested on my back and she said nothing for the longest time. She just sat, humming and stroking my hair. "You're a good boy, Lucca."

"No, I'm not..."

"Yes, you are"

"I'm not.... I'm really not." I wasn't, but for the first time in my life I wanted to be. I lay with my head in my lap and her stroking my hair for the longest time. Her chest rose and fell, and my head pillowing on her breast was the most heavenly feeling ever. Then I realized something. My head. Was on her breast. I had my big stupid head on a nun's breast. I was going to hell for sure.

I leapt away from her like a scalded cat. "I'm sorry… I didn't mean… I mean……

She covered her mouth with sticky fingers. "Oh, yes. Well…. that's quite all right. No harm done. It's past my bed time. Yours too." I reluctantly pulled my blanket around me. She slipped out without another word, taking the candle with her and leaving my cell in total darkness. It seemed a lot colder, too.

What sleep I got that night came in short chunks of oblivion interrupted by panic-inducing dreams. Each time my eyes popped open, I struggled to remember exactly what knife-wielding, fang-toothed monster pinned me down, trying to devour me. I vaguely recalled a Hospitaller Knight wearing a caliph's turban and a veil threatening to make a meal of me, starting with my boy parts, but that image was only one of too many that came that night.

The never-ending drought had sucked any remaining moisture from the air and even before the sun popped over the courtyard wall I knew the day was going to be merciless. As relentless as the sun promised to be, my instructors were worse.

"Are you sure you don't want to take a rest?" I looked up at Vardan from my usual position on my back. "You look tired."

"Of course he's tired. You try throwing 75 pounds of shit across the yard over and over. You're wearing him out." Sergeant Jacques sat on the bench in a sliver of shadow, digging his three good teeth into a wrinkled, but not completely rotten, golden persimmon. He impatiently waited his turn at me.

The big Armenian wiped a hand across his chest fur and smeared a dark wet line across his trousers. He just grunted and nodded at me in the universal sign for, "come here and let me beat on you some more." I nodded in resignation and took another run at him.

Ordinarily, there was a playful air to his thumpings that made them bearable—even enjoyable—compared to the more determined beatings I took from the Sergeant. Today, though, my companion was all business. Apparently, coming as close as possible to killing me was meant to keep me alive. It must have been the same principle they used in the Hospital; to drain all the blood from someone in an attempt to wear out the disease. I could only hope the results would be better in my case. For sure leeches hurt less. He didn't even bother to let me close this time, just gave me a backhanded swat that sent me sprawling even further away than usual.

"All right, take a break you hairy bastard." Jacques reluctantly rose to his feet.

Sister Fleure ran over to Vardan with a cup of water and his crutch, which he accepted with a shy smile. "Thank you, Sister." The large nun dropped her eyes and, so help me God, giggled before skittering off. With a sigh of relief, my wrestling instructor put the wooden cross piece under his arm and shifted the weight from his bad leg. He waved in my direction. "He's all yours. What's left of him."

This garnered a sarcastic "huzzah," from Sergeant

Jacques, who was wrapping an extra layer of bandages around his bad hand. If he was hurting more than usual, that would put him in a worse mood than usual, and that didn't bode at all well. I hurried over to grab my wooden practice sword but he ordered me to stop.

"Won't need that today. We have something else in mind."

"What's that?" I asked. From his belt he drew a dagger. The thin blade was about seven inches long and dulled with age. The knife was ancient, but the hilt was wrapped in dark brown leather that looked brand new.

"Haven't got time to make a swordsman out of you. Let's see if you can handle something a little easier. Even a woman can handle a knife."

"Like that whore in Joppa?" shouted Vardan.

The soldier snorted. "She outweighed this one by a hundred pounds… And I was drunk."

"You should have wrapped something other than your hand that night… as I recall…." Vardan's reminiscence was interrupted by a slap to the back of his head from Sister Fleure.

"Enough of that. The lad doesn't need to hear about all of this. He's still an innocent—unlike the two of you, who are beyond even God's help."

My instructor ignored her and held the knife out to me, hilt first. "Go on, take it." My fingers wrapped around the leather. I felt the ridges against my palm. The knife was heavier than it appeared.

"God help me," the sergeant muttered. He took my

fingers, nearly ripping them off my hand. He roughly rearranged them so my palm was down, the blade flat, and my arm bent. "That's how you hold a knife, understand. Every time. Like that."

I nodded. He took my wrist in his good hand and slowly lifted it to his eye, then across his throat, and finally he traced a diagonal line across his stomach. "That's where you slice a man. Eyes, throat, stomach. Anywhere else and he'll have his chance at you. Understand, you don't want to fight him. You want to end him. Now, come at me."

I weakly thrust my arm forward, and Jacques' thickly bandaged arm flashed out, catching me across the wrist. The dagger flew ten feet and landed in a puff of dust. The throbbing in my arm told me there were, indeed, places on my body I hadn't bruised yet.

"Don't poke at your man. Slice him. That way even if he blocks you, you'll hurt him. Remember this isn't a duel. There's no such thing as an honorable knife fight. Open him up, thrust hard and twist. Understand?" The image of al Sameen slitting Charles' throat in an eye-blink reinforced the message. I nodded and bent my knees for the next, probably useless, attempt.

"Are you sure you're ready?" One thing I learned in my time training with Vardan and Jacques, is that when a teacher asks if you're ready, you're not. *What in God's name am I doing wrong this time?* I adjusted my feet and looked into Jacques' face. Instead of the usual contempt, there was a worried expression I'd never seen.

"What's wrong?" I asked.

He shook his head and offered a quiet, "Nothing boy, there's just so little time…" he paused, then in a normal tone barked, "Come on. I haven't got all day. Open your man up, thrust, twist." He set his feet and beckoned me forward.

This time I brought my weapon in from the right side in an attempt to slice, rather than poke, and again he blocked it. Despite the lightning bolt running up my arm, I didn't drop the knife. Without pausing, I swung my arm back the other way as fast as I could.

I don't know which of us was more surprised by the drops of blood that landed beside the Sergeant's feet. I think it was him, because he gaped dumbly for a second, before lifting his elbow to inspect the three-inch gash in his fore-arm. "Damn it to hell," he spat.

"I'm sorry, I…."

"Don't be sorry, you little idiot. That's what you're supposed to do when you've a knife in your damned hand." Jacques pressed the bandages on his other hand against the wound and took a deep ragged breath. "You may live to be eleven yet. Assuming I don't kill you first."

Vardan shouted from the bench. "You'd best let Fleure take a look at that." Jacques lifted the bandages away. He didn't argue the point.

"Suspect so." He said. I held the knife out to him, hilt first, and he gave me the first real smile I'd ever seen from him. "No, that's yours. Keep it. Keep it close." Then he walked inside.

I stood in stunned silence watching the toughest man I knew walk away with a wound—shallow and harmless as it was—I'd given him. I probably should have felt pride, or happiness, or at least relief that the beatings had momentarily paused. I didn't. I felt awful.

"Lucca?" Brother Marco's voice penetrated the fog in my head and I turned to see him standing there in his beggar's rags. "Come on, we have to go."

"Where to?" I asked. My mentor bit his lip and waved me on.

"You're not going to like this."

He was right.

Chapter 13

Marco was absolutely right; I didn't like it. First, I didn't want to leave the House of St Lazar at all. Secondly, I didn't want to live outside Acre's walls with Count Raymond's people and sleep in a tent with a dozen or so of his servants. Maybe most of all, no one told me that work was really hard, and water deceptively heavy.

"Careful, you'll spill again." Ahmed was just about out of patience. He was no happier being my leash-holder than I was, but he'd tried to be friendly and supportive up until a full pail of water soaked him. To be fair, as a boy my age, he'd never been in charge of anyone or anything before, and certainly not anyone as completely useless as me.

About my age, Ahmed was half a head taller than I and about as big around as Marco's oak staff. That didn't stop him from effortlessly shouldering heavy earthen jugs or slinging a pole with full skins of water at both ends across his neck like it was nothing. It was not nothing. I managed to do it twice before my arms ached like I'd trained with Vardan all day and could barely lift anything to shoulder height.

Our job was to fill all the available buckets and water skins around the camp before it got too hot. I was slowing things down considerably, so I was a little surprised when Ahmed called for a break. "Lucca, stay here. I'll be back in a few minutes."

"Can I come?" He was pleasant enough company, and as long as he was on a break, I supposed I was too.

"If you want. I have to go to prayers." I knew the monks went to chapel multiple times a day, but I'd never met anyone—at least anyone who wasn't a priest—voluntarily drop everything in the middle of the day. Even at St Lazar the various services, except for morning mass, were more or less suggestions.

"Where's the chapel?" I asked. Then it occurred to me. "Wait. You're a Mohammedan?"

"You're not?" he asked, equally incredulous. I suppose I should have been insulted that he couldn't discern my obvious Christianity just by looking at me. His open apostasy in a Christian army camp surprised me, though.

"Does Count Raymond know?" I whispered so as not to betray his secret to any soldiers passing by.

"Of course he knows. There are ten people from my village here plus a few others." He sped up, joining several older men trudging through the dust towards a ramshackle tent at the eastern edge of Raymond's camp.

I followed quietly, looking everywhere for signs of trouble. I thought we were dead when several of Raymond's guardsmen walked up to us, but they didn't roust everyone and throw them to the dogs like good Christian knights would. Instead they took a standing rest position at the four corners of the canvas as maybe half a dozen men and boys entered, faced the cloth wall at the back of the hovel, and knelt on the rugs that served as a floor. They appeared to be standing guard, which confused me more.

One of the men began to recite in Arabic, and everyone else followed with a series of bows, salaams and responses no less bewildering, and only slightly more ridiculous, than I'd seen the monks do in the Hospital Chapel.

I watched, and eventually curiosity turned to boredom like it always did during religious services. I asked the least intimidating—which meant shortest and youngest—guardsman what that was all about. "Do you know what they're doing in there?"

He turned his head and looked back at me slightly confused. "Praying, right?"

"Are they allowed to do that?" The question was met by knitted brows.

"I think they have to. Five times a day, if you can believe it."

"No, I mean... won't they get in trouble? Does the Count know?"

"Course he knows. It's why we're here. Some of the men don't much like them doing that so we watch out til it's over. Then they go back to work. The Count and them have an agreement."

The guard—Pierre it turns out--explained it was a matter of practicality, although a word that complex certainly never crossed his thin lips. "You ever been to Tiberias?" he asked. I didn't want to tell him that this exact spot was as far from Acre as I'd ever been, so I simply shook my head. "They outnumber us by plenty. Couldn't kill them all if we had to.

And then what would we do for workers? So the Count, he leaves 'em alone to do as they please. Long as they pay their rents and give him his share of the crops, he doesn't much care."

The Count I met seemed like a good Christian, his taste in furniture aside, and no idiot. "But aren't you worried? I mean, don't they all want to kill you?"

Pierre just sniffed. "Most of 'em are too busy working and living and taking care of their squawlin' brats. Women are prettier too, what we can see of 'em. We don't bother them, they don't bother us. Least until lately. There's been some trouble makers, some say Salah-adin is sending in spies to stir things up." I thought about a fat merchant somewhere beyond the camp and realized it was more than likely. "That's one reason the Count brought some of them with us. Just to ensure everyone behaves. Well that and they cook a whole lot better than soldiers so long as you don't like pork."

The chanting and muttering inside the makeshift mosque went on for a while, and though I didn't understand all of it, I translated enough to know that, far from sinister and arcane, their appeals to Allah sounded exactly as boring and mundane as those we Christians made to Mary and Jesus. Not one word about eating Frankish flesh or driving us into the sea. It all seemed a bit disappointing.

The men emerged blinking into the bright noontime sun. The oldest one lowered his head in thanks to my friend Pierre, who maintained a professional demeanor and offered a grudging nod in return. Ahmed walked close beside the man, and there was a slight resemblance, although the older man was more bent and worried-looking than his years warranted. My friend waved me over.

"*Khal*, this is Lucca. Lucca, this is my Uncle Ahmed" The older man, a maternal uncle judging from the title, gave me a polite toothless smile and touched his heart in greeting.

"Salaam Al-aikum."

I touched my own heart in an automatic response. I almost offered my own "wa-Alaykum," then remembered some took it as a great insult for a non-Muslim to return the greeting. My hesitation only brought another smile that crinkled his brown face, so much like my own.

"It's quite all right to greet one another in peace, young Frank, as long as one means it." Well that was a relief. I hadn't insulted him. Lately it occurred to me that being polite to adults was a much better policy than I'd ever thought. Obviously, Ahmed had explained my situation.

As we walked back to the water wagons, we chatted about nothing in particular. At first, the two Syrians spoke in Outremer French, but I figured it would be politer for me to speak their tongue. I managed pretty well, except for the occasional slip when I wasn't sure of the word.

The afternoon passed easier, now that I had more than one person to bother with stupid questions. When the others saw how comfortable Khal Ahmed was with me, they felt at ease enough to laugh at my shoddy work openly, rather than up their sleeves. The easy camaraderie made me feel less lonely, and a tad less homesick for my friends at the House of St Lazar.

Quickly the cisterns were loaded on wagons and covered

with thick cloth and tied down. Ahmed—the uncle not the youngster—*and why is every other Syrian named Ahmed?*—had me reef hard on the rope as he tied it down. He hummed ceaselessly as we worked. At last I worked up the nerve to ask something I'd wondered all afternoon.

"Uncle, may I ask you a strange question?" He wiped sweaty hands on his robes.

"Strange questions get strange answers, but go ahead," he offered with only the slightest hesitation.

"Do you want to kill me?"

"Why, what have you done?" he asked, looking surprised. I gulped, but he couldn't hold back a smile. "I admit, that is a strange question, boy. Why would you even ask it?"

"Well, the Brothers tell us that all Saracens want to kill Christians, and it's a Christian's job to kill infidels. But you live and work with Count Raymond. His guards even help you pray."

"Do you want to kill me?" he asked. I shook my head so hard it nearly flew off my shoulders. "That's a relief. Leave war to the warriors. I'm too busy taking care of my family. If God wants me to kill someone, I'm sure he'll give me a reason. Besides, if everyone killed everyone they were supposed to, we'd all be dead a long time ago. Especially you, since you are rather an affront to both sides, no?"

That took me aback. Until that moment I assumed both Christians and Muslims would have been proud to claim me. "The Count is wise enough to know that if he wants peace, he has to be peaceful. We know that if we want to be left alone, we leave him alone. Live and let live. Besides, he protects us from Salah-adin's people."

Now I wasn't sure if he was making fun of me or not.

"Hey there. Give us some of that water." A loud voice boomed in very proper French. I saw two Templars, both a head and a half taller than any of us sitting on Arabic horses so massive they blocked out the sun. The animals were panting, covered in white lather. Their hooves shifted nervously, no doubt looking for bare toes to trample.

Before I could stop myself, I heard my mouth say, "But we just got everything tied down".

That was met by a stern eyeball warning from Ahmed, who slumped his shoulders a bit and nodded meekly to the knights. He held up his hands, pleading for a moment and began to untie the tarpaulin we'd just lashed down.

One of the Templars, a huge dark-haired man with a square beard that reached to his collar held his helmet under one arm. Glaring at me, he harrumphed, "Teach that young one some manners, or he'll learn them somewhere else." Uncle Ahmed bowed repeatedly.

"Yes, yes. Of course, Sir Knight." Ahmed took a ladle of water and held it out to the man, who carelessly grabbed it and poured it over his head and let out a huge sigh, relishing the slight relief from the heat. Then he handed the ladle down again, and once more Ahmed filled it and handed it back. This time the huge man slurped it down, at least half of the water spilling in streams of water winding through his beard and dripping to the ground.

The second Templar silently held his hand out. Ahmed handed me the ladle and with his eyes suggested I make myself useful. I took the handle in one hand, steadied the other from below and ran over. As I drew near, that huge brute of a horse snorted, dropped his head and slammed it into me. It knocked me, the water and whatever dignity I had left into the mud.

To make things worse, the evil brown horse nipped at me as I lay on the ground. From atop the demon, the second Templar glared down at me. "God's sake boy, look what you've done."

I knew perfectly well the right thing to do. I should have said nothing, or if I had to, groveled in Arabic.

"It's not my fault, that ugly thing tried to kill me," I yelled. In French. Then from my back in the dust I threw a useless, frustrated kick at the horse. I'd have thrown a second but I heard a "thunk" and the point of a lance stuck in the dirt two inches from my face. Somewhere I found the good sense to lay on my back and shut up.

Square-beard's voice was calm and deep, in tones that implied a very serious threat with very little fear behind it. "If he wanted to kill you, you'd be dead and that'd be one less heathen bastard we'll have to kill down the road."

"Is there a problem here?" Pierre, my confidant from earlier, stood beside the water wagon with another young soldier. To his credit, his voice hardly shook at all as he and his friend—dressed only in a guard's uniforms with a simple lance and sword each, faced two mounted and fully armored Templar knights.

"No problem at all," the second Templar growled. "Seems my horse is willing to do more to keep your master's pets in line than he is. But then, look what he has to work with."

Pierre stiffened, and he gripped his lance until the knuckles whitened. His partner—slightly taller than he and with a red, extremely pimply face-reached for his sword. Thankfully, he demonstrated the good sense not to draw it. Square-beard and his friend grinned at each other and calmly dismounted.

I took the opportunity to scramble like a crab to the safety of the wagon and I'm not ashamed to admit took refuge behind both young Ahmed and his uncle. The two Brother Knights confidently strode within a few feet of the Count's men, and stopped with their arms crossed calmly across their massive chests.

Standing as tall as he could, which wasn't very, and keeping his voice as steady as possible, which was only partly successful, Pierre croaked out. "You know the Count's people are not to be molested."

Square-beard's partner hocked a huge phlegm ball and spit it on the ground at Pierre's feet. "My horse didn't receive the orders. Take it up with him."

"I'm talking to you… sir." Pierre was certainly trying his best to be brave. "You know no one is to bother Count Raymond's people… any of them…. While they are here on his business."

A second spitball from Square Beard landed a little closer to Pierre's feet. "Do you really want to fight over these cursed pigs? If that coward would do his Christian duty you could make yourself really useful to our cause and rid the whole country of them. Instead he acts more like a Syrian than a proper Christian and makes you protect them. How does that feel, boy?"

The other soldier reddened and looked down at his feet but Pierre never dropped his eyes. He took a slow, shaky breath and replied, "Doesn't matter. We have our orders, No one is to bother these people while they're under his protection. Move along. Please"

The second Templar unleashed yet a third phlegm projectile that landed precisely between Pierre's feet. "Fortunately I've had my fill of killing Saracens for one day. Keep your dogs on a better leash, or teach them better manners."

The two Templars remounted and continued on towards Acre, but not before that stupid horse locked eyes with me and stomped angrily. Pierre and his partner stoically watched them pass. Square-beard's mount flicked his tail in passing, catching the lad square in the face but he never moved. Both watched quietly until the knights were safely out of hearing.

"He's right you know," the pimply soldier offered.

"Shut up," Pierre turned to the group of grateful water workers. "What the hell are you waiting for? Get your asses back to work before you cause any more trouble."

Uncle Ahmed bobbed his head in gratitude. "Thank you, young sir."

Pierre just held up a hand and avoided his gaze entirely. "Just…go. Move your asses. Go on." Old Ahmed bit his lip and motioned for us to get moving. The afternoon's pleasant mood had evaporated like the water I'd spilled on the dusty earth.

Ahmed jammed an elbow in my ribs as he plodded past me. "Ow, what was that for?" I asked.

"I knew you'd be trouble. Just keep me out of it." They all picked up the pace, leaving me in the rear echelon following the wagon back to camp. Uncle Ahmed was ten or so paces behind, and I slowed enough for him to catch up. We walked in companionable silence for a while.

"So, let me understand, Uncle Ahmed. Christians and the Saracens want to kill each other... for God..." That got me a nod, so I continued. "But some Christians are protecting some of the Saracens, so the two groups of Christians hate each other as well?"

"Yes, that's right."

I knitted my brow, mentally went over what I'd just said. *Why would Saracens want to kill each other when they are all fanatical killers and united in wanting us dead?* I continued. "But those Saracens are afraid that Salah-adin's Saracens think God wants to kill them, so they help the Christians, just not the ones that want to kill them."

"Precisely."

"But that makes no sense at all."

Ahmed placed a callused brown hand on my shoulder. "Then you understand the situation here perfectly. So young to be so wise. That's rare in a *firengi*. Come, let's get these barrels back safely before anything else happens, *inshallah*."

I set to work. My brain hurt too much to argue.

Chapter 14

"Lucca. Lucca." A voice drifted gently to me through the fog of a very welcome sleep. I ignored it. Then the soft voice was accompanied by the hard gritty sole of a sandal pushed insistently into my midsection. "Lucca."

Reluctantly, I opened my eyes to see Ahmed bent over me, silhouetted against the faint light from an oil lamp "What?" I asked in French. Then I remembered who I was speaking to and switched to Arabic. "Is it morning already?"

"No, we just finished dinner. You fell asleep before we could eat. Someone wants to speak to you." That didn't seem like reason enough to wake me so I rolled back over into my pillow. "It's Count Raymond. He's asking for you." That was a different matter entirely.

I stretched, managing not to scream as my abused muscles came alive. Shaking my head in an attempt to become fully functional, I looked around for my sandals, then realized they were still on my feet where they were when I passed out. Out of habit I asked, "What did I do now?"

"I don't think you're in trouble. He was very careful to ask me to keep it private and to get you right away." Being wanted was mysterious. Being wanted and not being in trouble certainly made it more appealing. It was best not to keep him waiting. "I'm supposed to come with you," Ahmed added.

"Why?"

"He said you have…" Ahmed looked up as if the exact words were written above his head, "…a tendency not to get where you're going without trouble." Then he threw up his hands. "His words." I couldn't argue, so I nodded and we emerged from the servants' tent into the dusk.

An army camp is a very different place when everyone's been fed and the day's work is done. It's less dusty, for one thing. Most of the men were off duty and disinclined to move much. A few of the more diligent types squatted around the fires, sharpening weapons or sipping tea. Many more were gambling, or telling filthy stories in small groups. Whatever they were doing, it allowed the dirt to settle for the day. Clean, cool evening air had just a hint of moisture in it as a sea breeze managed to fight its way over Acre to those of us in the flat desert beyond. Inside Acre, the walls and buildings of the city seldom allowed a good wind to really build up. It felt good caressing my face and bare arms.

Ahmed and I wound our way through the groups of men towards Count Raymond's pavilion. A bright lantern shone inside, making it glow eerily in the otherwise pitch black. My curiosity was driving me to move a bit faster than my friend, so I was surprised to see him move to the left and wave me to him. I whispered, "I thought we were going to see the Count?"

Ahmed jerked his head past the tent a bit to the north. "We are." Then he picked up speed. I shrugged and followed. This was getting more mysterious all the time. My mind invented all kinds of scenarios, ranging from the ridiculous (I was about to be adopted by the Count and made his heir) to the mundane (he just wanted to know how my day was, which come to think of it was maybe more ridiculous, since it would imply the Count really gave two damns.) Finally, we saw a low ring of stones at the back edge of the camp. The fire had burned to coals and gave off a soft red glow, but not much real light.

Squinting, I saw only one figure there; a man in dirty, ragged clothes. *Was Ahmed playing a trick on me? Was he betraying me?* I halted, unsure whether to draw any closer but the figure looked up and said, in heavily French-accented Arabic, "Thank you, Ahmed. That will be all."

My friend gave a polite bow to his Lord, for it was his face that peered out under the cowl, and practically evaporated into the night, leaving me alone. Count Raymond gestured me to pull up a comfy rock. "I would have a private word with you, my little louse."

I looked around at the camp, at the men gathered around a dozen or so fires and the dark blue desert stretching out behind him. I nodded, tried desperately to remember the right way to address the second most powerful man in the Kingdom and managed to croak out, "As you wish.... Your Grace. But wouldn't it be more private in your own tent?"

This drew a most un-noble snort of laughter, and Count Raymond gestured to a flat surface near him. "There's no place less private than a leader's 'private' chambers, Lucca. Besides, I like this country at night." He looked around him, taking a deep breath through his nose, drawing the desert into his lungs. "It's beautiful isn't it? And look at those stars…" I followed his gaze skyward. The stars reached from horizon to horizon in thickly clustered lines, as if God scattered them like chicken seed. For someone who'd never left a city's walls, there was an unnerving amount of empty space.

"It's moments like this I can almost bring myself to think the Lord actually cares about this land. The rest of the time…" His voice trailed away. Hearing him talk like that made my stomach ache a bit. After spending so much time among warrior monks sworn to mouthing holy platitudes incessantly, it was a little jarring to hear grownups like Marco and Count Raymond say such things. If they weren't completely sure what they were doing and why they were here, what were we regular people supposed to think?

I realized that I missed the firm, unquestioning belief of the Brothers—at least a bit. It left little room for doubt and unanswerable questions. Without the comfort of unassailable facts, life would be nothing but an endless series of Brother Marco's interrogations. How exhausting.

The Count's voice dragged me back to the moment. "Do you know what Brother Marco told me about you?" *That I'm a scatterbrain who can't do what he's told? That I have a brain like a sieve?* Judging from how he spoke to me most of the time, those were the leading contenders, but I had no idea what he said when I wasn't around. I just shook my head, awaiting judgement.

"He says that you are smarter than you know, and see more than anyone he's ever known. What do you think of that?"

Was Brother Marco drunk? "I don't know, my Grace…"

"Yes you do, it's true or it isn't." His smile was still in place, but the voice carried a harsh tone of command that was missing a moment ago. I hesitated. Through my whole, short life the question 'do you think you're clever' was usually followed by a slap to the head. I'd never been asked it as a real question before. Fortunately, I didn't have to come up with a response right away.

"False modesty is a sin, too, lad. I rather hope it's true. I need someone smart who can see what's beneath the surface of things."

"No, I'm smart," I blurted, sounding anything but. "Uh, what do I have to do?"

Count Raymond breathed deeply, puffing out his cheeks, then let the breath escape in a long slow whoosh. "War is coming, Lucca. Salah-adin has decided the time has come to stop toying with us and we aren't prepared. Or at least I don't think we are. I don't really know."

He stood with a slight groan and turned his back to me, staring out into the desert to the East. Without looking my way, he continued. "I need to know what's going on inside Acre. The Orders are up to something, and there's a rumor the King is coming. But apparently I don't need to know anything except to march when told." Somewhere, God only knew how far in that direction, was his castle at Tiberias, along with his lands, his servants and his wife.

"I need someone inside the city to be my eyes and ears. Brother Marco seems to have the idea that you're the man for the job. Unless, of course, you're having a good time hauling water around. It looks like glamorous work; I can see why you'd enjoy it."

He wanted me to go back inside Acre. Where Brother Idoneus hunted me and al Sameen could be waiting to slit my throat. Where the rats and the fleas outnumbered the stars in the clean desert air. Behind the city's walls, the safest place I knew was a leper hospital. The smell of the open sewers and unwashed thousands could make maggots gag. But there lived Brother Marco, and my friends...and Sister Marie-Pilar. I couldn't wait to get home.

The words gushed out of my mouth. "Yes, Your Grace. Of course...."

He offered a curt nod. "Good. Marco will meet you inside the walls. You will spend the night letting me know what's really going on, and report to me each afternoon. Agreed?"

I tried to pay attention, but my eyes kept drifting over his shoulder. Squinting against the red glow of the embers into the darkness, it looked like the night air was moving in small ripples. I squeezed my eyelids harder, but couldn't make it out. The air shifted and moved like heat waves, but the night was too dark and cool for that. The silence did nothing to dispel the tingling at the back of my neck.

"Am I boring you, Mr. Louse?" Count Raymond asked. The sharp command in his voice momentarily brought me back to the moment.

"I think there's someone out there." I could barely hear the words myself but Count Raymond was on his feet, hand on his sword before I'd finished. He held his palm up to shut my mouth, scanning the desert beyond us.

The shape rose from the ground before Raymond saw it. A shadow dressed completely in black leapt at the Count. Ember light glinted off a curved dagger as the attacker wrapped strong thin arms around his target, taking him to the ground with a horrible thud and a frantic gasp.

Straddling the body, the dark figure reached down to pin the knight to the ground with one hand while the other lifted the dagger above his throat.

I shouted in French as loudly as I could, "Help. They're trying to kill Count Raymond!" I had no idea if anyone heard me. The whole purpose of being out here was to be out of earshot of anyone who could conceivably help. The attacker brought his blade down, but Count Raymond managed to grab the man by the arm and jerk his own head out of the way as the dagger struck nothing but sand.

For a moment I stood helplessly watching the struggle. Then I remembered my own knife, tucked inside my robe. I grabbed Sergeant Jacques' gift and sprung at the attacker, frantically trying to remember the old bastard's instructions.

I heard that growl in my head. *Slash wide to open him up.* So I did. While I struck only air, the assassin had to dodge my clumsy attempt and he pulled away. The hand holding the dagger was now away from Count Raymond's prone body.

Move inside and stick him deep. With tightly closed eyes, I thrust with all my strength. My opponent's eyes flew open in shocked agony as a blade pierced his stomach. It wasn't my blade, though.

I'd missed by a good half foot and my momentum

brought me to the ground in a frustrated heap. The feeble distraction, though, allowed Count Raymond to grasp his own sword and plunge it deep into the man's gut. Over my shoulder I saw the attacker shake, and what looked like sausages spilled from his stomach onto his intended victim.

A voice barked, "What the hell?" and the night erupted into torch-lit bedlam. First one guard, then a dozen arrived. Two of them grabbed the dead attacker and threw the body several feet. Two more attended to Count Raymond while another stepped on my hand and tripped over my body, landing right on top of me, forcing every bit of air from my lungs.

I thrashed around, vainly trying to catch my breath. My efforts to breathe simply earned me a backhand across the head from the soldier, who thought I was trying to fight him. He slapped a gloved hand across my face a second time. "What did you do, you little shit?"

"Enough." The Count's ragged voice had enough command left in it to make the guardsman jump off of me to attention. "Lucca are you all right?" My first attempt at a reply didn't have nearly enough breath in it, so I just nodded, managing to rise as far as my knees.

The lifeless body lay on the ground a few feet away, guts and blood spilled on the dirt. I saw it and immediately pitched forward. Over the sounds of someone—probably me—puking, I heard Raymond's voice. "See to him, make sure he's okay. The lad saved my life."

The man who'd struck me was immediately replaced by a familiar face. Pierre, the young guard from earlier bent over me. "Take it easy. Pull your legs up to your belly. There you go. Breathe deep." It was easy for him to say, but I made the effort. I managed to drag a little air into my body, then a little more on the next attempt until I truly believed I would live. "Christ's sake, I've never seen a kid get into so much trouble in one day."

"Me either," I groaned.

While I recovered, two of the guards searched what was left of the attacker. "He's a Saracen, sure as shit," one voice offered.

"Yeah, but not one of ours. He might be *hashishin*." The more senior of the two searched the body as he spoke. "This knife isn't for amateurs."

His partner seemed puzzled. "Why would someone go to all the trouble of hiring an assassin when we're already at war with the bastards?"

"That's two hashishin attempts in two weeks," Pierre offered.

"Two?" One of the soldiers asked.

"Yeah, this one, and that sanctimonious Hospitaller with the..." Pierre made a zigzag motion over his face. "... what's his name... Idoneus. That prick."

Count Raymond picked up the assassin's dagger from the ground. In the torchlight we could clearly see Arabic engraving on the blade and handle. "No, there's just the one. This one is legitimate. A real *hashishin*. Somebody wanted me dead."

"Then what happened to... the one with the scar? At the Hospital?" The Count pointedly ignored the question with a snort and turned in my direction.

Bending slowly to one knee, he gently took my chin in his hand and drew my head first to one side then the other, checking for permanent damage. He must not have found any, because he sucked his bottom lip thoughtfully and said, "You're right. It's been a long night. What do you say we begin tomorrow, eh?"

That sounded so good. One more sleep in the cool clear air couldn't hurt. Acre could survive without me for another day.

Chapter 15

Back inside Acre, two things were immediately noticeable. First, war was inevitable; a final push against Salah-adin was coming sooner rather than later. Secondly, my beloved city stunk— it really smelled awful. It only took a few days in relatively fresh air to sensitize my nose to it.

The usual city reek of open sewers, animals and stale salt air was made worse by the drought. Latrines and gutters weren't being rinsed clean, and the shortage of water meant that bathing, always an optional activity for most Franks but a pleasure for those born in Outremer, became a luxury few could afford. That made sneaking through crowds and brushing against people singularly unpleasant. The home I always considered something of—if not a paradise at least a haven-- seemed a lot less enticing.

The first evening at sundown I headed for the harbor to see what was going on and was stunned to find only two or three vessels—all Venetian of course—bobbing in the sea. One ship—I don't know what kind but it had both oars and sails—was tied to the pier and was being loaded with goods as well as people. Well-dressed women and a few of their spoiled offspring stood sniffling and confused among piles of their possessions. Merchants attempted to console their families while keeping one eye on the lading process. They winced as rough sailors picked up trunks and bags, heaving them unceremoniously onto the deck.

A stout woman sweated profusely in a heavy Frankish dress and too much jewelry watched in horror as a heavy cloth bag was ripped from her hand and heaved end over end, where it landed with the unmistakable crash of broken glass.

"Please… oh for…. Watch what you're doing." She protested. The sailor just glared at her.

In guttural French with a heavy Venetian accent, he growled, "Be quiet. You're lucky you and your God-forsaken brats aren't going aboard the same way. If you don't like it, I'm sure we can find someone else to take your place…" This brought elaborate protests of confidence in the man's ability and pleas to be perhaps just a bit more careful. I'm not sure he heard either as he heaved another trunk onto the boat and her protests were drowned out by grunts and crashes.

A few yards up the seawall, near the Templar House, I watched three knights; newly arrived judging by the neat beards and lack of filth on their robes, drilling their squires. The boys were maybe a year or two older than I, but a head and a half taller. I'd never seen their like. Their hair was almost orange, and their arms and legs were a pasty, sickly white. Sweating, bug-eyed faces glowed ember -red with exertion and one of them looked like he was ready to drop at any moment. None of them… and likely only one of the knights… would have passed muster with Sergeant Jacques.

Their commander yelled at them in some unintelligible language I'd never heard. It was full of rolled "r's and phlegmy "achs", and the Templar was apparently as unimpressed with their efforts as I was. While I couldn't make out a word of what was said, I recognized the activity well enough. The knights were trying to train these lads up as best they could in a short time in an attempt to help them survive, and despairing of the effort. It was the same frustrated expression Vardan had on his face the last time I'd seen him.

"They're from Scotland," I heard a familiar voice over my shoulder and there was Brother Marco in his beggar gear, leaning on his staff.

I tried to stay cool, as if I hadn't missed him at all. "Where's that?"

"I'm not really sure, except they say it's cold and rainy there all the time, and the people grow big as trees and half as smart and you can't understand a word they say."

"They're still Templars, yes?" I asked.

"Supposedly, although they're more like Norsemen than good Christians, in my humble opinion. Good men with an axe, complete crap with a sword. But those are the only new arrival in weeks. Whatever happens, it seems we'll have to make do with the fighters we've got."

"What will happen?"

This drew a non-committal shrug and he looked off over the darkening sea. "Chatillon and the king are on their way. After that, assuming we can't talk sense into them, we'll march on Salah-adin."

"You don't think we should fight the Mamelukes? Isn't that why everyone is here?" We, I asked. Like I was going to pick up a sword and shield.

There was a long pause, then he said, "It doesn't matter what I think, lad." He must have heard the same melancholy in his voice I did, because he took a deep breath and clapped me on the shoulder a little too hard. "Enough of that. What have you seen since you've been back?"

I took a deep breath and began to list what I'd observed. More people were leaving Acre than arriving—the only newcomers were military, Hospitallers and Templars, and a small, sorry lot they were.

"Really, is that your considered military opinion?" Marco grinned at me. I just pointed over to the three knights and their squires, two of whom were on their knees, panting in the warm night air.

"Those are some of the good ones." He bit his lip thoughtfully.

"Hmmm. What else?"

What else? It seemed everyone in the city was on edge and miserable. The odors of violence and fear permeated the air. Simple tensions were magnified. But how could I explain that?

"You know 'Cretia and Mario? The oil merchants near the King's Gate?" Marco nodded. Everyone knew them. Their constant verbal sparring made for great entertainment, and listening to her harangue her husband while he tried to conduct business was always amusing, and often resulted in people paying more than they should out of pity. That, of course, was probably the plan all along. I always enjoyed the show immensely.

Tonight, though, she'd said something mild by her usual standards and Mario backhanded her. Hard. In moments she'd pulled a knife and went after him, screaming and slashing like a maniac as people stood watching. When the City Guard showed up to regain order, she turned her attention to them, as did her intended victim and two or three bystanders. What should have been an amusing bit of street theater held the promise of ugly mob violence and potential murder. The entire city seemed to vibrate with the same black energy. After a couple of hours I could feel the tension rippling through my own gut.

"People are frightened, Lucca, and fear never brings out the best in people."

"But we're the best guarded city in the world. We have the Hospital, the Temple… there are more fighting men than …. normal people," I protested.

"As long as they stay put, yes."

"Brother Iago always said that if the Devil hasn't taken Acre by now, no one ever will."

"Salah-adin isn't the devil, despite what you hear." That's not what every breathing soul I knew said, but I let it go. Brother Marco didn't say anything else, he simply scanned the harbor from North to South and back again. "Oh, Sister asked me to give you these." In his unscarred left hand he pulled four good-sized dates from his pocket. "There were more but…. Well consider it a tax."

I didn't begrudge him his small commission. I took the sticky fruit and popped the first one in my mouth, savoring the gooey sweetness, sucking the pit as clean as possible before spitting it onto the ground. "Thank you."

We continued examining the harbor. "We... They miss you. Even Sergeant Jacques asked where you are. Apparently he needs more exercise."

"Does that mean I can come home?" I asked, hopefully.

Marco, shook his head. "The Count is waiting for your report. I'll see you tomorrow." He patted my arm with his glove. "Best be getting back. Take your time and make sure you tell him everything. No matter how small, understood?"

"Yes, sir." This earned me a curt nod of dismissal and Brother Marco hobbled off, pretending to rely on his staff for support. I watched him for a moment, then turned towards the city, the seawall at my back. I had come in through the King's Gate, and would have to go back that way, but once entering I made my way in kind of a semi-circle around the south side of town. It would only make sense to complete the circle. This would bring me past the Hospital, but it was nightfall now, and the odds of being seen dropped with each moment of growing darkness.

I kept my distance from the Scots Templars, although I sympathized with the pale boys. They kept getting knocked down by their increasingly angry masters and struggled to get up again, prepared for more. A faint ache in my gut reminded me of Jacques and Vardan. *And Sister Marie-Pilar*, I thought, popping another date into my mouth. I missed her most of all.

To the north of the Templar House were the shops and homes of those who served them—the clerks, farriers, armorers and other human cogs in the machine of war. The clang of hammers on metal echoed off the buildings. Normally the din ended at sundown but with battle in the air, the demand for new and better weapons meant late nights for those men and their families. The extra cash would compensate, assuming they lived to spend it.

While there was plenty of activity going on in the homes and shops and businesses, very little of that activity spilled into the street itself. The alleys and boulevards were completely empty. The problem with blending into the crowd, is there has to be a crowd to blend into. I settled for staying as close to the buildings as I could, letting the shadows wrap me in darkness. I passed the Templar chapel, then the stables where those ridiculously big stupid war horses were kept, and on to the Hospitaller district.

From the South, the Hospital looked abandoned. Most of the dormitories were on this side, and the devout knights were already down for the evening. The less saintly hadn't yet returned from wherever their compulsions took them. Rounding a corner, I was surprised to find bright light flooding from the Hospital itself, through slatted windows. Ominous shadows played against the walls across the street. From within, I heard a loud anguished moan and the low murmuring of prayer, the only real assistance the poor patient could expect.

Looking at the Hospital House, I felt an unexpected pang of homesickness. I remembered, with more fondness than accuracy, sleeping in the dormitories with my fellow orphans. I achingly recalled the unexpected kindnesses most of the Brothers—like good-natured Iago—bestowed on us, and the comfort of knowing where I'd be sleeping every night—when I took advantage of the blessed opportunity.

The clip-clop of horse shoes on stones pulled me out of my reverie. Two Hospitallers in their everyday robes pulled to a stop. The door to the hospital flew open I was surprised to recognize young Brother Josephus—those eyebrows were unmistakable—step out.

A tall monk sat on the first horse. He handed something down to Josephus. The younger man dipped his head and crossed himself fervently before accepting it.

"You can feel its power, can't you?" The monk on horseback said. I recognized the silky smooth voice immediately. It was Idoneus. "I'll bet someone like you has never held such a thing have you?"

"No, Brother." Josephus nearly fell to his knees, looking in wonder at the reliquary with the True Cross. Idoneus held it just a moment longer, running his thumbs up and down the sides, then passed it down to the younger monk.

"Few have, because so few are worthy. I'm truly blessed to be its keeper, even if only for a short time."

The second horseman, who up til now had remained silent, just harumphed sarcastically. The man was huge—wide at the shoulders as all knights who specialized in the broadsword were—and obviously more useful for his brawn than his piety.

"You don't think so, Brother?"

"Doesn't much matter what I think. Your audience tonight believed it. That's what's important," the big man growled.

"Your lack of faith doesn't serve you well, Gregory." This elicited another snort. "Still, I appreciate your help tonight." If Idoneus was really perturbed by the lack of respect, it didn't show in his voice, which was smooth as satin.

Big Brother Gregory, said nothing, but dismounted with a grunt. He took his horse by the bridle and led it towards the stables. A tall, thin figure ran out of the door as if chased by the Devil himself and nearly crashed into Brother Josephus.

"I'm so sorry, Master. I just now heard you arrived. Please, let me help you." It was Gilbert, who took the reins from Idoneus and held the big roan close so the warrior monk could dismount, which he did with far more grace than Gregory exhibited.

"You couldn't know exactly when I was arriving, Gilbert. The Lord's work doesn't stick to man's schedule." Gilbert kept his head down and nodded gratefully at his master's kind words.

As soon as Idoneus was on solid ground, Josephus thrust the True Cross back into his hands. "Were you successful tonight, Brother?"

Idoneus craned his neck to rid himself of a kink and I heard it crack from my spot in the shadows. "Ahh, that's better. Yes, I think so. Some of Raymond's men stay loyal to him, but many more are recognizing the time for appeasing the Anti-Christ is over. After all, who could argue with such a sign of God's grace?" He held the reliquary up, as if examining it for the first time.

Josephus crossed himself with even more devotion than

before, while Gilbert did the same, although less enthusiastically. Idoneus laid a hand on Gilbert's shoulder. "Gilbert, please make sure he's well fed. Doing the Lord's work should earn rewards for everyone, even the beasts of the field, eh?" My friend didn't look up, just nodded quickly.

"Yes, sir." He patted the horse's nose, which got him a warm nuzzle as a reward and shuffled towards the stables. The moment Idoneus and Josephus turned to the door, I darted to the next dark patch, trailing Gilbert and the horse.

As soon as the door closed behind the monks, I ran across the street and nearly scared Gilbert to death. His nerves hadn't noticeably improved in my absence.

"Christ's sake, Lucca. You scared the devil out of me." His head nearly spun in a complete circle as he looked around us like a panicked rat. His voice dropped to a terrified hiss. "What are you doing here?"

As was so often the case, the truth probably wasn't going to serve me well. "I was homesick. Are they still looking for me?" I admit I was a little disappointed when he shook his head. "Nobody has really asked about you, except for…. I think as long as you stay far away and don't interfere he'll stop looking."

I took a step sideways to put the other boy in between me and the jittery horse. You never knew when they'd just up and take a chomp out of you. In the faint glow of the stable lamp I looked Gilbert up and down. He seemed even taller and thinner than when I left, if it was possible in such a short time. I noticed two lone blonde hairs protruding out of his weak, trembling chin. "You can't stay here. You need to stay lost. Go back to your lepers, or wherever you've been hiding." My heart sank. Idoneus knew where I'd been.

"What about you?" I asked. "Do you…." Did he what? Did he want to leave the comfort of the only home he'd ever known? Take shelter with me in a leper house, or even worse, a Syrian tent in the middle of an army camp? Finally, I settled for simply asking, "Are you all right?"

"As long as no one sees me talking to you, then yes. I'm fine." That wasn't true but I let it drop. "I have to get this stupid…. Piece of shit…. Put away before I can get to bed. I have to go." I actually gasped. It was the first time I'd heard Gilbert swear, and it sounded clumsy coming from him. He really needed to practice. I knew who I'd start with if I were him, but I knew he'd never speak such thoughts aloud.

"Can I help? Do you need anything?" It was a stupid question, met with the stony silence it deserved. Gilbert just clicked his tongue and walked the horse toward the stable, shaking his head. I started north towards the next district, but after a couple of steps I stopped and looked back. From the stable door, I saw Gilbert standing, watching me. I raised my hand in a half-hearted wave and walked quickly away from him, deeper into the darkened city streets.

Block after silent block, I walked. My head pounded with thoughts trying to escape my thick skull. How can Gilbert stand it…? What was Idoneus doing stirring dissent among the Count's men? Was it working? How would I describe this to Count Raymond? Most selfishly, will I ever be able to go back to my friends again if Idoneus knows about them?

I trudged on, enjoying the solitude and not in any great

hurry to get back and report to Count Raymond.

I worked my way north then east past the Montmusard gate. I managed to pass the tannery without gagging, which meant my nose was readjusting to the city, even if my heart was not. I stayed lost in my own thoughts, not really noticing anything until noises from the caravanserai caught my attention.

At this hour, the animals should have been down for the night. Instead, the usual gentle lowing and bleating was drowned out by the annoyed honks of donkeys and stubborn moans of camels. The pens and corrals were full of men and boys herding the animals into corners.

I watched one young boy tug on a rope attached to the most stubborn ass I'd ever seen. The grey and white beast had its feet dug deep into the mud of a pen, leaning back on its hind legs and protesting loudly. The boy gave the rope a mighty tug, which only resulted in burning the palm of his hands and annoying the donkey even more.

"Ouch. Come on you miserable…" I recognized Fadhil's voice. I smiled, remembering how much he hated that donkey. So did his father, which is no doubt why old Firan gave him the assignment. I watched the boy struggle for a few moments, then snuck up behind him and picked up the mucky end of the rope.

Fadhil tensed up for another futile attempt at moving the animal, and I did the same. When he pulled, so did I—as hard as I could. Our combined efforts must have surprised him as much as the donkey, because the stubborn ass lurched forward. The rope went slack and my friend fell backwards against me.

"What would you do without me?" I asked as he turned around to see who it was.

"Lucca!" He threw his arms around me, then stepped back, embarrassed, and inspected me head to toe. "Are you okay? Where have you been? Everyone's been asking...."

"I'm fine. I've just been..." What had I been doing, at least that I could share with even my best friends? "...laying low. What are you doing here this late?"

He wiped his mucky hands on his tunic and picked up a switch from the ground. "We have to move all our animals to the far corral." He strode with bad intent to the donkey, who must have realized the game was over and began to walk towards its young master. Fadhil gave it a gentle swipe on the haunches, more out of revenge than a sense of purpose, because the stubborn animal walked obediently to the far end of the corral.

"Why now?" I asked, slipping in the mud and who-knows-what-else of the pen.

Fadhil looked at me as if I had three heads. "Haven't you heard? King Guy is arriving tomorrow and we have to make room for all his animals and things."

"What are you supposed to do with all your stuff?" I asked.

"Whatever they tell us to," he said with a world-weary shrug. He gave the donkey another half-hearted swat just to keep him moving. "My father says it means more business."

"How's that?"

"If there's going to be a fight, someone has to help bring

205

the supplies. He says we'll go with them when they move out."

"And your father's going?" I could imagine Firan weighing the danger and the money, and where the scales tipped. Of course he was going. Fadhil smiled.

"I'm going too. He says it's time I learned the business. I'm going to help haul food and water." My friend's face beamed with pride. "If we can get this idiot to do as he's told." The donkey brayed as if he took the insult personally and kicked a clod of mud back towards us. We dodged it and moved along. Fadhil caught me up on my friends as well as all the gossip of the Royal visit. I tried to follow it all and nodded appropriately. Most of it buzzed past my head as I was lost in my own thoughts.

War was coming, and my friends—all of them—were going to be swept up in it.

Chapter 16

I returned to camp long after midnight and was immediately ushered into the Count's tent where I found him slumped at his desk. He obviously hadn't slept any more than I had, and from the looks of him hadn't shut his eyes since we'd last seen each other. Bloodshot eyes were small red bullseyes surrounded by dark purple-black circles. His hair hung limply and his robes were thickly coated in dust.

"Lucca, welcome back. What have you brought me tonight?" Then Count Raymond took a second look at me and rose from his desk. "Sit down, boy… water?" I nodded and gratefully sank into a cushion.

"Thank you…. your Grace." I managed through dusty, chapped lips. He gave me just enough time to take a single, grateful gulp and heave a sigh of relief.

"So?" He dropped heavily into the cushion by my side? "What have you learned tonight?"

I sat straight up, and looked heavenward, like I always did when trying to remember something.

"The King is arriving tomorrow." I hoped this was what he was looking for, but he waved my bombshell away.

"I know that…. Everyone knows that," he sounded exasperated. "What else?"

If he already knew the important information, what did

he expect me to tell him? "Some new Templars arrived…from Scopeland, I think it's called." My companion sat up straight.

"How many?"

"Three… and their squires." I watched the air go out of his lungs and Count Raymond slumped back into the brocaded cushion.

"Three. And from where did you say?"

"Scopleand, my lord. It's North… I think. The palest men I've ever seen. And big, though, good fighters with an axe, I'm told," I added helpfully.

"Well, they'll blunt a Mameluke sword as well as the next man, I suppose. What else?"

I strained to think of what he'd consider useful. 'Cretia and Mario's battle in the square was beneath his notice, and I doubted he'd see the humor in the fight. "Everyone seems to be in a terrible mood."

"They should be. Troubled times are on us, Lucca." I'd never heard anyone sound so sad and tired in my life. "Still, they'll get to sit safe behind the walls while we march to glory, eh?"

"But a lot of them are going, too." I said. Count Raymond managed to pry one eye open at that. I told him about Firan and Fadhil, and how the citizens were being hired to carry water and supplies.

He shook his head in disbelief. "That's a lot of supplies and men. Where do they think they're going?" Now it was my turn to look surprised.

"Well, Tiberias. They're going to relieve your wife

and…."

Raymond slapped his hand down on the tabletop, scattering several documents. "Damn it to hell. That's the stupidest…." He jumped to his feet and began pacing. He spoke to the cloth roof of his tent as much as to me. "What do those idiots think they're doing? This is no time of year to…"

"But your wife and…" I couldn't imagine anyone not rushing right off to rescue his family.

"She's perfectly safe in Salah-adin's hands. He won't harm a woman… unless we force his hand. And that's exactly what they're doing. Blast them…" He looked at me. "When are they supposed to head out… your friends… how long before they leave?"

"As soon as the King arrives, I guess." The look he gave me let me know that guessing was not going to help either of us. Raymond crossed his arms, turning away from me and staring at a spot on the pavilion wall until I thought a hole would appear.

"Three days at the most," I said, taking a wild guess and sounding far more confident than I felt. He nodded.

"Too soon, and in the wrong bloody direction. Typical of those idiots. You can bet this is Reynauld's idea. He and that horse's ass de Ridefort." The hatred between Count Raymond and Reynauld de Chatillon was legendary. Each was regularly cursing and causing trouble for the other, but I had never heard an adult—at least a sober one—so much as mention the Grand Master of the Templars, Gerard de Ridefort, by name. Like the Devil, if you said his name he might appear.

"Three days…" Raymond said more to the walls of his tent more than me, "All right, Lucca. Thank you." He gave a tired wave of dismissal and I took the opportunity to head for bed. My head throbbed, my stomach growled and my feet hurt. My eyes burned with the need to sleep as I staggered to the tent I shared with Ahmed's family.

I tried to be quiet, but must have woken up a rooster on the way because no sooner had my head hit the blanket than a cock crowed and I sensed people stirring around me.

"Get up, you lazy dog." By now I knew the feeling of Ahmed's sandal digging into my side.

"Noooo, please. Let me sleep." I groaned.

"Can't. We have to load up. Uncle is waiting for us" Ahmed was already at the flap of the tent, impatiently glaring over his shoulder at me.

I had never had a hangover, but the way my head weighed a hundred pounds and my temples throbbed, this must be what they were like. "Where are we going?"

"Home. Today." Then he was gone.

I managed to find some fruit and bread and shoved it into my face before heading to the wagons, where everything was already in full roar.

Uncle Ahmed greeted me without his usual smile. Without really even looking, he handed me a rope and gestured to loop it over some boxes stacked haphazardly on the back of a cart. "About time you got here. Help me with this."

I leapt on the back of the cart, or at least managed it the

second time. The first time I misjudged the height of the deck and scraped my shin, falling into the dirt. The next effort was successful, and I looped the rope over the crates and pulled it tight. Meanwhile, Ahmed shouted orders in Arabic and pointed wildly in every direction. Everyone but me seemed to understand what was going on. I just stood on the wagon deck looking confused.

"Are you just going to stand there all day?" Old Ahmed demanded. Actually, it sounded like a really good idea, but I shook my head.

"No, Uncle. Of course. I'm just so tired."

"Then you should sleep at night instead of wandering off doing whatever you *Firengi* do." I couldn't even begin to imagine what that might be, but if the lies Muslims told each other about Christians were half as wild as we told about them, it probably involved devil worship, whores, and alcohol, even if ten was a bit young for all that. "Come on, we have to leave for al Majdal today."

"Why are you going to al Majdal? I thought you were going to Tiberias with the army?"

He shook his head and handed another crate to the wagon's edge, where I was barely able to keep it from falling off. "The army *is* going to Tiberias. We're heading home to our village at al Majdal, praise God. And you're coming with us."

"I can't go. I live here."

"Count Raymond says we are to take you with us, and to keep you safe. By noon we have to be on our way, so make yourself useful, or I'm the one you'll need saving from." I gripped the edge of the crate and rocked it slowly into position, only pinning myself between the wooden boxes once.

At last the cart was dangerously overloaded but somehow met Uncle Ahmed's standards. I was dismissed for the moment and immediately went off in search of my friend. It took me a moment to orient myself, because the camp had changed overnight. Soldiers had grouped closer together, and the civilians, who were leaving soon, found ourselves in tents scattered crazily outside the main circle.

I tried to remember what Ahmed told me about their village. al Majdal wasn't anything much, apparently, just a few small huts and farms, but it was on the shores of *Bahr Tubariya*. It took a bit of discussion to learn that was the same place we Christians called the Sea of Galilee. And it wasn't a sea at all, but a small lake. I thought it was no wonder people couldn't get along. They couldn't agree on what to call something even when they were all looking at it.

Ahmed was in charge of breaking down our tent, which was a shame since I wanted nothing more than to crawl inside it, but as I approached I saw him standing with his hand on his hips, looking exactly like his Uncle, and barking nearly as loud. Two men were rolling the material tightly, while another stood beside my friend. Deep in conversation.

This other man was dressed in nice but not overly fancy robes, his head covered with a keffiya, and he was quite broad at the shoulders.

In fact, he was broad all over. Fat, in fact.

He looked an awful lot like al Sameen.

It was, indeed, the huge spy. I stood rooted to the ground about thirty feet away, looking for an escape route when Ahmed turned around and saw me. His face lit up.

"There you are, come on over. I want you to meet someone." He gestured to the fat man at his side. Al Sameen's smile was wide as his back and he salaamed without a trace of irony. "Nurad al-Fatin, this is my friend, Lucca. Lucca, Mr. al-Fatin is joining his caravan with ours on the way home. Uncle Ahmed has put me in charge of the arrangements," he added proudly.

The man's eyebrows raised ever so slightly. His wide smile never changed as he put a hand on Ahmed's shoulder and greeted me in Arabic. "*Salaam alaikum*, young man."

I meekly offered, "*wa alaikum salaam*, sir." Those squinty eyes bore holes into my skull. I'd always been good at staring contests, and damned if I was about to lose this one. Ahmed was droning on about something or other, but I didn't dare let my eyes drift for even a moment.

"And then once we're back in al Majdal...." Ahmed's voice penetrated my brain.

That seemed to startle al Sameen as well. "Al Majdal? I thought you were going to Tiberias."

"Oh, we are. But we have important things to do before Lord Raymond's troops arrive home. Of course, I can't talk about it. You understand." Ahmed was reveling in his importance, and his stupid smile nearly cracked his face wide open when al Sameen clapped him on the back.

"Of course, my young friend. Duty and all...." He kept his hand on Ahmed as he turned to me. "Young man, I have some documents I need to get back to Ahmed here. Would you be kind enough to come with me and run them back?" He moved only slightly, but his outer robes parted and I could see the dagger at his belt. His eyes darted from me to Ahmed and back.

I gaped stupidly. "Well, I really…"

"Please," oozed the smooth talking merchant. "I'd take it as a great favor, and I'm sure you can be spared for a few minutes." Ahmed shifted a bit as the hand on his shoulder seemed to get heavier all of a sudden.

"Go on, Lucca," my friend said, trying to sound like the boss. "It's not like you're much use to us here."

"There, you see? Come along then" the big man said happily. "Thank you, Ahmed…. I look forward to speaking more on our journey". He offered an oily salaam to my friend and beckoned me forward. I couldn't speak nor think. Without wanting to, I stood within a few steps of Saladin's spy master. That grip transferred from one young set of shoulders to another—mine.

A soft voice came from between clenched teeth, so quiet only I heard it. "Move very slowly and don't draw attention. I don't want to hurt you, but I will, and your friend with you. Understand?"

I managed an almost normal sounding, "Of course, how may I be of service sir?" Shooting Ahmed a quick, desperate look over my shoulder, my heart sank when he'd already turned to harangue the men folding the tent. He clearly enjoyed being in command.

I wasn't having nearly as much fun. Al Sameen's talons

dug into my bony shoulder. "You're a hard man to find," he hissed.

Not hard enough, apparently. "What do you want with me?"

"Answers to questions. Then we'll see." We walked slowly towards the city. My eyes desperately sought a chance to escape among the crowd and where I knew the ground, but we turned short of the gate and continued north. In the shadow of Acre's wall, it was cool and relatively uncrowded. As we walked further, I swiveled my head, desperate for any opportunity to make a break.

"Don't," al Sameen said wearily. "I am too fat and tired to run after you. If you disappear again, I'll be forced to ask questions of your friends. I know exactly where they are... and where they're going." For a split second I imagined either of the Ahmeds in a pool of blood. "They deserve to die anyway for choosing sides with the *Firengi a*gainst their own people, but that day of reckoning is coming soon enough, *Inshallah.*"

The world-weary manner in which he said "God willing" sent a shiver down my spine. I gave up the notion of escape and just focused on doing whatever I could to appease al Sameen and stay alive.

"Are you really Nurad al-Fatin?" I finally asked. I couldn't continue to call him Fat Man, at least to his face, and stay on his good side. My companion raised an amused eyebrow.

"I am called that, among other things. It's as good as any name I suppose. And what should I call you? Lucca, I know, but Lucca what?"

"Lucca…. "I thought for just a moment about telling him the truth—the actual, factual truth, but I wouldn't admit that I was Lucca Nemo--Lucca Nobody. "Le Pou. Lucca Le Pou."

A loud laugh started somewhere in the fattest part of his belly. "Le Pou, is it? Your father must have been awfully proud of that name. So your father was a Frankish louse, and your mother was… what, a Syrian caterpillar? But, when you do what we do, one name will do as well as another." He studied me as we walked. "Still, I wonder how someone as brown as you ever found yourself among the Christians. I'm sure there's quite a tale there."

He wouldn't hear it from me. In fact, he didn't hear anything from me for a while. I kept thinking about what he'd said. *When you do what we do.* I wasn't anything like him, was I? On the other hand, how was it any different?

After about another hundred yards, a tall man came towards us leading a big black Arab horse. "Ah," said al Fatin. In my mind I'd already stopped calling him al Sameen. It was no longer funny. "Your transportation." The horse stomped its hoof, kicking up dust. He was obviously no happier to hear that than I was. "Take this one to Baisan. I will meet up with you there as soon as I can. And watch him closely, he's a slippery little bastard. Which reminds me…" He roughly shoved his hand into my robe and pulled out my dagger. "And watch out. This louse bites."

The tall man had the biggest, most crooked nose I'd ever seen. He bowed obediently and said nothing else.

"I can't ride a horse…" I protested.

This drew another laugh from al-Fatin. "You're not a passenger. You're cargo." With that Crooked Nose hoisted me up and laid me on my belly across the horse's black haunches. My eyes suddenly filled with dust, horse hair and flies. The briny smell of sweat nearly gagged me. The black monster reared up a bit too, just to make his opinion of his passenger known.

Crooked Nose leapt nimbly into the saddle despite his height. I was facing the wrong way, but I heard the fat man tell my guard, "He'd best be there and in one piece when I arrive. Do you understand me?"

"Yes, *Ustaaz*, I understand. As long as he behaves himself, he'll get there all right." Big Beak had a surprisingly high squeaky voice for someone so intimidating. The horse shifted to the right, and the air was squeezed from my lungs as I bounced up and down on my stomach.

"That doesn't look comfortable at all," the rider squeaked at me.

"I could use a pillow." I said, trying to be charming.

"If you promise not to be a nuisance you can sit up." I felt strong hands grab my arm and I was suddenly in the air, then plunked down in front of my guard facing forward. The big horse turned and made a feeble attempt to snap at me but I was too close to his neck, so he settled for shaking his head violently to rid himself of the additional burden.

"Stay there, all right?" Before I could even nod, my pilot let loose a piercing whistle between his teeth and the horse took off at a fast trot.

My bum immediately flew off the horse, up to about my

shoulders then slammed down again. I'd never actually been on a horse before, let alone one going this quickly. I'd seen countless knights and soldiers ride, and it didn't look that difficult. That turned out to be a misjudgment. I didn't have to time to worry about how much it hurt to land, because I was skyward again on the next bounce and the next landing was just as painful and awkward.

Crooked Nose gently reined the monster to a stop. "First time on a horse?" he asked.

"Yes, Ustaaz." I replied as politely as I could. He shook his head in disbelief and dismounted long enough to take a blanket from his roll. He shook it open and folded it over.

"Lift up." I complied. He slid the blanket over the horse's withers. I settled down on it gratefully. "This will help a bit, but you're going to be awfully sore by the time we get to Baisan."

"How far is it?" I asked.

"About fifty miles or so." Since I'd never been anywhere, ever, I had no idea how far that was. "We'll be there tomorrow mid-day. If we ever get started that is." Another whistle and we took off again, with me bouncing just as high but landing just a little less awkwardly.

Fifty miles. I'd never been out of eyeshot of Acre's walls before. I was being taken to the ends of the earth by a crooked-nosed giant and a fast dark horse straight out of Hell and there was nothing I could do about it.

Chapter 17

I have no idea how long we bounced across the desert. I do know my face was caked and dry where tears and snot mixed with trail dust had turned to cement. My tailbone ached horribly and if I thought the night before I was as tired as a person could be, well I was wrong. Now I wanted nothing more than to sleep for three days. Even when safely on the ground, I felt dizzy and sick.

My crooked-nosed companion did stop from time to time so we could drink some warm water and choke down some dried meat and fruit while his horse rested in whatever limited shade we could find. It was during the first of those rest stops that I discovered his name. Turns out, he loved to talk.

"I'm Ali bin Yusuf bin Ali," he told me. Syrians who loved to yammer on usually started with as much of their lineage as they could spit out in one breath. "Who are you?" I tried to maintain a stoic silence, even though I suspected I looked pouty rather than defiant. He gave a shrug. "Suit yourself, but it's a long way to go, and you won't find anyone else to talk to in the desert. Besides, there's no reason to be rude."

"Rude? You've kidnapped me. Why shouldn't I be rude?"

He shook his head sadly. "Not kidnapped. No. You're a

prisoner, there's a difference."

I sniffed. "What's the difference?"

"If we kidnapped you, we would either sell you as a slave or return you for a ransom, if anyone would pay for you." An arched eyebrow made it a question of sorts. From my reaction he knew that was highly unlikely. He offered an empathetic shrug. "You are a *jasus,* a spy… or at least that's what *Al Jasus* says, and I guess he'd know." It seemed even his countrymen didn't call him al Fatin, just "The Spy." Maybe he didn't have a real name after all. "So, we will treat you as a captive until it's decided what to do with you."

"Then what?" I asked.

"He probably kills you, but only Allah knows."

That didn't sound at all promising. "Who decides?"

"Al Jasus is taking you to Baisan. That means you will probably meet the Sultan himself." The very idea turned my insides to water and I fought the urge to mess myself. "Salah-adin likes to question all spies himself. That's why it's so important you arrive in good shape. And I'd loosen that tongue a bit, if I were you." I heard myself swallow.

Ali looked at me closely. "Speaking of which…" he rummaged in his little bag and pulled out a dusty cloth and quickly tied it around my head, making a *keffiya* out of it. "There. Now your brains won't fry."

"Thank you," I said, truly grateful. As long as I had my head, it may as well be cool. I decided given the circumstances I needed all the friends I could get. "I'm Lucca." That earned me a nod and a big grin.

"That's better. No reason we can't be polite. Lucca

bin…?" he prodded.

"Just Lucca."

He shook his head with a sympathetic "tsk" and said, "A man should know his people. No wonder you fell in with the Firengi. Ready to go?" I wasn't really, but nodded to be as agreeable as I could. He gave me a friendly smile. "Good."

Ali whistled again, although how his mouth was moist enough I have no idea, and the horse took a few bored steps towards us, then stopped and eyed me hatefully as if to say, "him again?" I didn't have time to glare back because I was suddenly hoisted by the waist and perched painfully, and precariously back atop his withers. Then my companion leapt up and we were off again.

The dust kicked up from the road and the pounding hoof beats made conversation difficult, which was just as well as I had plenty to think about. I knew that there were other cities and villages besides Acre, of course. But I had no idea that there was so much *nothing* between them. We were on our way from a big city to a village, a day and a half apart, and yet we hardly saw anyone, and nothing resembling a real town. We saw scrub brush, the occasional two or three camel caravan, and a village or two, if you could call them that.

When people back in Acre talked about this or that village, I'm not sure what I expected them to look like. Mostly they were a collection of three or four mud brick farmers' huts, owned by members of the same family, with a dried up and useless well in the center. The inhabitants were always Syrian and Mussulman. Christians tended to gather together for protection and companionship in the larger towns where there was a military presence.

Bouncing along across the featureless desert, my brain kept inventing scenarios where I would miraculously escape. These alternated with equally vivid daydreams of being caught and summarily executed. Between the physical discomfort of being on the horse and the very real concerns for my life, I found myself near tears most of the day.

Eventually, though, my fear as it usually did, turned to boredom. I began to take an interest in my surroundings. If I were to report back to Brother Marco, what would I tell him? There was no way of judging distance or time. In Acre, I never got lost because landmarks were everywhere. How would I tell someone where I was? *Turn left at the second hill with a dead tree on it.* He'd be spinning forever.

Every time we approached a settlement, our arrival was met by a panicked shout from one person, then an explosion of chicken squawks and goat bleats as the villagers ran inside their huts. Only when there was no perceived danger did the oldest male dare poke his head out the door to address Ali. The conversation was almost always the same as the first one I witnessed.

After a polite exchange of *salaam alaikum*s, Ali asked for water.

"I'm sorry, the well is dry... has been for weeks."

"Are you sure you can't do anything for me? My son here is very thirsty." A strong hand on my back reminded me this wasn't a good time to argue about parentage. While the old man protested and tried to assess how much danger they were in, a wrinkled crone emerged, shouting loudly, berating the old man for his thoughtlessness. She gave me a toothless smile and told me to get off my horse and come inside.

As much as I wanted to oblige, Ali had other plans. "I'm sorry Mother…. We must get to Baisan as quickly as possible. But Allah has seen your generosity. And Salah-adin will remember you and your family as well."

At the mention of the dreaded name, a cloud passed over the head man's face, then quickly twisted into a nervous smile. "So he is near then?"

Ali nodded as he gulped down a ladleful of brackish water that had miraculously appeared. "You've lived under the *Firengi* dogs long enough. Soon you will be under the protection of the Commander of the Faithful, *inshallah.*" The family didn't look nearly as relieved as expected, and I remember what Ahmed said about some of the Mussulman families fearing Salah-adin more than the Christians. None of it made any sense. I was getting used to that.

The mother offered a soft and unconvincing, "inshallah." It occurred to me that Mussulmen use inshallah, like Christians use "God willing". Some mean it, some are being sarcastic, and the rest use it when you're expected to have an opinion but there's nothing left to say, almost like a verbal shrug.

There was a pleasant enough exchange between the two men. Yes, the weather had been hot, and Allah hadn't blessed them with rain for months, but what can one do? The goats, it appeared, didn't like the heat any more than the people did. Ali pretended to care and nodded sympathetically.

"Take care for your family. A Christian war party will be

coming through here soon."

The old man's fake smile disappeared. "How long?"

Ali shrugged. "Three, four days."

"How big?"

Ali helped me back up on his horse, leapt up himself and looked down at the family. "All of them, little Father. Every cursed Christian in the world will come marching through here and straight into hell. Take care of your family." With that, we headed east again.

This scene was repeated three more times until it was late in the afternoon. The sun was at our back now, and it looked as though we were trying to ride down our own long shadows. My eyes and head were heavy, and I must have dozed off, uncomfortable as I was, because I remember suddenly hearing a sharp long whistle and forcing myself awake.

Ali pulled that foaming black monster of his to a halt and nearly blew out my ear drums with an equally sharp whistle of his own. From over a small hill, nearly dead ahead of us but slightly south, three men on horseback appeared. Their shiny helmets glinted like stars as they stood still on the top of the hill looking down at us. On hearing Ali's signal they rode our way at a relaxed trot, not bothering to look around for signs of trouble.

The three were Mameluke soldiers in full armor. Besides their round, pointed helmets, they wore quilted jackets, with long swords and small round shields dangling at the sides of their long skirts. Strung bows hung loosely behind them. All three were tall, although not as tall as Ali, and thin; a lot leaner than the knights I knew. Their armor also seemed completely ineffective and I wondered how these skinny men on skinny horses ever expected to beat trained Templars and Hospitallers, twice their size, fully encased in steel chain mail and riding huge war destriers. A drop of sweat ran the length of my nose and dripped off. It occurred to me being comfortable might be a bigger tactical advantage than sweating inside a metal suit.

"These are friends of mine," Ali told me sternly. "They aren't nearly as civilized as I am, so don't speak unless spoken to. And be polite."

I could tell they were good friends, because like all soldiers I'd ever met, they started insulting each other's' mothers and manhood, and the likely manhood of their mothers, as soon as they were in shouting distance. Except for being in Arabic, it could have been any soldiers meeting anywhere in the world.

Ali halted and waited for his friends to arrive. One of the men looked at the others, then let out a shout and kicked his horse in the side. The animal took off as if shot from a bow, and the others realized they'd been challenged to a race and did the same. Laughs and curses mixed with the pounding hooves and snorts of their mounts. They closed the distance in no time at all and nearly rode past us before they pulled up.

"As usual, you're too slow, boys," shouted the lead rider, an unsavory looking Turk with a thick rug of a beard. He leaned over his horse and made cooing noises, patting her neck appreciatively.

"As usual, you cheated." The speaker was a young man, his reddish beard more ambition than finished product.

The Cheater, as I instantly named him, just chuckled. "Never confuse playing fair with good strategy, boy. Besides, I had to get away from the two of you for a minute. You both smell like camel farts."

I couldn't help myself, and laughed, which immediately drew all four sets of eyes to me and put an end to that. The Cheater's shifty eyes darted from Ali to me and back in an unspoken question.

"I'm bringing him back to Baisan. He's a *Firengi* spy."

"Right, and I'm the King of Jerusalem." The youngest soldier, Scraggly, said with a laugh.

Calmly, my captor replied, "Well, your highness. I'm under orders from *Al Jasus* himself." Ali hadn't used the fat man's name, just called him The Spy, and I noticed two things. First, every man there knew exactly who he was referring to, and secondly, the color drained completely from Scraggly's face. It seemed others were as afraid of the man as I was.

I heard the ring of a sword being pulled from a scabbard and in the same motion the horribly sharp point stopped within an inch of my face. "Really, lad, you're a spy against your own people for the…. them?"

Ali turned his attention to the man with the sword. "And if he says this one is a spy, and should go to Baisan, and get there alive and safe, then don't you think that's what should happen?"

The Cheater inspected me from head to toe and back up

again, then re-sheathed his blade. "He doesn't look like much."

Ali just shrugged. "That's because he's a spy. Wouldn't be much good if you could tell from looking at him, would it? All I know is he's given Al Jasus quite the run around, and he thinks this boy is dangerous, so don't be stupid."

Really? He thinks I'm dangerous? I thought I saw a grudging look of respect pass over Scraggly's face, and I sat up taller on the horse, trying not to wince at the soreness in my backside.

The third soldier hadn't said anything up to that point. He was older than the others, with a nearly triangular face, huge ears and a beard that ended in a sharp point. His small dark eyes moved slowly from face to face, and I felt like everything he heard was chiseled onto his brain. He probably never forgot anything. Despite the threats from the Cheater, and Scraggly's doubts about me, this one was the man I'd have to watch out for.

Cheater jerked his head towards the hill. "Come on. We have a camp not too far. You can spend the night and get your precious cargo to Baisan tomorrow. There's even a little water, although it tastes like shit." If Ali was reluctant to stop, that changed his mind.

"All right, as long as we're there before Al Jasus. The Firengi are getting ready to move." This got Big-Ear's attention.

"Where are they headed?" The deep voice sounded like a wooden wheel scraping over gravel.

"Everyone knows they're going to Tiberias to rescue

Raymond's bitch." Cheater smirked. "If I had my way, they'd just find smoking ruins and dead bodies. I don't know why the Sultan hasn't just burned the place to the ground and be done with it."

Big-Ears shook his head. "They're not that stupid. There isn't a drop of water between Acre and Tiberias… it would be suicide. They'll come for us further south, along the river." I knew the truth, but bit my tongue. Why let him know he was giving the Christians far too much credit.

Ali's voice was like the piping of a seabird compared to Big Ear's bullfrog drone. "That's what this one is going to tell us when we get to Baisan." Then he gave a little clicking noise and his big black horse trotted off.

Maybe it was spending so much time alone in the desert, but the four men—except for Big-Ears, who remained silent as a stone—seemed to compete for who could speak the most. Ali and Cheater traded stories of women and enemies conquered, with Scraggly chiming in from time to time with what even I knew were obvious lies, but the older men let him prattle on.

For the first time in my life, I quit talking and listened. It sounds obvious now, but I realized how much you can learn if you just kept your mouth shut. For example, Salah-adin had indeed captured Tiberias. Out of respect for Count Raymond—weakness Scraggly called it, which earned him a sharp cuff on the back of the head from Big-Ears—his wife and people were fine. One of the neighboring villages had been put to the torch as a lesson to those who collaborated with Enemies of the Faith. I didn't know which village, but hoped it wasn't al Majdal.

By the time we arrived at the campsite—nothing more than a few stones forming a fireplace and a patch of dry thatch that used to be a pasture—I'd also learned that Salahadin's men were better informed than Count Raymond about King Guy's plans.

As the soldiers rummaged through their bags for food, The Cheater filled Ali in on what had happened while he'd been in Acre. "That honorless bastard Rayno," he spat as he said the name. At first I didn't know who he meant, but realized he meant Reynauld de Chatillon, "got exactly what he wanted. First he broke the truce by attacking the Commander of the Faithful's sister, and then he managed to get King Guy to leave Jerusalem and come at us."

Scraggly laughed. "I'm going to charge in, fast as I can, and kill me a knight. Maybe even a Templar." He swung an imaginary sword with great skill and a lot of grunting.

Big-Ears spit out a date seed. "I keep telling you kid. Walk in and kill them all." Ordinarily, boasting of killings and promises of future slaughter were just so much soldier's talk. Whenever I'd heard Christian knights say similar things I either chalked it up to mere boasting or felt a little tingle of excitement and envy. This time, though, the killers were deadly serious, and the intended victims my friends. I stayed very quiet.

Every time I looked up, I could see Scraggly staring. Finally, he asked Ali, "What's this one supposed to have done?"

When soldiers get together you can be sure of a couple of

things. Tales best left untold would be related with relish, and those tales may or may not be based in actual fact. The fewer facts, the more gusto in the telling.

Ali told a vaguely accurate version of my stealing the map from al Sameen, (which apparently I did knowing exactly what it was, who he was, and what I was doing--none of which was remotely true) and the first attempt to capture me which ended with Rafi's death in the marketplace. In Ali's version, which he heard from someone who heard it from Al Jasus himself, I struck the fatal blow with a hashishin's skill. Possibly with my bare hands. Oh, I was also a confidante of both Count Raymond and the Grand Masters of both the Temple and the Hospital. The story was so fascinating I forgot it was supposed to be about me.

Scraggly's attitude changed from highly skeptical to outright hostile. When it came time for bed, it was left up to him to tie my hands and stand guard. He wrapped a strip of cloth around my hands so tightly that they immediately began to turn blue.

I let out an involuntary, "Ow," which made the others look up from the fire.

"Damn it, man. Not so tight. You want to his hands to fall off?" Ali walked over and ripped the strips from my captor's hands. "Tight enough he can't get out, but don't cut the blood off. Like this…" A few simple motions and my wrists were bound. They didn't hurt nearly as much, but I knew there was no escape, either. "There." He paused for a moment, then asked Scraggly, "Did you let him pee first?"

The look on the lad's face told him the answer, and Ali

cursed again as he untied me, roughly walked me over away from the campsite a bit, let me do what I needed to do and brought me back. He handed the strips to Scraggly and watched him retie my wrists.

I laid down on the ground, facing the stone barrier. Laying there, trying to imagine reporting everything I'd experienced back to Brother Marco, got me wondering about him and the others at St. Lazar. Eventually exhaustion overcame fear, and I fell into a deep dreamless sleep.

Morning came far too early. After a little brackish water, stale bread and a few dates, I was back on the black bane of my existence. This morning, time was of the essence, so there was less idle chatter and more bouncing. My saddle sores hadn't improved overnight.

As we neared the valley, we saw more Saracen soldiers and fewer civilians. A few of the little hamlets were deserted and ominously quiet. There wasn't even a squawking chicken to comment on our passing.

The ground became more rolling. Small dips in the road became low hills. A little moisture in the air meant more plant life, some of it still alive. As we neared the crest of the tallest hill yet, Ali said the first thing I'd heard from him in hours. "Here we are, boy."

Scraggly picked up speed and outran the rest of us to the top, then turned with a huge smile on his face that made him look even younger than that sparse excuse of a beard.

All four riders pulled their horses to a stop. Down the other side I could see the glint of sunlight on the legendary River Jordan. It was actually a disappointingly narrow stream with a flat valley between us and the water. I couldn't see much of the valley floor, though. Every square inch of the ground was covered in tents, horses or soldiers. As crowded as Acre was, I don't think I've ever seen so many people gathered in one place.

I tried to count the number of unique banners, since that's what you'd do with enemy troops, but I simply couldn't. There were too many to count. And every single person there was determined to kill Crusaders. As far as I could tell, I was the only Christian for miles around.

"Remember what I said, Lucca. Speak when spoken to and mind your manners." With that Ali and I rode down the steep hill into Salah-adin's camp.

Chapter 18

We approached the camp at a slow walk. From my perch atop the horse's neck, I saw the glint of sunlight off the river, almost indistinguishable from the gleam of morning sunlight on armor and steel. Even on Acre's market days, I had never seen so many people assembled in one place, and each and every one here was intent on killing me and those like me.

Ali pointed around us. "See this? For too long the Firengi kept us fighting with each other. Now Salah-adin has us all fighting together for the glory of Allah. We'll push them into the sea once and for all. I think you picked the wrong side, my friend." I said nothing, partly because counting troop flags and remembering details gave me a reason not to panic, and partly because I didn't recall ever having a choice. I never purposely chose to be Christian any more than I suspect Ali chose to be Muslim… we were what we were born to be. It didn't seem the right time to discuss it, though, so I kept my mouth shut.

Ali's hell-black mount was the rock against which the river of sun-browned soldiers and hangers-on changed course. Slowly but inexorably we pushed through the throng to the very heart of the camp. The din and dust rose, and the tents became bigger and more opulent.

About a hundred yards to the north of us was a huge

pavilion constructed of rich scarlet and black cloth and a stream of people running in and out like ants; only ants didn't bow from the waist when they entered and left their hill. That had to be Salah-adin's headquarters, and I felt my breath catch in my chest.

Scraggly and Big-Ears passed us on either side, pushing towards the pavilion. A richly dressed man in a black turban and unbelievably white robes stood quietly, hands folded at his waist, right above where a sharp wickedly curved sword hung. The soldiers dismounted and dropped immediately into a low bow. I couldn't make out the discussion, but there was a lot of head shaking by the important-looking one, and a lot of pointing at us from our companions.

"Is that Salah-adin?" I asked. Ali laughed.

"No, just one of his Imams." So, he was a priest. The Templars and Hospitallers always had priests with them, many of whom seemed more important—and always a lot cleaner—than the actual fighters. Apparently, the Saracens worked the same way with God's representatives mingled among actual combatants for support, encouragement or punishment as the situation commanded.

Scraggly got back on his horse and unhappily rode off towards the river. Big Ears walked back to us, shaking his head. He took Ali's horse by the bridle, giving the animal an affectionate scratch behind the ears. "Says we're to take this one over there." He gestured with his chin somewhere behind him. Apparently, it was specific enough for Ali.

"Really?" He sounded more surprised than concerned. I took that as good news.

"That's what he said." Big Ears glared at me as if expecting me to explain the mystery. I felt myself squirm under that gaze. If I'd know anything I'm sure he'd have gotten it out of me, but since I was completely clueless I just dropped my head as if fascinated by the horse's dark mane.

I felt Ali shrug behind me. "All right then. Lucca, seems you get the royal treatment today," and gave his mount a gentle kick towards the far side of the camp. I bounced along in confused silence as we approached a large but plain-looking tent. Two of the biggest soldiers I'd ever seen squatted in front of it and stood to immediate attention on our arrival, looking very serious indeed.

The horse shook his giant head, huge drops of foamy sweat flying everywhere, but the guards never changed expression, just stoically wiped their faces with a finger. Ali got off the monster and stretched gratefully. Then he reached up, grabbed me by the waist and pulled me to the ground. My legs were so chafed and sore, I could barely stand. Each guard grabbed a flap of the tent and pulled it open for us. My companion shepherded me inside.

The tent was a blessed relief from the sun, heat and dust of the camp. I blinked a few times to help my eyes adjust. At first it appeared completely innocent. Comfortable cushions lined the far wall, beckoning my aching behind like a siren's song. Plain carpets covered the floor. A low table was pushed to one corner, covered in unlit lamps. The only ominous sign was a metal post, about a foot and a half high. A light metal chain was connected to it, and the chain lay harmlessly on the ground, leading to a pair of shackles inches from the cushions.

Ali pointed to the plush ground coverings. "Sit there. Make yourself comfortable." When I had settled my grateful bottom into the cushion, he took one of the shackles and clamped it around my ankle.

"What are you doing?" I squeaked. The metal felt cold against my bare skin, but my leg was so skinny I could have easily slipped out of the restraints, which were obviously made for full-grown men. Ali thoughtfully ran a finger inside the shackle, bit his lip and then opened it again. He wrapped a strip of cloth above my foot, then put the shackle back on. This time it fit snugly.

"This is where the important prisoners are kept. They are doing you a great honor." Ali offered as if that was a comfort.

The idea seemed hard to swallow. "What do they do with the prisoners that aren't important?" I asked him. His sad eyes told me there were only two types of prisoners; important ones—like me apparently—and unimportant ones. The less important probably didn't require much shelter, at least not for very long.

I looked down at the metal around my leg. "What's going to happen to me?"

Ali bit his lip and shook his head. "I don't know. I imagine they will question you, and then they'll decide." He paused, then put two fingers under my chin and forced me to look into his eyes. "Lucca, do what they tell you. Say what you know, and don't cause trouble. There may be a way out of this yet. You seem like a good boy, and a brave one. Don't make al Jasus angrier than he already is. And you don't know

236

who you'll meet, so keep a civil tongue in your head." I nodded silently. It was good advice, but not making adults angry wasn't my strength, and I doubted it would be as easy as Ali made it sound.

Just then the tent flap flew open, and a spear point of sunlight pierced my eyes. Two small shapes entered, and as I blinked away the glare, I realized they were girls. Both slightly older than me, and rail-thin beneath their gowns. Their heads were covered in glossy cloth, and thin veils concealed their mouths and noses. For just a moment, the image of Sister Marie-Pilar shot across my mind's eye and then vanished. One girl carried a tray of fruit, while another carried a pitcher of water and a cup.

Round dark eyes flew open in surprise. "Apologies," the one carrying the food stammered. We were told there was an important prisoner…"

Ali smiled. "So there is, little one. This is a most important guest of the Caliph. And a dangerous one, can't you tell?"

The smaller, probably younger, girl sniffed. "He doesn't look like much. He's just a stupid boy. His hair isn't even white." This earned her an elbow to her skinny ribs from her partner and a loud barking laugh from Ali, who was well aware of all Syrian girls' fascination with the blonde—and especially the redheaded—foreigners. I looked like just another worthless boy—just like everyone they'd ever met.

"Until we decide what happens to him, you will treat him with honor. Understand?" The girls both nodded. The younger one, whose thick eyebrows almost met at her nose, eyed me suspiciously over the top of her veil. She shoved the plate of food at me, or at least in my direction, and I managed to grab a couple of dates before she pulled it away again. I almost grabbed for them with my left hand, but remembered how scandalized Ahmed always was whenever I did that, and switched to my right. Chained to a post in the middle of an enemy camp didn't seem like a good time to offer offense.

I managed to nod politely and mumble "thank you", although it would have sounded more heartfelt if I wasn't shoving the food into my mouth at the same time. I've heard men tell tales of their adventures, of being "too frightened to eat." I've never experienced that. The body needs fuel if your heart is going to race that quickly and you feel the need to shake all over. No matter how sick, or nervous, or sore I have ever been, my stomach demands its due.

The older, thinner girl poured me some water and I gratefully gulped it down in one long pull.

"You're thirsty." She poured me another cup, and I took a more civilized sip and offered what I hoped was an ingratiating smile and another thank you. She bowed ever so slightly, and I thought her eyes crinkled in a slight smile but that could have been the blazing daylight, because Ali stood at the door with the flap wide open, pointing outside.

"All right, ladies, that's enough. Out with you." Eyebrows gave him a meek bow and hustled out without paying me any more notice. Pretty Eyes, on the other hand, turned and nodded in my direction before hustling out after her friend, who immediately began to chastise her with a tongue worthy of any Armenian merchant.

"Sit there and be quiet." Ali pointed to the cushions.

"For how long?" I asked.

"Not long, *inshallah*." Perfect, I was at the mercy of God's timing again. So far, He hadn't seemed to be in much of a hurry. I watched Ali duck through the flaps and looked around me. The tent was large, but with nothing in it except cushions and me, it practically echoed.

I gave the chain an exploratory tug. The peg was firmly embedded in the ground, and since it was made to hold fully grown knights in place, I knew there was no chance of pulling it out.

The cushions were very comfortable compared to the horse's withers, and my bruised, raw buttocks sank gratefully into a brocaded pillow. I laid back, staring at where the tent material reached a peak. Outside, I could hear the expected sounds of a military camp. Except for the fact everyone was shouting, laughing, or cursing in Arabic the clangs, crashes, groans and shouted orders could have emanated from Count Raymond's camp. Except, of course, there were more soldiers. An awful lot more.

My bored eyes scoured the tent, top to bottom, and along the perimeter. In places, there were gaps of an inch or two where the segments of cloth didn't quite meet. I glimpsed shaky shadows of the occasional sandal or slipper through the openings. A hot breeze caused the flaps of the tent to flutter, and bright beams of sunlight would flash through against the far wall of the tent. Since it was afternoon, we must have been facing west. I thought Brother Marco would have been pleased at my figuring that out, and then tears blurred my vision. I wiped them away on my sleeve and cleared my nose at the same time. He wouldn't be as proud of me if I cried like a girl and fought to stay brave.

Time dragged, and I must have dozed off out of boredom, exhaustion or the suffocating heat inside my prison. My eyes flew open as horse hooves pawed at the ground outside. I heard snorting and whinnying and cursing. The silhouette of a horse played across the tent wall and I watched it rear up, front hooves flashing and nearly decapitating one of my guards. There was a lot of yelling and shouting. I thought I recognized one of the voices, but couldn't place it until the tent flaps parted and, silhouetted by the late afternoon sun, was a familiar round shape. A visibly angry al Sameen (he was back to being Fattie. Al Jasus seemed too good for him) stood in the doorway glaring at me.

Whenever I'd seen him before, even in disguise, he was always immaculate and well-dressed. Now the man was a dusty, sweat-soaked mess. He must have ridden like crazy to catch up to us so soon, and for once in my life I felt pity for a horse. No wonder the creature was so foul tempered. The trip had done nothing for the mood of the rider, either. I could feel his eyes burn into mine and his fat grimy cheeks puffed up when he attempted a smile.

He took a couple of steps forward, then one to the side as the tent opened and another man strode in. This man was slim—maybe half as wide as my tormentor, and half a head shorter. His beard was still neatly trimmed and dark so it was difficult to tell his exact age. Dark eyes, deeply set in a bed of crinkles, seemed more ancient than the rest of his wiry soldier's body.

The stranger examined me for a minute, then let out a hearty laugh. "This is him?"

My old nemesis didn't join in the levity. He dropped his eyes to the floor, head bowed, his cheeks burning in shame and barely contained anger. "Yes, my Lord." Whoever this stranger was, he was important. And powerful. I tried to imagine the spy being intimidated by anyone, even Salah-adin himself…. And that's when it dawned on me.

I dropped to my knees and bowed so low I bumped my head on the ground, hoping to strike an appropriately submissive pose. My brain spun inside my skull. How do you address the most powerful man in the world?

Salah-adin put his hands behind his back, rocking on his heels as he studied me. He barely concealed his amusement, but knew his spy master didn't find anything humorous about the situation. Instead, the Commander of the Faithful allowed himself one last smirk before becoming more serious.

"So, you are the cause of all this trouble are you?" I hoped the question was rhetorical, because there was no way I could possibly speak. I kept my eyes on the embroidered slippers directly in front of me, slippers that took several steps forward. "What's his name?" Salah-adin asked.

"He says his name is Lucca, o Commander of the Faithful. He's an orphan of no particular importance. He's been living with Raymo…" al Sameen used the nickname the Saracens used for Count Raymond.

"He doesn't look like a spy. Or a killer for that matter.

241

Look at me, boy." I meekly complied. The most feared man in all of Outremer looked down at me with more curiosity than menace. You look Syrian. How did you come to live among the Firengi? They're not exactly known for their kindness to our brothers and sisters."

Answering his questions, at least as much as honor would allow, seemed like the wisest course. "My mother was Syrian, my lord. My father was a French Knight.... Your Highness." I had no idea what his appropriate title might be, so I aimed as high as I could so as not to give offense to someone who could have my head cut off if sufficiently irked.

"He's also working with the Knights of St Lazar, and the Hospital, and the Templars and even the Devil himself, as far as I can tell."

"What do the Lepers have to do with anything?" The King addressed the spy, but his eyes never left me.

"I was just about to.... question him about that, among other things." The spy made the simple word "question" sound more like 'chop him into small pieces and eat him'.

Salah-adin nodded. "Question him as you see fit, but don't hurt him.... Too badly, at least. He might still prove useful to us."

"I don't think...." but the smaller man silenced the angry spy with a raised hand.

Salah-adin switched to pretty good French. "Lucca, you know I could use a young man of your talents. Allah welcomes everyone to the one true faith. You could be with your own people, and on the winning side. In just a few days, inshallah, we will drive all the Christian infidels into the sea."

Was it really that simple? All I had to do was say I was what most people assumed I was anyway and they'd let me live? I could feel the blood rushing through my temples. It would be so simple. *Maybe they'd let me live in al Majdal with Ahmed and...*

"Leave him to me, my Lord." The way Fatso said that made it sound like a really, really bad idea, but Salah-adin nodded.

"Yes, fine. Think about what I said, Lucca."

I was thinking about it, and in that moment it didn't seem the worst idea. "Yes, your highness. I will think about it."

"He's all yours," Salah-adin turned to leave. He must have seen the evil leer on Fatso's face because he added, "and go gently." The smile faded but the spy nodded meekly and bowed low as his master left the tent.

Suddenly I was alone with the spy master. Just in case God was going to grant me a miracle, I gave a futile pull on the chain. The clinking of the metal links only made the man grin wider. "Now, you are going to tell me what I want to know. Do you understand?"

I nodded mutely. I would try to be brave. I'd try to hold out and not give anything away, but what did I even know? My heart pounded as he took a step towards me.

"Now, who are you?"

"I…. I told you. My name's Lucca."

The huge figure loomed over me and he leaned close in to me. I could smell the sweat, and the garlic and the evil come off him in waves. "I didn't ask your name, I asked who you are. Your name doesn't help me. I've got four or five names of my own, but I am what I am. Now, who… or what…. are you?"

"I'm no one. I just…" A meaty hand shot out and struck me so hard I flew back onto the cushions. I had received blows from the Brothers for misbehaving. I'd taken some hard shots from Vardan and Sergeant Jacques while training, but until that moment I'd never been hit with really bad intentions. Fatso had some very bad intentions, indeed.

My captor rubbed his hand and flexed his fingers unhappily. "Ordinarily, I don't like hurting people. Especially children. But you have caused me a lot of trouble, and we don't have much time. The Christians are already marching on Tiberias, but you already know that."

I didn't know it, of course, and it occurred to me that the man thought I knew much more than I did. That would make it really hard to provide satisfactory answers, and that meant I was in real trouble.

"Let's try again. How did you come to work with De Riggio?" He could see the ignorance on my face. "Marco. The Leper. What are you to him?"

"He took me in and gave me a place to live." I flinched against a blow that never came. I'd given an answer that was true… and didn't reveal anything. Maybe I could be truthful enough to stay alive without betraying my friends.

"And made you a spy."

"I'm not a…." He slapped me across the face and took a fistful of my hair.

Calmly, he said. "Don't lie to me, Lucca. You'll only make me angry. Now, how did you know I would have the map?"

244

"I didn't. I was following Charles…. Mohammed, for fun. Then I saw you and him together…." I closed my eyes, prepared for another blow.

"Does this seem like fun?" I shook my head frantically. "You play some very dangerous games. Why were you living with the Lepers instead of the Brothers at the Hospital?"

"I ran away." It was true. True enough, anyway. There was no need to tell him the whole story.

Al Sameen gave a heavy sigh and shook his head. "And Raymo? Why were you in his camp?"

I said nothing. He said nothing either. We just looked at each other for the longest time. Once he raised his hand and I flinched, but he simply scratched his head. "I'll tell you why you were there. Because you were spying for Count Raymond… on the other Firengi." I hadn't really put that together, but he was right of course. My widened eyes were all the confirmation he needed, so he went on.

"Rayno and the King are intent on ending the truce and think they can defeat us. They think Tripoli is too friendly with Salah-adin so they're using him as an excuse but don't tell him anything. They might be right…I think Salah-adin should have burned Tiberias to the ground and killed the infidel's bitch of a wife but as God wills. He needed you to tell him what was going on inside the city."

He neither wanted nor expected a real answer. He straightened up with a groan. "You're a lucky boy. If Salah-adin hadn't ordered me to keep you alive you'd be just one more dead Christian by now. Consider his offer. Accept the true faith and come work for me. I could grow to like you."

And I could grow a second head with purple hair.

A tall, incredibly ugly soldier stuck his head inside the tent. "Forgive me, but The Commander of the Faithful has asked for you."

The big spy nodded. "Yes, I'll be right there." He turned back towards me. "I'll leave you to think about it. But you don't have much time. We'll be breaking camp in the morning, and once the battle starts it will be too late to do the right thing." Then he left me alone.

By now the far wall of the tent glowed bright orange. The sun had nearly set, and soon it would be completely dark. I was all alone in the growing gloom, without a candle or a single happy thought to offer any comfort.

Chapter 19

The tent wasn't all that large, but as night fell and the dark gradually swallowed every inch of it—and me—it felt cavernous. Through the thinnest of cell walls I heard the noises of the army camp, but in my solitude those familiar sounds may as well have been miles away. On the other side of the cloth was life and excitement. On my side, only heat, darkness and growing despair.

At first I nestled into the cushions, grateful for the softness and the fact they didn't bounce up and down like Ali's nasty horse. Then, as the heat grew, they began to become sticky, and odors wafted up from the cloth. Given who this prison normally housed, I tried not to identify the scents. It was bad enough I smelled like dirt and horse sweat. I tossed and turned, vainly trying to sleep.

When it was obvious I wasn't going to be able to sleep, I began exploring my cloth cage. First, I pulled the chain as tight as I could, and realized I could reach the pillows, but not quite get to the walls of the tent itself. I was about an arm's reach away. If I kept the chain fully extended, I could make a circle around the tent. I also realized that when the chain clinked and clanked, it caused a large ugly head to poke through the flap.

"What are you doing in here?" the guard demanded.

"Nothing...." I realized that was both untrue and sounded stupid. "I'm just walking around." That was at least a more honest and slightly more intelligent answer. He grunted at me.

"Knock it off. Just sit there and behave." The man must have had ears like a hound, because every time I made the slightest noise, he would stop talking to his partner with a quick "Shoosh". Just my luck to get the one soldier in a million who took guard duty seriously.

I tried sitting very still and listening, determined to learn whatever I could on the very remote chance I ever got out of there. *What would I say?* Mostly I heard the night-time noises of a military camp. There were the same jokes, the same shouts of outrage over loaded dice, the same slow metallic hiss of blade and whetstone that hung over Count Raymond's camp, as well as the barracks of the Hospital. The laughter tonight, though, was a little louder and less harsh. If there was a difference from what I'd heard back outside Acre, it was this; these men were confident of victory.

I thought of the soldiers fighting for Count Raymond, and those of the Orders inside Acre. *No, they aren't inside Acre, they're on the way here.* Brave fighting men I always thought of as invincible, who before long would be sword to sword with the Saracens. *Do they have any idea how many of the enemy they face—and how likely they are to die?*

Those thoughts eventually turned to Sisters Agnes, and Fleure, and Marie-Pilar, of great fat Berk, and Fadhil and his shit-heel of a father. Did they know the dangers lying ahead for them? What were Brother Marco and Vardan doing? To my surprise I found myself even missing Sergeant Jacques, and hoping he was safe. Odds were the very disease that destroyed their lives as soldiers was keeping him safe behind the city walls. That no doubt irritated the hell out of them. Had the two Ahmed's managed to get back to al Majdal, or had they been attacked on the way? I tried without success to will away the vision of Scraggly chopping the head off of my friend's uncle.

In a bored, thoughtless way I picked at the band of cloth around my ankle. It moved the metal shackle up and down, which amused me enough to do it again. Then a second time, and then with a soft thunk, the restraint fell to my ankle, and I realized I could lift my foot right out of it. In a panic, I tried to shove my skinny foot back into the metal circle, lest Hound-Ears find out. After holding my breath for a frighteningly long time, I removed my foot again and wiggled it in delight. Now I could explore my prison in silence.

I climbed over the little hill of cushions to the very back wall of the tent. As I said, in places there were inch or two-inch gaps. I dropped to my stomach to peer through the opening, and was rewarded with a breath of cool, fresh air. It was almost as good as water in the sweaty, close quarters.

Just as I began to concoct various fantastic plans to burrow out the back of the tent, a giant sandal-covered foot appeared about three inches from my nose. Some soldier was wandering around and I was reminded that even if I could get out of my cloth confinement, I was still dead center in the largest Mussulman force ever assembled. Where was I going to go?

That realization took all the fun out of exploring, and I crawled back to my pillow bed. Before trying to sleep, though, I carefully put my foot back inside the shackle and pulled it up to the cloth so that it appeared secure. I'm sure that panic made the slight tinkle of the metal sound like a blacksmith pounding on an anvil, but my guard never even hushed his partner.

I lay back and tried to think positively. My world had expanded by about a yard and a half in all directions, but I was still trapped. And alone. The loneliness threatened to overtake me completely. I buried my face into one of the least-smelly pillows and forced myself to get some sleep.

The camp awoke with the buzz of gossip. Arabic voices whispered to each other at first, slowly growing louder and more confident, then insistent as the innuendo and guesses became facts and orders. "They're coming."

"They're not coming."

"They're over the next hill."

"They're holed up like rats in Aleppo." The sounds of action: meals being prepared and equipment collected, horses fed and equipped for battle, all added to the growing chaos.

I slipped out of my shackle and pressed my ear to one of the walls. Two young squires stood nearby, and I managed to make out most of what they were saying, although between their accents—maybe Egyptian—and the growing din I couldn't make out everything, just snatches of conversation, most of which was guesswork or boasting.

"…. the Infidels are nearly to Tiberias, maybe half a day's

march."

"Have they finally gone crazy? Where did they find water?"

"We're going to come up behind them…"

"I'm going to take a Templar's head…" There was a lot of that. The Templars were a popular target.

Then I heard a deep barking voice, like Sergeant Jacques' long lost Saracen brother. "You'll be lucky if there's anything there for you to take by the time we get there…. Quit prattling on like old women and move it. These tents won't pack themselves…"

They were breaking down the camp. That meant my home away from home would be coming down. What did that mean for me? I looked around me as a familiar round shadow grew ever larger against the far cloth wall, then turn towards the flap. Al Sameen was coming.

And my foot wasn't in my shackles.

I dove for the chain and pulled it towards me. The darned thing flew up and nearly brained me, but I caught it, slipped my foot inside and pulled it snug against the rags just as daylight, and the fat spy master, entered. He stood, hands on hips without saying a word.

I was dying to ask what was going on, but I knew this game. Adults played it all the time, and usually lost. The only way to shut me up was to expect me to speak first and I saw no reason to make the big man's life easy. I plunked down on the cushion, crossed my legs with a soft tinkling of chain, and stared back. I'm pretty sure an unintentional smirk crossed my face. It must have, because at the same time a nasty scowl passed over his, and I was afraid I'd pushed him too far.

"Bah, we don't have time for your stupid games, boy. The Commander of the Faithful still thinks you can be useful to us, but I want you to see something first." Al Sameen— because he would always be Fat Man to me—stomped forward and grabbed my ankle. He roughly tore at the cloths, and my shackle fell away. His eyes narrowed, but he either didn't have time or couldn't be bothered with unnecessary details. He simply grabbed a fistful of hair and yanked me to my feet.

I let out a yowl of pain, which he either ignored or enjoyed in silence. He shook me by the handful of locks. "Hold your hands out." I obliged, and he wrapped a leather thong around my wrists, binding them together.

A quick shove to my shoulder propelled me through the tent flap, and I found myself outside, blinking frantically. After the darkness of the tent, my eyes burned and teared up. The morning sun was already at full boil. Metal glinted everywhere that dust didn't obscure it.

Finally, I couldn't take it anymore. "Where are we going?"

"I want you to see what you couldn't stop. What no one can stop." That was the only answer I got before a timid-looking squire led a short shaggy poop-brown horse over to us. It seemed stupider but less vicious than most of its peers. The squire nodded at me with his head. "Front or back?"

I groaned and dropped my head in resignation. "Front." I was then hoisted up, legs kicking frantically, over the animal's neck. The way I landed reminded me how much I was going to miss those cushions. With surprising grace, the spy leapt up behind me. The pony buckled under the burden, although less than I expected, and we headed out at a trot through the crowded encampment.

We were going north, near as I could tell, as quickly as the teeming army around us allowed. It seemed that no matter how long we rode, we never ran out of armed company and it took a long time before the desert opened up ahead of us. Finally, though, the crowd thinned, and the horse sped to a trot. Several skins of water slapped against his brown backside as we bounced along.

We turned away from the river, and across a broad field of broken rock and scrub plants. Ahead of us, two rocks loomed. They weren't high enough to be called mountains, but they towered over the valley. The rider reined the horse towards the easternmost outcrop and left the trail.

The poor horse plodded along as the ground became more uneven. His hooves scattered stones and gravel with every step as we neared the steep slope leading up to the rock. The beast stopped and looked over his shoulder at us, as if to ask, "you're sure you want to do this?" That only earned him a sharp kick in the ribs, and if horses could sigh, that's what he did. Then he picked his way up the goat path ahead.

For the first time in ages, my captor spoke. "They're called the Horns of Hattin. It's the shortest way to Tiberias from Acre. They must pass through here." I remained silent, looking around. From our elevated position, I saw the main road winding west, a more or less straight line scratched in the sand, just as it looked on the map I'd stolen.

If Tiberias was, in fact, north of here, then the Crusader army would have to pass between these two giant stone sentries. I knew from snooping that there was a smaller Turkopole army already awaiting them at Count Raymond's castle, and every Mussulman in the world who wasn't there, was making their way from Baisan in the South. I knew nothing about military tactics, but this looked like a spectacularly bad idea by King Guy and the Christian armies.

At last, our mount delivered us nearly to the top of the hill and came to a dejected stop. He looked back at me sadly, and despite myself, I couldn't resist offering a gentle pat on his brown, sweaty neck. Al Sameen slipped off, stretched with an audible crack of his spine, and then pulled me down. I managed to land more or less on my feet.

The blood pounded in my hands where the leather strap cut into the skin. Holding my wrists up in a silent request to be cut loose, I got a disbelieving shake of the head and a "hmmph" for an answer. The big man then took several steps towards the summit and looked out. Then he turned west. "Seems as good a place to watch as any doesn't it?"

I looked around us. There were a few yards of bare stone ahead of us to the actual top. Unlike its partner, this "Horn" had a reasonably flat top, perhaps thirty paces across. From up here we could see a good distance—miles I supposed— in all four directions. More importantly, whatever was happening below us, we'd be safely above everything. It certainly seemed more secure than down in the valley where every soldier in creation was going to meet. I looked behind us to see the droopy horse munching on a dry stick and watching us. He shook his head to scare off flies, but it looked more like he was offering an opinion.

Al Sameen didn't notice. He stood, hands on hips, and gestured around the hilltop. "People like us don't fight. We watch. It's what we do. Salah-adin would very much like you to watch for him. After today, maybe you'll change your mind about which side you want to be on." I didn't respond, so he just shrugged. "Come with me."

He led me back down to the end of the trail and took one of the water skins he'd brought from the pony's back. He enjoyed a long draught of water, gulping it down as if it were the last wine on earth, then held it out to me.

I managed a very reluctant, "thank you," and took a long swig of my own.

"Did riding up here make you thirsty?" he asked in a friendly manner. I couldn't see the harm in agreeing, so I nodded suspiciously. "That was less than an hour. Imagine riding for a day and a half with no water at all. That would be awful, wouldn't it? How about marching with armor and equipment…. that would be really thirsty work." Again, I saw no reason to argue.

"There isn't a drop of water between here and Acre," he continued. "The Christians will be hot and thirsty, and half-dead before they get here. They hope to get to Tiberias where there's water. Raymond's people are waiting for them there. Our soldiers are well rested, well-fed and have a river at their backs." He said nothing else. He didn't have to.

Was that why Ahmed and his family left early? To bring

water back to the troops from the Raymond's territory? If so, where were they?

The smug look on his fat face infuriated me, and I'd been quiet and respectful for two long days, longer than any time in my life and I couldn't take it anymore. "You can't beat them. They have the True Cross with them…"

"So I've heard, but you can't drink relics, can you? King Guy should have paid more attention to his supply sergeants and less to his priests, I think." I couldn't argue that point, so I just turned mopily away, watching the horse forage for anything edible among the gravel and dust.

The bedraggled animal somehow managed to find a few dried twigs here and there, and wandered a few feet further away in search of more. My eyes drifted off towards the west, when a startled snort and the stomp of hooves made me look. The horse's eyes were wide, and he backed off a few steps. The big man and I both moved closer to see what had startled him.

It took a moment of scanning the rock and brush to find a slipper. Then a boot. Then we saw the two corpses who had worn them. A Seljuk scout dressed in black, and his Frankish counterpoint lay dead amongst the stones, their arms wrapped around each other. Two swords, one curved and delicate looking, one heavy and straight, lay on the ground near their hands. A dark cloud of flies circled and buzzed loudly as the ugly insects dropped down into the bloody gaping holes in their mid-sections then took off making room for their brothers. The reek was nauseating.

I immediately gagged and fell to my knees. More out of

reflex than piety, I tried to cross myself only to find my swollen bloody hands still tied together. I settled for bursting into tears instead. Huge, steaming, unmanly tears ran down my cheeks. I could hear myself sobbing, unable to control the tears or the heaving in my gut. I didn't even know who I was weeping for, only that it seemed like the only reasonable thing left to do.

From over my shoulder I heard a disgusted, "tsk", but Al Sameen said nothing else. He just stepped back up the rock, leaving me alone with the bodies and my misery. I could barely see, between the boiling tears in my eyes, my heaving shoulders and retching gut. Through the blur, I saw something glinting against the stones.

It was a dagger. Intricate etching on the handle told me it belonged to the dead Mussulman, rather than the Christian, although it was no longer any use to either of them. I bowed further, pretending to retch again, and closed my hand over it.

From behind and above me, I heard a voice say, "They're dead, boy. Don't waste your tears. Allah will judge them and they will get the reward they've earned. Nothing you or I do can change that." He stepped closer. "It's God's will. Weeping is a waste of time." He climbed back to the hilltop and sat cross-legged on the sun-warmed stone.

He was right. Words couldn't bring these men back. Nor would they do anything for the people I'd already seen killed. Charles, Rafi, who knows how many others. Words wouldn't prevent the coming disaster. More importantly, talking and tears wouldn't set me free. I wrapped my swollen, throbbing fingers around the handle of the dagger.

Through the buzzing of the flies and the blood pounding in my ears I heard the spy master drone on. None of it made much sense. Vaguely I heard words like "duty," and "warrior", and "honor" and of course, "Inshallah."

I was a boy of ten with a knife against a huge man with a sword. I tried to imagine what Jacques would tell me.

He'd tell me I was as good as dead.

But I also heard his commands as I joined the other man. *"Open your opponent up. Step inside. Thrust like your life depends on it—because it does."* I took a long sniffly breath and turned towards al Sameen.

He rose to his feet and looked down at me, arms crossed impatiently. "Are you done crying like a woman?"

I nodded. Yes, I was. Very much done. I joined him on the flat hilltop. The sun was behind him and he was a huge black smudge against cloudless blue sky.

As I slowly approached him, the scabrous old soldiers' voice echoed in my head.

"Open your opponent up."

My opponent stood above me, though. There was no way to swing at him effectively. Then I looked down and gritted my teeth. Lifting my hands, I drove the blade downwards as hard as I could into the top of Al Sameen's foot. A single thin spray of blood shot across my face, hot and sticky, but it opened him up all right. The big man's eyes flew open in pain. His arms waved furiously and he staggered backwards across the rocky slope. In horror I realized my dagger was stuck in the top of his slipper. I was empty handed.

With the roar of a bull, he kicked at me viciously with his wounded foot, but I rolled to my right. The huge spy cursed and grasped his own blade. He swung it at me in unfocused, vicious arcs that made the wind whistle over my head. His vision was blinded by the searing pain in his foot. But it opened him up.

My dagger was buried deep in the fat man's foot. He continued to swing at me, hopping up and down until the knife dislodged and skittered across the rocky surface, leaving a crimson trail. I ducked low to avoid another thrust and picked it up. Now I held it in my bound wrists, facing my enemy.

"Step inside," the voice in my head shouted in guttural French.

Staying low, I felt the sword pass overhead again. I crouched low between his feet and looked up at him.

My head echoed with the next order. "Thrust like your life depends on it... because it does."

For the first time, I followed the Sergeant's orders without question. I took a two-handed grip at gut-level, directed it at my opponent's belly, and jumped forward. Al Sameen let out an outraged roar from the deepest part of his belly and jumped back safely out of range. Or at least he tried to.

His damaged foot couldn't support that much weight moving so awkwardly. My momentum carried me past my target and I landed belly-first on bare rock so close to the edge that I looked down and saw nothing but air and sand. I flipped onto my back, expecting to see al Sameen but just saw blue sky.

While the force of my attack drove me to the ground, it propelled him backwards as well. Two or three lurching steps back to where it was nothing but slick weather-worn stone.

I watched his eyes widen in panic. He flailed wildly, struggling for balance. With a dagger wound in his foot, he couldn't stop rocking back and forth. For a moment, his arms wind-milled furiously. A rock skittered over the edge where the mountain met the desert sky and vanished. Al Sameen bellowed a curse, then toppled backwards and disappeared from sight as well.

I lay stunned, then clawed towards where he vanished. Loose rock skittered over the edge of the precipice and I gripped hard to a boulder for support as I peered over the edge. There, a hundred feet down, the body of the spy master--al Jasus, or al Sameen, or Nurad al Fatin--whoever he really was—formed a misshaped X against the light sand. All I could do was stare silently. I didn't feel satisfaction, or relief. Nor did I feel any guilt, God forgive me. I just felt so very tired.

Crawling slowly a few body lengths away, I flipped onto my back, gasping for breath. Somewhere above me a hawk screamed and circled. Wind rustled a few twiggy branches on low bushes. I heard a whinny from beneath me and the pony stared at me as well, looking very bored and cranky.

After a few eternities to catch my breath, I looked at my hands. They were still tied together, and I was losing circulation. Clumsily pulling myself along and using the boulders for leverage, I stumbled down towards the two bodies. Sure enough, the Christian had a dagger as well. I found it a few steps away from its owner, who wouldn't mind if I borrowed it. It took more effort than expected but I managed to wedge the sharp blade between some rocks to hold it still. Then I slowly, clumsily cut through my leather bonds.

When I was finally free, I looked down at myself. I was covered in blood and God knew what else, but I was alive. I sat on the ground for Christ only knows how long before staggering to my feet. The stupid old horse tossed his head then took a couple of steps towards me and nuzzled his nose against my neck. I wrapped my skinny arms around his neck and wept again.

Finally, I took one of the water skins and gulped greedily, then washed my face. I had no idea what to do or where to go. I walked to the western edge of the rock, avoiding looking directly down, sheltered my eyes from the sun and looked off toward home. A cloud of dust obscured the view and I squinted to see better. The cloud was moving.

The Christian army was arriving. I wanted to shout a warning. I wanted to cry out for help. All I could do, though, was sit on a windswept rock and watch in frustration as the arrogant bastards walked into Salah-adin's trap.

Chapter 20

From my perch on top of the eastern-most Horn, I could see the world in a complete, never ending circle around me. Off to the east was the Sea of Galilee, or Baharat Tabarīyā, and the River Jordan draining away to the south. To the North were the Sultan's troops that had taken Tiberias, eagerly awaiting the rescue attempt. Coming from the west, slowly and inexorably, were the Crusaders. To the south, not yet visible but coming far too quickly, were countless thousands of Salah-adin's troops.

Too exhausted to move, and afraid of running into anyone, I hid in the dry scrub and watched helplessly as the Christian army marched forward. It was impossible to make out individual figures at this distance, they were simply small black dots moving through an enormous camel-colored dust cloud.

That cloud was making a straight line for the river, and its precious water. I did the only thing I could do. I crossed myself and offered a heartfelt, but futile prayer for their relief.

From behind and below, I heard faint voices on the breeze. I stumbled a few feet over to the other side of my perch and looked down towards the Jordan. I could see them a little better. Across the track to the river, a few dozen men in turbans ran back and forth, pointing and screaming around heaps of something brown and indistinguishable. I could make out bright flashes where the sunlight bounced off armor and weapons, and pinpricks of orange that I couldn't distinguish.

Those pinpricks were torches that touched the brown heaps of scrub, tar and grass. They quickly turned into tongues of flame shooting in a straight line for a hundred feet or more. Thick black smoke filled the sky creating a barrier of hellfire barring the only way to the river and its life sustaining water. If the Crusaders intention was to stock up there before relieving Raymond's castle, that dream now laid scorched and dying.

The Crusader procession stopped. The black blob was now motionless but growing as an endless line of stragglers reached the main party and halted. I could only imagine the arguments and blame sharing. Reynauld and the King would be all for heading to Tiberius and liberating the castle, regardless of what awaited them. The Templars and Hospitallers wouldn't much care which way they went as long as they got to kill Saracens. After all, if God was with them, who could stand against them—besides countless Turks, Syrians and Egyptians? Count Raymond would uselessly protest all of it and fight anyway.

From the south, there appeared fast moving figures. I guessed—and later found out I was right as if that matters at all—they were Turkopoles on horseback. From my perch I watched them ride close to the Christians, then circle back again and again, their war cries barely audible from where I sat.

Of course they were doing more than riding and shouting. The Turks were elite troops of bowmen. While they'd have gladly killed as many of the Crusaders as they could, their main job was to settle the inevitable arguments in the Christian camp and make it impossible not to veer northeast into the jaws of the Syrian army. In order to avoid being picked apart by arrows, which the Knights of the Orders considered the weapon of cowards, they'd march straight into a head on battle with a superior force. Just the way God intended men to fight and likely die.

A whinny and a thin trickle of horse snot running down my cheek pulled me away from my obsessive observation. The brown nag nuzzled at my neck and wouldn't take "get the hell away from me" for an answer. I unwillingly patted his head, but that only encouraged him to nudge me to my feet.

Beyond despising all of them, I knew nothing about horses except that this was a particularly unattractive specimen. While most of the Arab horses were sleek and fast, and the Hospitals mounts either sturdy ponies or huge destriers, this poor thing was shaggy and slow. Its huge brown eyes reflected sadness or mild bewilderment rather than any kind of martial spirit. Still, it was a living thing that so far at least, hadn't tried to kill me. Grateful for small mercies, I patted his velvety nose. He must have liked it, because he let me keep my hand and digits.

One of those mercies was the saddle bags that were still draped across his back. Besides plenty of water, there were sacks of dates and dried meat. I should have known that al Sameen wouldn't set out on a trip without plenty of food. Suddenly I was hungry enough to eat his share as well as my own.

"Thank you," I said and my companion just offered a slow, spit- and-sweat showering head shake in return, but stepped closer. I took down one of the food bags as well as a water skin and settled in. Who knew how long I'd be up here, and I wasn't going down until I knew it would be safe. It might take days.

Once the path to the Jordan was irrevocably blocked, King Guy's army had two options. Three if you considered retreat, which no one seriously did. They could stay on the flat, sunbaked, wide-open plain and fight or push north between the two "horns" directly beneath me into the waiting teeth of the men holding Tiberius.

Everything, even the birds and my snorting grumpy companion was quiet. The world seemed to hold its breath while the army made the decision as to where they'd make their stand. The slowly growing dust cloud to the south told me it wouldn't matter much either way. Salah-adin was going to win. The only question was how long it would take.

If you know your ballads, then you also know the whole "Battle of Hattin", grand and glorious as the poets make it sound, was over in less than an afternoon.

Another bank of fires was set in the north, and apparently, Allah controlled the winds here, because the smoke blew directly into the King's troops. Choking soot and fumes added to the heat, sunstroke and thirst that already tortured the Franks.

After a long parley, a small troop set off at a quick pace towards Tiberias, the others turned to face the enemy coming from the South. I guessed the smaller force was Count Raymond, who at last decided to rescue his wife regardless the odds of success. I ran to the northern corner of my roost to check on their fate hoping more than praying for some sign of victory. They burst through the thick line of smoke, and were instantly set upon.

One by one, black dots fell to the sand and lay there while other dots, probably the surviving riderless horses, ran off in every direction until they, too dropped. Soon the sand looked like someone had ground pepper all over a bowl of hummus.

An even smaller subset of the troop, carrying a banner I couldn't make out, broke off and ran. Part of me wanted to curse their cowardice, a bigger part of me wished them Godspeed and hoped they'd live to see tomorrow.

The breeze picked up, and carried with it isolated shrieks of horses and men. By now the southern plain was a dark mass with a clearly defined front line, like ink spilled on a sloping floor, slowly but inevitably trickling towards the Crusaders.

The army of Jerusalem bulged and a black bubble broke off the main body—Templars, doubtless—and charged the Saracen line. The perfect formation lasted two minutes or so until it began to elongate and leave thin dotted lines on the ground. The Mameluke line began to shift, two small crescent shaped horns extending past the charging Christian forces, then folded in on itself again.

From my height and distance, it wasn't long before I could no longer distinguish one troop from the other. The Templars were swallowed by the enemy's forces. Before that first wave of attackers was properly digested, the rest of the beast that was Salah-adin's army charged.

Poets, monks and people much smarter about such things have written about the details of that day. I wasn't close enough to observe anything that would have satisfied Brother Marco, and what I do remember, I wish I could scrub from my memory. It's enough to say that many hours before sunset, the desert floor was black with bodies, and Salah-adin's great wave of an army had crashed over the Christians and began receding again. Horses, loot and the noblest of prisoners—or at least their heads— returned to their camp near Baisan.

I'd seen men fight—even die—before, but had never witnessed real battle. All the songs, poems and drunken soldiers' boasts made it seem glorious and wonderful; something about which the rest of us made up games and aspired to experience for ourselves. I no longer believed that. It was an awful game; and final. Whoever left the greater number of black dots on the ground, won. Seldom was there a rematch.

I squinted as the landscape far below me changed. More black dots appeared out of nowhere. It took a moment to realize what was happening, but at last I figured it out. Vultures and crows who couldn't believe their good luck filled the air with invitations to their brothers to join the feast. The caws and cackles were as terrible as the cries of the dead and dying. I turned away and sought the shady side of a lichen-crusted rock. When you spend a lot of time on the street, watching others eat is never entertaining.

What was I supposed to do? Tempting as it was, remaining on the top of a rock wasn't a long-term plan. I could live among the Syrians. It sounded easy enough, you simply had to say the words; "there is no God but Allah, and Mohammad is his prophet." Everyone knew the words. I don't suppose it mattered much whether I really meant them…I'd been saying Hail Marys my whole life and it didn't impact my soul or my day to day life very much. Maybe I could go to al Majdal and change my name to Ahmed and never be found.

Eventually the sun grew larger and glowed bright orange low over the desert. Still further to the west it was sinking into the sea, about to plunge Acre into darkness. Acre. The thought of home brought short, sharp images to mind. The smell of fruit in the stalls, the briny taste of salt in the thick air, all seemed like a dream. I closed my eyes and experienced them again. I recalled big, dumb Murad's good natured laughter and Fadhil's friendship, which led immediately to Brother Marco, Sergeant Jacques, Vardan, Sister Fleure, Sister Agnes and, inevitably Sister Marie-Pilar. I pictured her eyes peering warm and dark over her veil and her picture changed to the girl in the prison tent and back. No, it might not be safe, or even pleasant, but Acre was home and I needed to get back.

Deciding was the easy part. I still had to get there across

over 50 miles of territory no longer protected by Christian knights.

The good thing about port cities is that long as you know where the sun and sea are, you can only go so wrong. If I traveled due west, I'd be fine. As if he heard me talking about him, the sad, silly pony walked over and nudged me looking for more pats on the nose. The poor saggy thing seemed overly grateful for the grudging kindness I showed him, but then he may have been expressing thanks for relieving him of the burden of his previous rider.

"All right, Droopy," I said, giving him a friendly scratch. I decided he was Droopy, because I can only spend so long with someone before giving them a name and it was wildly appropriate. "When it's dark, we'll go home."

The idea of navigating that treacherous gravel-strewn trail at night wasn't appealing, but I couldn't be sure who I'd run into. "Want to go on a trip?" I swear he nodded, but might have been just chasing away the fat biting flies that found live food more tempting than the feast down below.

When only a thin strip of purple defined the horizon, I stood and stretched. "Come on, you." I slid the Crusader's dagger in my sleeve, slung one of the water skins over my shoulder and took Droopy's reins. I took a couple of steps and found the pony stubbornly resistant. "What? Come on you stupid mule."

Droopy merely dropped his shaggy head and walked in the opposite direction, which of course was the head of the trail we'd taken up the hill. I am not proud of the name I called him as I elbowed past. At first I led the way, gingerly testing each step lest I skid on the gravel or walk off the side of the rock. Eventually, my four-legged guide nudged me out of the way and slowly, sure-footedly, wound his way to the bottom of the trail. There he waited patiently for me to arrive scratched, bruised and sweaty.

By the light of a crescent moon—only appropriate given Salah-adin's victory—I could make out the hump of a body and the small amount of open desert floor before the next corpse. Faint groans of pain and pleas to either or both Gods hung in the hot, still air. Occasionally one of those humps would move, lifting a hand in a mute cry for help. I just put my head down until I passed the poor man, and the hand would drop again, probably for the last time.

Once in a while I saw something stooped low, darting from hump to hump. Grave robbers, no doubt, probably local Syrians. I suspected there was enough dead prey they wouldn't risk attacking the living. At least I hoped so.

I took Droopy's bridle and stumbled west. After a while, he yanked me backwards and looked over his shoulder, as if perturbed I didn't climb on and save us both some trouble. I had never ridden a horse by myself before, and felt far more comfortable on my own feet but I had a feeling the silly nag wouldn't let the matter rest, and to be fair, he hadn't steered me wrong yet. I led him over to a large stone, stepped on it and then managed to climb aboard on my second attempt.

Without waiting for a command, Droopy plodded away in approximately the right direction, which is fortunate since I wasn't exactly sure how to direct him if I had to.

From the ground, the desert was less flat and featureless

than it looked from above. There were plenty of rocks and wadis. Soldiers of both armies had used them for cover, for all the good it did them. In the lee of one rock was a pit, where a sword and the arm—and only the arm—that held it marked the final resting place of a Templar knight. I crossed myself and we trudged on.

Ahead of us and to the right, two large stones loomed. A black hole between them indicated a cave, or at least a deep crevice. I heard a hollow sobbing sound, which at first I shrugged off as ghosts, because if there were spirits this is exactly the kind of place they'd lurk, but it seemed to be coming from there. I didn't want to stop, I swear I didn't, but then I heard a voice moaning in French. "Oh God, oh God... help me..."

I tried to remember how to stop a horse. Most men yanked on the reins. Ali simply whistled and his charger obeyed. I gave a half-hearted tug on the leather straps and whined, "Droopy, stop... Please." He graciously halted a few yards from the rocks.

Now I could make out the faint voice and individual words.... "Help me... Mother of God... Now and in the hour of our deaths..." I slid off my horse and cautiously drew near.

When I thought the person in there could hear me and no one else would, I hissed, "Who's there?" Stupidly, I added, "Are you all right?"

Whoever it was gasped loudly. "Oh, thank God. Help us, please." There were more than one of them in there. This was a very bad idea. Of course, that didn't stop me.

"All right, give me a minute." I grabbed one of the water skins and slowly crept towards the black hole. I could hear sniffling, and a low moan that may have been another voice altogether. I couldn't help feeling this was one of my worst ideas ever, but the pleading was so pathetic I couldn't help myself. I dropped low to the ground and reached out to touch the smooth grey rock.

As I moved to the opening, a ghostly white thin hand shot out of the blackness and I heard myself let out a little scream. "Please…. Oh thank God…." The voice was louder now, and a head followed the hand, clawing at the sand to get out. It was a boy, blond and incredibly thin. And familiar.

"Gilbert?" The boy froze and then leaned in closer….

"Lucca, what are you doing here?" Then he saw my water skin and his amazement vanished. He made a half-hearted grab for the water but lacked the strength to take it from me.

I pulled the plug and held it out to him, then just said, "Here, let me. Open your mouth," and I poured a few drops into his mouth. When his tongue could move again, I poured a bit more. He uttered a grateful groan and lay panting on the ground. From behind him, I heard another moan. Deeper and far more anguished.

"Who's with you?"

Gilbert's shoulders bounced up and down, and he began to cry. "I told him I didn't want to be a squire. I didn't want to fight. I told you, didn't I?"

"Yes… yes you did." I couldn't remember if he had or not, and in that moment, didn't think it mattered much.

"But he had that cursed Cross…. We were in the front…

and…." The rest of his tale was swallowed up in huge gulping sobs.

"Wait. Is that Brother Idoneus in there?" My throat constricted and I wrenched the water skin away to take a big swig of water for myself.

My question was met with a moan from the darkness. "Gilbert, who's out there with you? Are we rescued? Praise God, I knew He wouldn't desert me…."

My friend's eyes widened, the whites as big as eggs. Gilbert took a couple of steps backwards. "He's hurt…. badly. He needs water…" I handed him the skin, but he shook his head and pulled away as though singed. "No, I can't… go back in there…"

The voice, weaker now, croaked from the blackness. "Gilbert, for the love of God, is there water?" Gilbert pointed feebly to the hole.

I hesitated. I went, but I needed to think about every step and each inch. Finally, I slipped feet first into the cool, black space. My eyes, always pretty good in the dark, were nearly useless. I could make out a body, curled up against the stone wall. The clouds must have passed from the moon, because the Hospitaller cross stood out against the filthy background of his cuirass. Gradually my sight adjusted and I could see a bit more of my surroundings.

Idoneus' helmet lay dented in the dirt beside him. His egg-shaped head was bare, but no longer shiny and perfect. It was bruised, and crusted with dried scabs and blood. His eyes were misty and dull. A jagged scar extended across his face and the gap for his missing tooth showed through cracked, bloody lips. I said nothing, but held the skin to his lips, and gently poured. Most of the water, along with a fair amount of blood spilled out both sides of his mouth, but he smacked his lips gently.

His huge hand dropped limply onto my arm. It was meant as gratitude but it was all I could do not to shake it off. Idoneus' head lolled side to side. The tip of his tongue ran over his lips. "Gilbert... where's Gilbert? I told you we'd be saved didn't we? God hasn't abandoned us... I told you..."

Outside, I watched the boy hold his head in his hands, rocking back and forth. "Shut up! Shut up! Stop talking... This is your fault."

"Gilbert, hush." I tried to calm him down, but whatever had been dammed up inside my friend finally burst its seams and there was no stopping the rush of bile. Idoneus moaned, feebly protesting but Gilbert just continued shrieking.

"I was supposed to be a priest. I didn't want to be your squire... and you're no knight. But you had the True Cross... and you weren't worthy. You really weren't..."

The warrior monk's eyes widened. "I was... I *am* worthy..." He tried to rise, but couldn't move at all. Confused, he turned to me. "Who are you?"

"No one. I'm no one." I muttered. That seemed to satisfy him for a moment, then he looked again, closed his eyes against the apparition confronting him.

"Lucca? It's not you. It can't be..." He leaned back, his head cracked against the stone wall. Silently, he shook his head slowly side to side. "No, this is not real. God wouldn't forsake me like this...."

I wanted to shout at him. Worse, I wanted to pull my dagger and stab him over and over. Instead, I offered him some more water. "Shhh, don't strain yourself."

Rather than accept the water, he slapped my hand away. "No, you're not real. You're a demon sent by Satan. Get thee gone… Get away." He crossed himself frantically, over and over, muttering in Latin.

His legs thrashed weakly, and as he stretched out, pinning me against the wall, I saw the black stain below the cross. His stomach was slashed open and he sat in a pool of his own gore. He grimaced in agony, and weakly repeated, "Get away, get away…."

"Gladly." I reached for the opening and braced myself. Halfway out, I looked back. I threw the water skin onto his heaving chest, then pulled myself up into the cool night air. Gilbert grabbed my arm and pulled. I landed in a heap at his feet.

He stood there, holding something long and thin in his hands. It was a Mameluke lance. His red eyes never left the opening as he lowered the tip and tightened his jaw.

"No. Don't do it. Please. You don't want to kill him." I hoped I sounded calmer than I felt.

"I do. I really do." His arm pulled back and I laid a hand on him.

"You're not a killer. You're going to be a priest, remember?"

"I wanted to be, but he ruined it. It's too late…"

"No," I whispered. "It's not. Not yet. He can't hurt you anymore." I hoped that was true. "We can go home. You can study. Maybe even go to Rome... away from here." Over his shoulder I saw something move. The grave robber had slunk closer to see what we were up to.

"Leave him," I said a little louder than necessary. The shadow stopped. "He has his armor and his sword, and we'll leave him some water. If God wants him dead, He'll take him."

"God will protect me... You'll see...." Idoneus' voice barely escaped the inky blackness.

Gilbert dropped the spear and stared at the ground. Nodding meekly, he allowed me to steer him away from the rocks. Over my shoulder, the robber came even closer, laying as flat as he could to escape detection. It's a good thing he robbed the dead. A living victim would have kicked his arse. A coward like him wouldn't last a minute in Acre. Not like me.

"You have a horse?" Gilbert stared at Droopy and my mount looked back more interested in some dry grass he'd found than in us. "He doesn't look like much."

"You'd be surprised," I said. "Get on." Gilbert was so much taller than I that he needed no assistance mounting up.

Droopy gave me a surprised look, but nuzzled my neck and meekly accepted the new rider. I turned back to where Idoneus lay hidden and half-buried.

And still defiant. From inside the rocks his voice still croaked. "Go back to Hell. I am protected by God. I am worthy... I was chosen to bear his True Cross..." The robber was almost upon him.

I couldn't resist. I yelled, "And you lost it, you idiot."

Gilbert gasped and tightened, awaiting retribution that never came. Droopy whinnied softly and took a few steps forward. I walked alongside, but backwards so I could watch the figure in black slowly approach the hiding hole. Indistinct shouts and curses floated towards us but we ignored them. With one last look back, I saw the robber dip down between the rocks.

We heard nothing else from Brother Idoneus.

I followed Droopy and his silent passenger west towards Acre and home, never looking back.

Chapter 21

We weren't alone on that road for long. Before sunup we encountered other survivors hobbling, staggering or slinking back to Acre. There were soldiers and the odd household Knight, of course. Not a single Templar or Knight of the Hospital were seen, and that didn't bode at all well. For one thing, it meant not many escaped the slaughter—who was left to protect the citizenry? Many of the stragglers needed medical attention.

Certainly, I wish someone more qualified than I could have taken a look at Gilbert. My friend sat on Droopy, mutely staring straight ahead. His skin was a ghostly white, and his eyes seemed to suck in light rather than reflect it. Occasionally his lips moved in a mumble so low I couldn't make out what he was trying to say. From the looks of him, the message wasn't intended for me anyway.

Whenever we encountered other travelers, we had to make a choice. Certainly there was safety in numbers; a larger group could ward off, or at least dissuade, attack. The more generous folk shared what resources they had and—maybe most critically—information. Some of it was actually useful; the location of wells or water stashes, medical advice, which trail to take when we reached branches and crossroads. Most of it was just gossip. Perhaps the most valuable commodity was companionship, the comfort of not being alone on the worst day of your life.

Other people decided their odds were better on their own.

If for no other reason than speed, we usually kept up with the larger groups for a while. Then we'd move on until we caught up with the next batch of survivors. Those moving in pairs or alone did so by choice. I simply gave them a companionable nod and a wide berth as we headed west. Of course, being alone meant not risking all our water. Strangely, most of the groups had water for the return journey, which made no sense. At first they were tight-lipped about where it came from. Eventually we learned that the villagers from al Majdal had managed to reach them with wagons full of water but arriving far too late.

We took a couple of short breaks to sleep and let Droopy find some nasty dead grass which seemed to make him happy—or as happy as he ever got. Just before sunup we saw several wagons up ahead. The bedraggled caravans were easy to overtake. The oxen, donkeys, and occasional desperate owner limped along slower than those moving on foot or horseback. From behind you could see a lot of those carts weren't going to survive the trip home. Broken wheels wobbled wildly, ready to fall off at any moment. Some wheels didn't turn at all, their axles busted and useless, and were essentially being dragged back to Acre.

By this time, I wasn't seeing much of anything. Exhaustion and dust rendered my vision blurry and everything took on the same shape. Heading due west meant the sun rose behind us. I simply followed my shadow, head down and determined, when I heard a familiar voice.

"Lucca?" I wondered at first if Gilbert had finally broken his silence, but he just sat there mumbling. "Lucca, is that you?" The voice called from the back of the nearest cart. Looking down at me from among half a dozen filthy survivors was a familiar face.

"Fadhil?" I led Droopy and our silent passenger over to the side of the trail so I could walk alongside. "What are you doing here?"

"I told you we were going with…" his voice trailed off.

"Whoa there. Boy, who are you talking to?" Firan turned toward us, angrily glaring from the front of the wagon. He recognized me instantly. Instead of his usual growl, his face softened and he offered me a sad nod of greeting. "Are you all right, lad?" It took me a moment to realize he meant me.

"Yes sir. My friend, though…" He saw Gilbert and immediately brought the cart to a halt.

"Quick, you lot. He shouldn't be riding, lay him down." Two of the passengers gingerly got down—nursing wounds of their own—and helped the boy off the horse, hoisting him onto the bed of the cart.

"Is that Gilbert?" Fadhil and I had frequently made fun of the taller, older boy. "Is he hurt?"

"I don't think so. I mean, he's not bleeding or anything, but he's not…right." He wasn't, but few of us were. Those who could offer assistance did so, those who needed it meekly accepted what help was offered.

As soon as we had Gilbert settled, I took the water and

food from Droopy's back. We'd have to share, but it was a fair trade for knowing Gilbert was going to be okay. I handed the supplies to a grizzled old tinker I recognized from home—he'd thrown a rock at me once for making fun of his wife's bum. Now he just uttered a quiet, "God bless you" and made room for me.

I settled on the rear gate of the cart, and looked back. Droopy stood there looking at me.

"That your horse?" Firan asked, sounding a bit more like his old self.

"I guess so."

"Well is he coming with us or not?"

I hadn't given much thought to the pony. I didn't need him to get home now, but it didn't seem right somehow to just leave him in the middle of nowhere after all he'd done for me. I reluctantly slide down, landing on two very sore, battered feet. A shaggy head nuzzled my shoulder. I gave the nag a reluctant pat on his soft nose.

"Come on, you big silly thing." I looked for a place to tie the reins, and couldn't find one. Droopy let me struggle for a moment, then gave me a gentle push with his nose and simply began to walk. I ran a couple of steps and jumped on, making it the first try this time. This earned me a congratulatory head shake and my horse whinnied softly.

Once I was safely aboard, Firan softly "tsk tsked" to his donkeys and they set off again.

We overnighted with maybe two dozen other people in a wadi a few miles from Acre, and before sunup we were met by a patrol of city guards, sent out to search for word of the army. What they found instead were bloodied survivors, and precious few of them.

By mid-morning the road was thick with people returning home. It took over an hour from the first glimpse of the city walls to the queue at the gate. City watchmen tried valiantly to maintain order, or at least stop people from trampling each other. Most wanted in as quickly as possible. A few others sought loved ones among the incoming refugees so the line of people would flow in then out, shoving and cursing and, inevitably bursting into tears.

One of the Hospitallers who'd tried to bring me back to the orphanage strode up and I stiffened, anticipating the worst. He didn't recognize me, though. His gaze fell on the pale shivering figure in the back of the cart. "Gilbert? Good God, boy... is that you?" He took my friend's head in his hands, conducted an inspection, then waved one of the Hospital squires over. "Hurry now, get him back home." He did a cursory triage on the rest of the people in the cart and ordered those who could walk to do so, and hollered for help those unable to fend for themselves.

Gilbert was loaded onto a litter and two youngsters trotted off. The knight stood shaking his head. "What the hell were they thinking? The boy had no business being out there." Then he turned away to the next group of travelers without directing another thought or word to me or anyone else.

Firan and Fadhil led their exhausted donkeys through the gate to the corral, where one of them promptly keeled over dead. Without my saying a word, Droopy followed them.

Firan climbed wearily down from his cart. Then he dropped to his knees and wept like a baby, hugging the dead animal's neck. Fadhil stood silently embarrassed. At last he turned to me and held his hand out to take Droopy's reins. "We'll take care of him for you."

It hadn't occurred to me in over two days across Palestine that I couldn't just keep a horse in the city. Perhaps they'd let me keep him in the stables at St. Lazar, assuming I was still welcome there. Droopy left me to figure it out on my own. He meandered over to a water trough and stuck his whole brown, furry face in it.

"Lucca... thank God you're all right." A voice boomed from across the corral. Brother Marco stood there in full armor, although he wasn't wearing a helmet. He took large uneven strides, dragging his left foot and exhibiting a limp I hadn't seen before. Two more steps and he was on me, holding me at arm's length for inspection. "Thank God you're alive. You *are* all right, aren't you?"

The relief on his face was better than any hug he could have offered. I nodded as vigorously as I could. "Yes... yes, I'm fine. I have a lot to report, though."

The knight chuckled, wiping something out of his eye with the back of his glove. "At ease, boy. There'll be time for that. Christ only knows who you'd report to. But I'll bet you have tales to tell. I'd like to know how someone got you on a horse for one thing. That's probably a ballad in itself." He put his hand on my shoulder, the glove heavy against my skin. "Let's get you some food and a bed."

He winced as he turned, and I looked at his dragging foot.

There was no blood or sign of injury, but he was obviously in pain. We hobbled forward a few more steps before he bent over and took a deep hesitant breath. Then he bit his lip, nodded to himself and off we continued down the familiar streets of Acre.

After a long, awkward silence, Brother Marco spoke. "We've heard some of it, of course, and we're getting the rest in pieces. What did you see?"

I paused, then said, "Everything. I saw it all."

"Christ's blood, I am sorry to hear that. Must have been a terrible thing."

That didn't require an answer. I just nodded. Then I remembered. "One small group got away. They headed…" I turned my body to orient myself and gestured with my arm. "North… they went north."

Marco nodded. "That would have been Count Raymond. He managed to escape and is on his way back to Tripoli."

"How did he get away?" I asked.

My friend looked up at the cloudless sky and sighed. "Good question. Some say Salah-adin let him go because of their past friendship. Of course others say he betrayed the King and ran off."

I shook my head in horror. "No, he didn't. He fought, I saw it…"

That might have made Marco feel better, but he didn't say much of anything the rest of the trip back.

It took longer than it should have, but we eventually reached the cellar door leading to the tunnel. He reached down with his two gloved hands and tried to open it, but his fingers—even those on his healthy hand--wouldn't grip. Instead of taking off the glove, he left it on, flexing his fingers, but they barely moved. I reached down and opened it myself, barely able to hold it long enough for him to pass through.

He must have felt my eyes on him, because he stopped halfway through the cellar opening and looked up at me. "Thank you, Lucca."

"What's wrong with your hand? Are you hurt?"

He didn't answer me, just dipped into the tunnel and beckoned for me to follow. "Lots of time for us both to report. Come along."

The dark and cool felt as good as a bath after being in the open for so long. Marco led the way, slowly, and I tried not to rush him or ask too many questions. Finally, we reached the door to the House of St Lazar. My companion reached for the handle, but I darted my hand in and opened it myself.

I lifted the latch and swung the door out. There were the familiar steps. Long shafts of sunlight crisscrossed the chamber. I reached back to offer Brother Marco my hand, but he avoided my grasp and gingerly clung to the door jamb instead.

From up ahead, I heard the swish of skirts and the gentle pat of sandaled feet. My eyes met Sister Marie-Pilar's and we ran towards each other. Her arms gathered me close and she kissed my forehead through her veil.

"Oh my boy…." Her voice quivered and then she let out one big sob before regathering herself and sniffing loudly. "Oh my boy, you came home to us." I smelled her freshly laundered robes and buried my face against her. Unashamed, I pressed my face against her breast and could feel her heart pounding.

After a moment, I looked up at her. "Can I stay?"

Her eyes crinkled above the strip of gauze that covered her face. "For as long as you want, Lucca."

I pulled her even closer.

I could stay.

"Inshallah," I whispered.

Obligatory Ending Stuff

This book, like almost any novel, was a long-time a-birthing. Maybe it started in 2007 when I stood in Old Jerusalem, looking down at the ruins of the Hospital of St John. One thought kept rattling around in my brain; "What the hell were they thinking?" (And by *they*, I mean all of them. All sides, all religions, all sub-sects of the offshoots of the religions, all of them.) Any reading of the Crusades, particularly the Battle of Hattin, should elicit the same question. As does even a quick skim of today's news.

Perhaps the seed was planted when I reread Kipling's "Kim" for the umpteenth time and wondered about that story set against other historical backdrops. Poor old Rudyard's thrilling and hilarious 19th century adventure of a boy without a country, caught between worlds and seeing the insanity of grown-up behavior, has stuck with me through multiple readings and countless bad movie versions. I swear on my daughter's head Dean Stockwell will never play Lucca. (Oh look it up, people. I can't do everything for you.) If we can't draw a few lessons from that period of religious and political turmoil, we're really not trying very hard.

Or maybe it was during a discussion with some members of the Naperville Writers Group. I remember ranting about the surplus of "YA" novels, and how many of the books I loved as a kid would never have found a place on the shelves. "The Three Musketeers" is a rollicking adventure I read as a thirteen-year-old, but there's some awfully grownup stuff in there. "Treasure Island" is still terrific fun—and became known as a "Boy's Story,"—but was written originally for adults. Somewhere in my tequila-addled brain came the question, "could I tell a story that was adult, but might attract the brighter more adventurous teen reader; definitely not YA, but not exclusionary, either?" I don't think we give readers of all ages enough credit for sniffing out good stories.

I guess you can decide whether I've accomplished my task. For what it's worth, I like Lucca and his friends, and I'm not done with them yet.

As usual, I've inflicted this book on innocent victims before you. My thanks to the Naperville Writers Group, especially Lou Holly, Loretta Morris, Jeremy Brown, Eileen Kimbrough, Ray Zeimer and Frank Fedele. Your support is appreciated, your collective kicks to the seat of my pants even more so.

A special thank you to two authors I greatly respect who gave me some last-minute notes that made this work much better than it would have been if left to my own devices. Pat Camalliere for her eagle eyes and Helena P Schrader deserve more than a line in the dedication. That's all they're getting of course, but they deserve more. Also, visit the Real Crusades History site.

Of course, Her Serene Highness and the Duchess deserve medals for sticking through the writing process, but if I haven't scared them off by now, I probably won't.

Historical fiction is a wonderful window to where we've been, how we got where we are, as well as our future. I am amazed at the number of people who bring the past to life in so many ways. I enjoy interviewing and learning about them at my blog, www.WayneTurmel.com. Please visit, and discover new reads from authors who need your support.

If you've enjoyed this work, please share the news by giving a review on Amazon, Goodreads or Twitter and telling others. The way things work today, it's the only way new and independent authors can find an audience, and the audience can find new cures for their addictions. Someone once said, "offering a good review online is like applause for the author." Word.

Remember, those who forget the past are doomed to repeat it. The rest of us are doomed, too, but get to smile smugly and say "told you so."

Wayne Turmel
Lisle, IL

Read more about me and my interviews with other indie Historical Fiction authors at www.WayneTurmel.com

If you enjoyed Acre's Bastard
Check out "The Count of the Sahara"

In 1925, Count Byron de Prorok was the most famous archaeologist and lecturer in the world. By spring of 1926, his reputation, his marriage and his career were in ruins. What happened?

Based on true events, The Count of the Sahara is the gripping tale of an extraordinary man's obsession, of America in transition and a naïve young man's first steps in an adult world.

"a great tale of adventure, with authentic and complex characters living in a series of unpredictable events. HIGHLY RECOMMENDED." Windy City Reviews

"the most interesting character is the fascinating Count de Prorok, a figure that any writer of historical fiction would be proud to have in their book." Peter Darman, author of The Crusader Chronicles

Available on Amazon in Paperback and Kindle from

The Book Folks

CPSIA information can be obtained
at www.ICGtesting.com
Printed in the USA
FSOW01n1830291216
28969FS